KILLING KATE

ALSO BY JULIE KRAMER

Silencing Sam
Missing Mark
Stalking Susan

KILLING
KATE

A NOVEL

JULIE KRAMER

ATRIA BOOKS

New York London Toronto Sydney

Delafield Public Library
Delafield, WI 53018
262-646-6230
www.delafieldlibrary.org

ATRIA BOOKS

A Division of Simon & Schuster, Inc.
1230 Avenue of the Americas
New York, NY 10020

This book is a work of fiction. Names, characters, places, and incidents either are products of the author's imagination or are used fictitiously. Any resemblance to actual events or locales or persons, living or dead, is entirely coincidental.

Copyright © 2011 by Julie Kramer

All rights reserved, including the right to reproduce this book or portions thereof in any form whatsoever. For information address Atria Books Subsidiary Rights Department, 1230 Avenue of the Americas, New York, NY 10020.

First Atria Books hardcover edition July 2011

ATRIA BOOKS and colophon are trademarks of Simon & Schuster, Inc.

For information about special discounts for bulk purchases, please contact Simon & Schuster Special Sales at 1-866-506-1949 or business@simonandschuster.com.

The Simon & Schuster Speakers Bureau can bring authors to your live event. For more information or to book an event, contact the Simon & Schuster Speakers Bureau at 1-866-248-3049 or visit our website at www.simonspeakers.com.

Manufactured in the United States of America

10 9 8 7 6 5 4 3 2 1

Library of Congress Control Number: 2011019958

ISBN 978-1-4391-7801-0
ISBN 978-1-4391-7804-1 (ebook)

3 0646 00177 8491

To my editor Emily Bestler,
who always says the right thing

KILLING KATE

PROLOGUE

The night began with a teenage dare. She followed reluctantly as he led her by the hand to the shadow of the Black Angel.

A full moon gave them less privacy than she would have liked. Her back now against the horizontal concrete slab, she waited for him to lay his body across hers. Her lips prayed for the encounter to be quick because out of the corner of her eye a raven watched them intently from atop a gravestone.

Unlike most cemetery angels, whose heads and wings lift upward toward heaven, this statue's face and wings bent downward over the grave it guarded—as if pointing straight to hell. And while angel sculptures are traditionally a golden bronze or white marble, this one's hue was black. Besides the figure's sinister posture and color, its stony eyes seemed to stare into hers as if issuing a personal condemnation.

Her feeling of doom was so strong, the girl struggled to move away. But he held her down, pushed her dress up to her waist, and there, at the hem of the Black Angel, they sinned.

The writer paused over the keyboard and reread the scene. Then with a smile, added sensory and sensual details about places the boy was hard and the girl was soft, and how their throaty moans were the only sound of life amid the dark tombstones. A final tweak when the female character closed her eyes tight to shut out the angel's glare completed the carnal passage.

CHAPTER 1

Waitresses were easy to research. For the price of lunch or coffee he gathered most of the information he needed.

First, he'd stall in the doorway of the restaurant skimming the menu. Then he might walk past the tables to the bathroom. Or maybe even pretend he recognized someone sitting on the other side of the room. All were opportunities to scan for a promising target—preferably a blonde—and note which section of the room she was serving.

Once he was seated, the rest came effortlessly. Often she wore a name tag. And if not, her name usually appeared on the bill. So no introduction was necessary. Her job was to be nice to customers. Even those she might give a cold shoulder to under different circumstances. Flirty charm meant the difference between twenty percent of the tab or being stiffed.

He could pretend they were new friends and practice making sociable conversation. Sometimes he even imagined they were married and she was preparing a home-cooked dinner for him after a long day at work. And he always paid in cash, so there was no check or credit card to trace back to him.

While she fetched water or restocked the bread basket, he recorded details in a small notebook to further the illusion his meal was business-related. Name. Physical description. And most important, how he was treated. If he detected scorn, he circled that entry with a red pen. That was his code for which ones needed to learn respect. He chose the color red deliberately.

Once, he stared so intensely at his server that she dropped silverware and backed away clumsily into another diner. He had meant his attention as a compliment. But instead of being flattered, she pointed him out to a coworker and even from across the room he could see her lips mutter "pervert."

He wrote down the affront. Then circled her name in red.

When she finished her shift, he was waiting in the parking lot to see which vehicle she drove. Women were always cautious going to their cars, and security cameras were mounted everywhere. He knew better than to approach her during that short trek. Home was where they felt safest, and there, it was simple to catch them off guard and out of sight of witnesses.

Patience was paramount.

He knew better than to follow her directly home, because the last thing he needed was a suspicious cop and a police report with his name and vehicle information on file. He stayed on her bumper only long enough to get her license plate number. Later, he popped her address from public records and watched to become familiar with her work schedule. It was important that she be dressed in the role.

To be assured of privacy, he also needed to learn the routine of her household. Whether she lived alone, with a roommate, or had a family. The journey to the end took weeks.

He also hungered for permission. But that blessing now came easily.

So one day when the garage door opened for her car, he followed inside . . . crouching low and close to the side of the building. When he cornered her, he was disappointed that she had no idea who he was, how he had picked her, or why he was wearing gloves and a hairnet.

"Say it," he told her.

But she was confused and didn't know what he was talking about. All she could mumble were a few shaky words that sounded like "please" and "don't hurt me."

But he'd heard similar stammers before. "Say it," he threatened her with a club held high.

She covered her head and sobbed, her shoulders quivering. She couldn't seem to hold eye contact with him. That wouldn't have changed anything, but he relished the fog in their eyes.

"Say it," he insisted, "say 'pervert.'" He smashed his weapon against the garbage can, denting the lid.

Finally, she raised her face and repeated the word.

Then he brought the club down. And when she was dead, he arranged her body just perfect and added his special touch. Turning her from devil to angel.

He was their salvation.

He never visited the same restaurant twice. He never cruised places in the town where he lived. He didn't mind driving long distances because he enjoyed the feeling of control behind the wheel. And on the special nights, he parked about a half mile away, carrying his tools in a backpack. After all, he had plenty of time.

He also had a formula that worked. But it soon grew unsatisfying.

So he broke the pattern. Ditched his distant waitress mania, instead focusing on a closer, more deserving target: Kate.

It was hard to admit to himself, because it meant acknowledging he'd made mistakes, but he'd come to realize he hadn't played fair with the first ones. Those women had deserved to know why he had come. Initially, he had worried that such a warning might alter the outcome, but he also savored the idea of them brooding over who or what or when or where.

Kate's transgression was plotted, not fleeting; so she had plenty of warning about his displeasure.

But the risk of discovery was worth the expression in her eyes as the club came down.

He would kill to see that look again.

CHAPTER 2

Until Kate Warner's homicide, it had been a slow news day in Minneapolis.

In the first hours after her body was discovered, media coverage was fairly predictable. Television live trucks and camera crews with tripods camped out along the street because the neighborhood where Kate had lived and died was previously regarded as safe and quiet—the Minnesota ideal of above-average income and below-average crime.

So when her neighbors learned she had been murdered in her own home, Kate's death became more interesting to them than her life had ever been.

My name is Riley Spartz. I'm a television reporter for Channel 3. Normally I'd describe myself as an investigative reporter, but those glorious days of long-term special projects are diminishing in the news business. While the word "investigation" still has promotional value, newsrooms simply don't have the budget for the real thing anymore. Now journalists are under orders to turn breaking news into "instant" investigations, hoping the public won't discern any real difference.

"Keep back, everyone."

A uniformed officer motioned to the curious to stay some distance from the crime scene tape. The yellow-and-black plastic ribbon was the only splash of color across the dried-up yard. If there were any spatters of blood, they blended invisibly into the grass—brown due to the summer watering ban.

The policeman then directed a terse "No comment" at me and the rest of the media. I made a note of his ID pin, "Stanley," but didn't press him further, because as a street cop, rather than a homicide detective, he probably understood little about what had happened inside the brick-and-stucco rambler. He might have secured the scene, but the homicide team would have quickly assigned him to the busy work of crowd control.

A large crowd hadn't gathered—that typically only happens with brutal crime in public places like parks or malls. Most of these onlookers were pretending not to look.

One man walked his dog up and down the block. A woman kept checking her mailbox. Another pushed a young child on a swing in her front yard even though the toddler made noises about wanting to go inside. And more folks than usual strolled past, feigning appreciation for the hot August weather.

But their eyes were all riveted on the homicide house.

I whispered to my cameraman to casually shoot video of all spectators, because sometimes the killer likes to watch the ensuing commotion. Occasionally the killer even volunteers to be interviewed for television newscasts. Researchers have no solid explanation for it, but know that for some psychopaths, the aftermath is even more rewarding than the actual deed.

"Why Kate?" one woman asked, looking with anguish into my photographer's camera. Her delivery smooth, as if she'd practiced in a mirror. "Who would want to kill her?"

Both legitimate questions—posed as a perfect sound bite that would definitely make air—but two separate queries that might never be fully answered. Such is the reality of violent death. "How" is much easier to explain than "why" or "who," and the medical examiner would likely release the "how" answer within a day or two.

Often, but not always, when a woman is slain in her own home, the murderer is someone she knows. From a career of covering crime, I knew the police would be looking for signs of forced entry, robbery, and sexual assault as a means of determining motive and focusing their investigation.

Two men were nailing a piece of fresh plywood over the front picture window when we arrived; while their actions resembled hurricane preparation often seen along the coasts, here in the Midwest they suggested a break-in. Though why an intruder wouldn't opt for a backyard entry seemed puzzling.

I knocked at the door of the two-story stucco directly across the street from Kate's place. No one answered, and I was about to shrug off the house as empty when I caught a glimpse of someone at an upstairs window. Most of the neighbors had been neighborly, likely hoping to hear whatever information I had without waiting to watch it on TV. This inhabitant was coy.

A woman a few doors down thought Kate had a boyfriend, but didn't think the relationship was particularly serious because she'd never introduced them. Once the police got wind of him, I knew they'd be pursuing the idea of a domestic squabble turned savage.

I glanced at a snapshot of Kate that a friend of hers had given me with the promise I'd return it later. I could have simply had my cameraman videotape the photo on her doorstep, but then other media might have landed the same shot. This way, I'd be the only reporter with this particular picture.

Kate's appearance was ordinary. Her hair brown. Her smile pleasant. No clues there. I weighed what details I had learned about the victim during the last couple of hours and saw no overt reason for anyone to want her dead. The script was practically writing itself. I made notes.

Kate didn't dress to attract trouble.

"Very modestly attired," said an elderly woman who cherished the deceased because she drove her to doctor appointments.

Kate sang lead in the church choir.

"A voice like an angel," said a man who regularly attended the same Sunday service.

If Kate had money, she didn't flaunt it.

"Frugal," said a woman in Kate's book club. "She preferred waiting for the paperback."

They confirmed that Kate worked at home as a medical transcriptionist, so it wasn't as if she upset retail customers or annoyed office colleagues. She didn't even have a dangerous commute.

Hers was a common case of Girl Next Door Gets Murdered. We all want to believe if someone dies violently, they must have done something to deserve it. That makes the rest of us feel safer. But a career of watching body bags being loaded in the back of medical examiner vans has taught me that nice people are sometimes killed for no good reason.

While it's not something we tout, the media appreciates a good murder, particularly if the motive contains some mystery— a disputed inheritance or a covert celebrity lover can bring an audience to a broadcast in numbers that robbery or rape can't.

If a case isn't solved right away, that can be okay as long as there are fascinating follow-ups and indications it will eventually end in an arrest. Cold cases frustrate families, police, and the public.

And, to be honest, we newshounds also want endings to our stories. You can argue that we don't care whether it's a happy ending or a sad ending, just as long as it ends. And that might be a fair assessment; we can't cover the same victims year after year without craving closure ourselves.

Our interest isn't just professional. Even we have a personal need to know what happened to the missing, whether it be eleven-year-old Jacob Wetterling, abducted two decades ago on a rural Minnesota road, or Iowa TV anchor Jodi Huisentruit, vanishing fifteen years ago on her way to work. Instead we settle for anniversary stories reliving the crimes.

So that night on Channel 3, I told viewers everything I could substantiate about Kate Warner's death. No sense in holding back a juicy fact for later, because you're only likely to get beat by your competition and reamed by your boss.

Right then, none of the other newsies in town seemed to have an inside track on the murder investigation, so I was sitting fine journalistically because it wasn't clear yet whether this homicide would have staying power with the media and the public. That status of a victim becoming a household name is awarded to only a handful of the more than ten thousand Americans murdered each year.

I didn't know yet that Kate had led a secret life, and that her secret did not die with her.

CHAPTER 3

Homicides were among the news stories my boss had recently banned me from covering, so Kate's murder wasn't assigned to me. More like I assigned myself, even though I suspected that move could bring me trouble.

Even reporters get tired of recounting heartache, so each morning I prayed for optimistic news stories to break. Maybe a cure for cancer. Or a solution to the state budget deficit. But miracles seldom happen, and most days the media has to get realistic and settle for a dog being rescued from a sheet of ice floating down the Mississippi.

In the midst of a deepening recession, happy news gets harder to come by.

Today was no exception. Earlier, a thousand miles west, a disgruntled man had piloted his small airplane into a government building, sparking a massive explosion and national debate on just what defines a terrorist. I'd been assigned to report that staple of local journalism: Could it happen here?

Newsrooms get a lot of mileage out of that question. A few phone calls later, I'd discovered yes—if someone's willing to crash his own plane into a building, then it's no more a security breach than any of us taking our car out of our own garage. Certainly less difficult than hijacking a jumbo jet. I was on my way out to shoot the story at a small airfield when the assignment desk yelled out the address of a homicide just coming over the police scanners.

"What was the location again, Ozzie?" I asked.

The last few killings I'd covered finished badly for me. I'd started off in my investigative journalist mode, then ended up a homicide suspect, and in one case, almost a victim myself. Those developments had taken some of the luster out of covering If-It-Bleeds-It-Leads crime.

It wouldn't have occurred to me that I even had a choice. My news director Noreen Banks was the one who suggested a change might be best, though she could have phrased it more diplomatically.

"Riley, you've become my biggest newsroom headache."

I was certain this was what being fired felt like, so was surprised she saw an alternative.

"We need to put you on less perilous stories," Noreen said. "You are becoming a distraction to the news we cover."

So she assigned me to white-collar crimes like embezzlement, Ponzi schemes, and fraud. And luckily, with the economy tanking, there were plenty of those to report—some even concerning public figures in the Twin Cities.

So when the word "homicide" was being tossed around the newsroom that day, I could have held tight to my airplane security story and steered clear of up-close violence.

But the address of the crime scene sounded familiar. I was fairly sure I'd been on that block before. And deep down, I wondered if I'd been inside that very house. Curiosity, and even a sense of duty, beckoned—not to the news of the day, rather a friendship of yesterday.

So I handed my airport notes off to a rookie reporter and to the surprise of our assignment editor, volunteered to check out the killing.

"Give it to me," I insisted.

Ozzie glanced toward Noreen's office, knowing our boss might disagree.

"I'll be done with the story before she even knows," I said. "Plus, I might have an inside line on this case."

The latter won Ozzie's collaboration because anything that gives us an edge over the competition is worth a minor misunderstanding with management.

When I arrived on the scene, I recognized the brick rambler, even though I hadn't been inside for more than a decade. I knew the layout as well as my own home, and wondered where the body rested.

"Please," I prayed silently to myself in the Channel 3 van parked at the curb. "Let them have moved."

"Come on, Riley, what's taking so long?" asked my cameraman, Malik Rahman. "We need to get going. Hit the dirt."

I'd been so eager to claim this story, Malik was puzzled why I was uncharacteristically slow getting out of the van.

"Just a second," I told him. "I need to focus."

"No, Riley, focusing is my job, the photographer's. Your job is to snoop. Now go nose around."

So while Malik sprayed the scene with video, I reverted to reporter form, knocking door to door until a woman holding a long-haired cat answered. She recognized me from TV, and I waited to see whether that carried pluses or minuses.

In this case she had enjoyed a story I did a couple weeks ago about owners who groomed and painted their dogs and cats for art shows. The fur certainly made an interesting canvas, but to me, the animal's eyes looked sad.

"Thanks," I said, accepting the compliment without debate. "It was my boss's idea." Noreen was fixated on animal stories as a way to win viewer loyalty . . . and station ratings.

"Be sure and tell her I liked it," the woman said.

"I sure will." Like hell. Noreen didn't need any more encouragement for fluffy features.

I craved sympathy for having to work for a rigid manager like Noreen, but these days of growing unemployment, almost anyone who still had a job hated their boss. And those out of work hated the bosses who'd fired them.

"Too bad you have to cover a murder," the neighbor said. "That's got to be rough."

"Yep." I nodded. Not the kind of consolation I was looking for, but I played along. "I wanted to cover that northern Minnesota story about the lost baby bear being reunited with its mother, but another reporter snatched it first."

Technically, that was a lie, but telling people something they like hearing often makes them more agreeable sources. Commiserating also allowed me to point to the crime scene and casually ask her the last name of the family.

She answered, "Warner."

My heart sped up at the familiar name, and I wondered, Which one?

But then she went on to say that Kate lived alone. "Do you think it was her?" she asked.

"No word yet." I got the neighbor's phone number by promising to call her if I learned anything—an effective technique to staying in touch with eyes on the block.

A half hour later, when Detective Delmonico confirmed that next of kin had been located, I officially learned that Kate Warner was the murder victim.

I'm ashamed to admit I felt relief. And then I felt guilt that I didn't feel more sorrow.

I had nothing against Kate. We'd first met when she was twelve. Her older sister had been a college roommate of mine.

Normally journalists steer away from stories in which we might know the players, because that can affect our judgment. Though having inside sources can sometimes trump conflict-of-interest concerns.

During our college days, Laura Warner and I were as tight as

Barbie and PJ or Bert and Ernie. Then we had a . . . rift. I hadn't seen her or any of her family members, including her little sister, in years. I juggled the math in my head and was surprised that it might have been as many as fourteen years without any contact. Didn't have her cell phone number. Or email address. Didn't even know where she was living these days, or what she called a job.

But I always sensed our paths would cross again, probably on Facebook or some other social networking site. I just never guessed it would be at a crime scene. And even though our friendship had ended badly, I knew that with her sister's death, Laura would need me.

The investigators remained tight-lipped that afternoon, confirming only what they legally had to under the Minnesota Data Practices Act: that a homicide had occurred, the victim's name, date of birth, and that no arrests had been made.

As far as murders went, it seemed routine.

CHAPTER 4

He enjoyed reading and clipping their obituaries.

He learned more about them there than from the news accounts. He was most interested in their genealogy. Who their parents were and whether they had children. He liked to sketch out as complete a family tree—spouses and siblings included—as he could for their files.

As for the murder scene, there was nothing a reporter could tell him that he didn't already know. Sometimes he watched TV newscasts to feel superior, other times to relive the crime in his head.

The hard part was waiting for the documents. They completed the project. He forced himself to wait at least a month before applying for the birth and death certificates of his victims.

When the mail finally arrived, he felt powerful . . . sliding a letter opener through the government envelope. He stroked his hands and face against the smooth paper typed with the name and official cause of death. Homicide. Blunt Trauma. The records gave him ownership of his deed.

Handsome leather folders finished off his work. Each woman's a separate color. Bonnie brown. Maggie black. Kathy blue. Kate would be tan. He liked to be organized in all things, whether at work or at home.

The Bonnie and Maggie files were finished and camouflaged on a top shelf with his other books. Kathy's needed more work. He wanted it to be perfect.

His genealogy hobby revealed from whence his own brutal streak came. What started as a quest to discover his roots became an obsession once he discerned the ancestral pattern of violence he shared. His family tree became his destiny.

His father died on the electric chair at Indiana State Prison for murdering his mother during a domestic argument.

When he reached adulthood, he tried to dismiss what happened in his childhood home as one very bad day. A family can't be judged by twenty-four hours, he reminded himself. But in the course of mapping his paternal bloodline, he discovered other very bad days that haunted his pedigree.

Generations of other relatives who had killed. In researching their deaths, he discovered sociopaths. Two died in prison serving life sentences for homicide. Others were executed for their crimes. One on the gallows. One by lethal injection. Another perished in a shootout with police. And one in a head-on car crash—trying to escape the cops—slamming into a family of five.

Eight whom society called scum, he called kin.

Plus, a mysterious legend.

CHAPTER 5

Back in Kate's neighborhood, the crime scene tape was down a few days later. The police cars were gone. Things looked normal except for the sheet of plywood still across the front of the murder house.

Laura was parked outside. I pulled in behind her rental car. The night before, I'd slipped her my business card as I went through her sister's funeral line.

"Let me know if you need any help, Laura."

Seeing her for the first time since college wasn't as weird as I expected. For one thing, she looked about the same. No extra pounds. No graying hair. Still unmarried, if I went by her ring finger. And still distant toward me.

She'd seemed noncommittal about my offer for a favor, so I was taken aback when she'd called this noon, telling me she didn't think she could go inside her family home alone and didn't know who else to ask.

"I'll come over," I assured her.

We walked to the front of the house in the muggy summer weather and paused while she rummaged through her purse. She pulled out a house key . . . back from the days when she also lived under that same roof, before their parents died. I let her walk in first, but immediately regretted my courtesy.

The crime scene had been cleared, but not cleaned.

A white outline seemed painted on the carpet, just a few feet from where we stood. I bent down to touch the white color and it smudged like chalk. It was chalk.

Laura's face paled as she realized this spot was where her sister lay dead. Philosophically, she understood that the house would be forever stigmatized by such a gruesome history. But being face to face with the tragedy clearly rattled her.

She made the sign of the cross and prayed. "I believe in God the Father, Almighty."

I stepped back to give her the illusion of privacy, but actually, I was scanning the room for clues. The outline was shaped like a human, but different. Where the victim's arms should have been were wide, pointed contours, as if Kate wore kimono sleeves.

"Maker of heaven and earth," her sister continued.

Near her head was a large reddish-brownish discoloration. A bloodstain. Numerous, smaller spatters had ricocheted over the surrounding floor and walls.

The room was dark because the picture window remained boarded up. Broken glass lay everywhere, and a steel lawn chair flung to one side seemed out of place in the room. I even wondered if it might have been the instrument used to break in. In that case, the killer would have dispensed with much element of surprise.

The next line of the prayer that I heard jarred me from such an interesting hypothesis. "He descended into hell."

He sure did, I thought. And he put Kate through it, too.

I'd seen bloodstains before, in the aftermath of other murders. Even crushed brain matter. But one thing you seldom see in real life covering crime is an actual chalk body outline. These days they exist only on TV dramas for visual effect.

Homicide investigators don't use them anymore because they can contaminate the crime scene with hair, footprints, and even

DNA from law enforcement rather than a suspect. Photographs and videotape better document the position of the body.

Chalk outlines are done by inexperienced police officers, often the first on the scene. They think they're being helpful and even feel important as they perform the artistic act. But they play dumb when a ranking investigator arrives and storms about, wanting to know who was playing detective. The investigators even have a nickname for them when no one owns up beyond a shrug.

"Huh, must have been the chalk fairy," I mumbled.

All this was explained to me by my cop beau Nick Garnett when he pointed out a "chalk fairy" to me once in a crime scene photo, telling me that's how the officers would razz each other when they'd come across an anonymous outline at the crime scene.

I wondered who got chewed out for drawing this one. Then thought back to Officer Stanley, the cop who played keep away with me and the crime scene tape. I considered looking him up and joshing him about the chalk fairy artwork, just to weigh his reaction.

Gazing at the wide arms, I realized the shape even resembled the wings of a fairy.

Laura faltered through the rest of the Apostles' Creed. Rushing down the hall the minute she reached "Amen." I heard a gagging sound, a toilet flush, then a door shut. While my old roommate was puking up her breakfast, I pulled out my cell phone and took a picture of the chalk body outline.

I felt sneaky doing it, but I also doubted Laura would let a Channel 3 photographer through the door. I told myself I wouldn't air the picture; I just wanted to have it handy. For research.

I took a second shot as backup.

Then I walked over to the bathroom door, and tapped gently. "Can I get you anything, Laura?"

No answer.

"I'll just wait out here," I told her. "Take your time."

I stared at the mess around the room. A small couch was knocked over. Fingerprint powder was spread in several places. I imagined the detectives put luminol on the walls to check for additional blood spatters under black light. Rubber gloves lay discarded in one corner. The cops must have left the pair behind; if they'd belonged to the killer, they would have been tagged and taken as evidence.

I figured that's what happened to the sheets on Kate's bed. No bloodstains on the mattress. No signs of scuffle in the bedroom. But forensic tests would look for semen stains to determine whether Kate had sex recently, and if so, with whom.

I also peaked into the kitchen where I saw shriveled-up veggies on a cutting board and dead lettuce in a bowl. Kate had been tossing a salad shortly before her skull was crushed.

Back in the living room, it felt creepy standing in a place that once held good memories, some belonging to me, but now reeked of terror. I could only imagine Laura's distress.

I thought back to years ago, me walking through the front door; Kate cheering my visit, acting happier to see me than her big sister.

"I want to sit by Riley! I want to sit by Riley!" she'd chant to tease Laura.

I wondered what her sister had told her when my visits stopped. And just then, I felt Kate's death more personally than I had at any time since her murder.

A door clicked, and Laura walked out of the bathroom. Her eyes were red and puffy.

Neither of us said anything. I used my body to block the death scene from her view, but that wasn't even necessary. She seemed to be purposely avoiding looking at her sister's final resting place. I wasn't sure what to say, and decided it best to keep quiet and take my cues from her.

Laura took a deep breath, looked straight into my eyes, and spoke. "Riley, will you help me?"

"Of course." I forced myself to make a small smile that I hoped looked reassuring. "Anyway I can."

I knew this was the kind of promise that could be trouble later on. But I also knew this wasn't the moment to negotiate the terms of our reunion.

"I'll make sure your sister's death gets publicity," I assured her. "I won't let Kate be forgotten."

"It's not that, Riley."

She stared over at the chalk outline, as if she'd decided to play dauntless in the face of heartbreak. Then she turned briskly and opened a hall closet, cluttered with a broom and mop.

"I can't clean it up by myself."

The medical examiner had removed Kate's body from the murder scene to conduct an autopsy. The homicide team took whatever they needed for their investigation, such as blood, fluid, and tissue samples. But lots of grisly things get left behind, things too icky for me to talk about on television.

It's not law enforcement's job to clean up the mess after homicides. That's up to the victim's family to arrange.

"Neither of us is going to do it, Laura." This was a job for professionals. "I'll call someone."

The expression on her face was a cross between relief and disbelief. "Who?"

"There are people." I explained that many crime scenes, unless a family was very poor, were cleaned by biohazard crews because of fears of infection from diseases such as HIV or hepatitis.

She shook her head angrily. "My sister didn't have any diseases. She didn't do drugs or sleep around."

"I'm sure you're right about Kate. But what about her killer? Who knows what kind of scumbag he was? I'm not taking any chances and I'm not going to let you."

Those words gave her something to think about.

"You'll call them?"

"Yes."

Crime scene cleanup is a fairly new occupation—and expensive, often hundreds of dollars an hour. But I knew of other homicides in which homeowners insurance had covered the cost and then there were crime victim relief funds. Otherwise the bill could be paid from Kate's estate. My guess was, Laura would be executor.

"I'll call them," I assured her.

So we locked the front door and headed for our vehicles. As Laura climbed in her rental, I promised to let her know the details for the cleanup.

"You're going to have to be here to let them in," I told her.

She nodded, but didn't look like she enjoyed the prospect.

"You can probably leave them to do their work, Laura, and wait somewhere else until they're finished. Then lock up."

"That sounds best."

Figuring I had nothing to lose, I asked to bring a photographer to shoot the crime scene for a future story.

She seemed more sad than angered by my question. "No, Riley. This can't be about that. I know you think publicity might help solve the case, but I'm not sure I want additional media coverage." Then she slammed the car door and drove away.

Seeing her for the first time after so long had been a little disconcerting for me. Neither of us mentioned the passage of time. She didn't bring up getting together again to visit or how great it was seeing me.

While sitting in my car, I checked my cell phone and noticed a missed call. My heart gave a pang when I saw the source. I hit Send, and he answered.

"I was just thinking about you a few minutes ago, honey," I said.

"I like the sound of that, Riley. Hold that thought a couple more days, and we'll go from thinking to acting." His voice held a playful tone, and I knew what game he had in mind.

"Not *that* kind of thought, Nick." Playing hard to get was easy, a thousand miles apart.

"You said I was to do the thinking for both of us."

"Humphrey Bogart, *Casablanca,* 1942."

In the last year, Nick Garnett had moved from a source of news to a source of affection. We had a long tradition of working famous movie quotes into our conversations and guessing the origin of the line.

"Ingrid Bergman may have put Bogie in charge of the decision making that night in Casablanca, but that hasn't happened with you and me," I continued.

"There's still time," he laughed. "So what *were* you thinking about?"

"I was thinking about what a smart cop you are." I emphasized the word "smart."

"And here I was hoping for something a little more intimate than intellectual."

When Garnett turned fifty, he left his job as a homicide investigator to run security for the world-famous Mall of America.

He now worked in Washington, DC, as part of Homeland Security, but we had an understanding that he'd finish up the year on the East Coast and find a job back in Minnesota.

And then if we were still on speaking terms, we might even get married.

"There's plenty of time for personal later, Nick. Right now I need a biohazard team to clean up a murder scene, and hoped you could recommend someone."

"Who'd you kill? That surly boss of yours?"

"Nobody you know. Actually the victim is the sister of a long-ago friend."

He wanted to hear more, but was apparently walking into an important meeting to Keep Our Country Safe. He gave me contact information for a company he'd seen handle similar jobs, then hung up.

Glancing in the rearview mirror, I realized I was smiling, and figured that was a good sign—on a whole lot of levels.

So I set up the crime scene cleanup time and texted all the details to Laura.

"Thanx" was her only response. I wasn't sure if she expected me to help supervise the work or not. I figured I'd have to wait for her to sort things out, just like back in college days.

CHAPTER 6

Laura and I didn't start out with much in common other than being paired together as college roommates. Because Laura's family lived twenty minutes from campus, I gained a second home to celebrate important events like birthdays and making the dean's list.

We had no classes together, yet shared a coming-of-age time in our lives when experiences were intense and friendships deep. I thought I knew her better than my own sister. We both had dark hair and lanky bodies, and some people even thought we looked like sisters.

Laura had more religious conviction than most of us living in the dorm. I benefited because I had a roommate whose loyalty would not be swayed by trends. On the other hand, her tendency to lecture people she felt lacked her own moral virtue when it came to sex and drugs could be irritating.

As for campus parties, I assured her she didn't have to drink or make out with anyone.

"Just carry a beer around and blend in."

"No, Riley, that wouldn't be honest. That's not who I am."

Who in college really knows who they are? That Laura was so sure of her place in life was something I admired as I struggled to find mine.

When the administration demanded the college newspaper retract one of my stories to appease powerful alumni, Laura was there to keep me from changing my journalism major in protest.

Everybody on campus knows what's going on," she said. "You're being made a scapegoat here. Are you going to let them win, or are you going to go on to become a big-shot reporter and someday make a difference in the world?"

So one weekend, while visiting my parents on the farm, I didn't hesitate to race one hundred twenty miles back to campus after getting a hysterical call. Laura had been raped.

She'd accompanied a friend back to his dorm room, where he'd acted like anything but a friend. His roommate and other chums walked in just as the crime was being consummated and hooted with glee.

She screamed for their help, and wrapped in a blanket she stumbled back to our room in tears.

The man in question insisted their act was consensual. "We both wanted it."

So for the next week, the campus police conducted interviews, including one with me in which they implied hers wasn't a "real" rape, rather a "date" rape.

"She's the most honest person I've ever known," I insisted. "I believe her."

Laura's parents got involved and called the "real" police. Sexual assault charges were filed. The man pleaded not guilty. A trial was set.

But a few weeks later, while we lay in our bunks, Laura told a different story. "Technically," the accused was innocent.

"What?" I asked.

"His friends walked in on us. I have a reputation to protect. I couldn't let people think my talk about celibacy was hogwash."

"But what about his reputation?" I asked. "You need to drop the charges before you ruin his life."

She refused, and I saw a hypocritical side to her. What I thought was righteous principle seemed a veil for selfishness.

"If you don't stop this, I will. I can't be part of such a lie."

"I don't believe you, Riley. You won't betray me."

I insisted I would; she insisted I wouldn't.

So I went back to the police and changed my statement. The case fell apart; the whole campus was abuzz about the scandal. A few months before graduation, Laura dropped out of college and my life.

I called her so many times because I didn't like the way things ended. But she either hung up the phone or didn't answer. My letters were returned unopened, marked "refused."

The split caused more pain than any of my boyfriend break-ups. I think that's why I have so few gal pals. A friendship gone bad can be a devastating thing. Because while Laura felt betrayed by me, I felt betrayed by her.

CHAPTER 7

A neighborhood liquor store beckoned on my way back to Channel 3. I didn't crave alcohol myself, though the stress of news competition has driven plenty of journalists to drink.

I was trying to snag a case of elusive Nordeast beer as a welcome home prize for Garnett. Brewed locally, it sells out soon after being unloaded from the truck—if a store is lucky enough to even score a shipment.

The temperature clock on the bank across the street showed ninety-three degrees, hot enough to make a run on cold beer. Even so, I gave a hopeful thumbs-up to the aging owner at the cash register as I walked in mouthing "Nordeast?"

Ed knew why I was there and had told me a couple of weeks earlier that deliveries were unpredictable, but he'd put a case aside for me if they got any. He smiled ruefully as he gave a big thumbs-down.

"Sorry, sweetie, nothing so far. Check back later in the week."

We chatted about neighborhood crime, particularly a recent headline in the Minneapolis newspaper that essentially told readers that, not counting all the recent murders, crime was actually down in the city.

"Reassuring, huh?" he joked.

Then, because the place was empty, and probably because he

was an old man who didn't get many chances to act macho, he showed me a small revolver he kept handy under the counter.

"Is it loaded?" The glint of metal reminded me that not long ago I weighed carrying a handgun myself for personal protection. But these days, if you want to do it nice and legal, there's lots of paperwork involved as well as firearms training. I never seemed to have time for either.

Ed's piece looked like it predated those kind of inconveniences. He flipped the cylinder open and revealed a full round of bullets.

"Ever had to pull the trigger, Ed?"

"Not in your lifetime, dearie."

"You're charming, but I'm older than you think."

"Not old enough."

We might have flirted back and forth a bit more, but we heard some commotion outside. Then an agitated woman rushed in asking if either of us owned the black pickup truck in the parking lot.

"There's a dog inside the cab. It was there when I went in the drugstore ten minutes ago and it's still there now."

We shook our heads and I followed her outside, even more aware of the heat. The temperature clock had climbed another degree and now read ninety-four. I knew her concern for the animal was valid from hearing Channel 3's veteran meteorologist annually lecture viewers that the interior of a car parked in the sun can reach a hundred and forty degrees in minutes, turning into a deathtrap for pets and children.

The woman pointed to a black-and-white mixed breed laying across the floor on the passenger side. The animal was panting uncomfortably.

The woman explained she had checked for the driver inside the corner cafe and the hardware store of the strip mall, but didn't have time to go into the other shops because she had to get back to her job. She wore a cashier's smock and looked like she might work in the drugstore down the block.

"But first, I'm calling 9-1-1," she said.

While she dialed the police, I phoned the station assignment desk, explaining the situation. I didn't own a dog myself, but had a history of turning hounds into headlines. Geographically, we were less than ten minutes from the station, so the odds were favorable a camera crew might be cruising nearby.

"Malik is out shooting weather video," Ozzie said, "I'll route him in your direction; he should be there in just a couple minutes. Keep us posted. This is the kind of real-life story Noreen prizes."

The woman relayed that police were also en route. She glanced at her watch. "I can only wait a little longer."

The animal seemed lethargic, its eyes now half closed. I opened my car trunk looking for a tire iron to break the windows on the vehicle. I found odds and ends including a sleeping bag in case I got stuck in a rural blizzard, but nothing with enough heft to break auto glass.

Suddenly Malik was peering into the cab with a camera on his shoulder. By now other shoppers were gathering to watch.

"Anybody got a baseball bat?" yelled the woman who first spotted the trouble. She looked in a mood to swing it, too.

No answer.

"Malik, where's the tripod?" I asked.

Tripods are virtually indestructible. The same can't be said for high-definition television cameras. My cell phone started buzzing, but I ignored it when I saw the station calling. Let them wait thirty seconds until we had something to report.

"We have to get the truck open," the woman insisted.

The crowd pressed closer, even more curious for a glance at the death watch inside the pickup. Even Ed, from the liquor store, pushed his way through to the front of the action. But instead of remaining part of the audience, he raised his revolver.

"Stand back." His voice wavered. The crowd moved frantically away. The first shot merely put a bullet hole in the windshield; his second shattered the side window on the truck.

I reached in, unlocked the pickup's door, and pulled out the pooch. He lay in my arms, breathing noisily.

Just then the cops arrived.

So did a live truck from Channel 3.

And everybody had a different mission.

"Who called the police?" a uniformed officer asked.

Again, no one answered.

"Noreen heard about the dog and wants a live shot for the five," the truck engineer whispered. "Something like Don't Do This At Home."

It was twenty minutes until the top of the hour when the newscast opened. I wanted to use the woman who called the cops as a live guest, but she was already gone.

And I was left holding the dog.

A bakery employee a few storefronts down brought over a pan of water, held it under the animal's chin, and we splashed its face. It took a few weak swallows, but that was all. We washed the foamy saliva from its mouth.

I noticed a tag on the collar that read "Buddy" and appeared to list a contact number. "Hey, Buddy, you hang in there."

A shopper brought back some ice from a gas station, and laid the bag across the dog's sweaty back. His eyes opened, but they looked bloodshot.

"Let's try to find the owner." I pulled out my cell phone and dialed as she read the number off the dog tag for me. No answer.

The cop motioned us over to his squad car, opened the back door and blew out some air-conditioning. I crawled in the back-seat with Buddy, and he seemed to breathe easier. We got him to sip the water again.

Just then a man in a suit, carrying a briefcase, started scream-ing, "Who smashed my pickup's windows?"

No one looked him in the eye, especially not Ed, who casually slipped back inside the liquor store to clean his gun.

By then the man noticed his dog was missing. "Hey, Buddy," he whistled. "Here, boy."

The ears on the animal seemed to twitch as the man got closer, and its eyes blinked rapidly.

His shadow fell over us. "Give me my dog." His voice was harsher than I expected from a man wearing a fancy tie. But the day was hot and so was his temper.

Now it was fifteen minutes before the newscast started. Malik was setting up a tripod in the shade of a building for my live shot. Hanging on to the mutt was awkward, but I didn't particularly want to hand him back to his owner.

"You almost killed your dog," I reminded him. I was careful to keep my voice matter-of-fact, not accusatory.

"That was an accident," he responded. "Some paperwork took longer than I expected at the bank."

More people gathered to watch the bustle, and several began to hoot when they heard his lame explanation. Classic mob mentality. The police officer waved them off, telling them animal control was en route. Then he asked the man if the pickup belonged to him.

"Yes, and I want someone charged with vandalism," he said. "Look at this mess." He waved his arms.

"May I see your vehicle registration?" the officer asked.

The man gave a snort of exasperation, then reached into the glove compartment for a piece of paper, shoving it at the officer.

"And your license, Mr. Avise?"

He flipped open his wallet, pulling out the plastic. Then he pointed to me and suggested I be held accountable for the damage.

"Some old man shot the windows out," said a member of the crowd, trying to be a helpful witness and probably hoping to get on TV. "It wasn't her fault."

I considered joining the verbal tussle, but airtime was now only ten minutes away, and I was organizing the story in my mind.

The animal control van pulled up, and a woman in coveralls opened the rear door of the vehicle while a similarly suited man took the dog from my lap. He looked in the animal's mouth and I could see its tongue was darkish-colored, rather than pink. Not a good sign.

"Just give him to me," the owner insisted. "I'll take care of him at home. I don't need all these people sticking their nose in my business."

But the animal control officers ignored him and loaded the dog into the back of their van, explaining they'd be transporting him to the University of Minnesota veterinary hospital for emergency care.

"You can follow us if you like," they told the owner.

"How about I give this to you first, Mr. Avise." The cop handed him a citation.

As the man read it, his face turned red—I couldn't tell if it was from anger or embarrassment. "Animal cruelty? What kind of joke is this? I love that dog."

I got in position for my live report, but could hear the officer lecturing the man about the hazards of leaving pets and children in cars on hot days.

I heard a "standby" in my ear, and within thirty seconds, Sophie Paulson, our news anchor, was introducing me as being in the center of a parking lot ruckus involving man's best friend.

((RILEY LIVE SHOT))
WITHIN THE PAST HALF HOUR LAW
ENFORCEMENT RESPONDED TO
A CALL ABOUT A DOG LOCKED IN
A HOT PICKUP TRUCK IN SOUTH
MINNEAPOLIS.

Malik had fed back some earlier shots of the dog trapped in the vehicle, the window exploding from gunfire, and me pulling the animal out. The producer rolled the video during my report, along with a sound bite from the animal's owner dismissing the incident as an accident.

>((RILEY CU))
>THE DOG'S NAME IS BUDDY AND
>THIS CROWD BEHIND ME IS
>ALL ROOTING FOR HIM TO PULL
>THROUGH THIS.
>
>((RILEY NAT))
>IT'S IMPORTANT TO REMEMBER
>THAT ON HOT DAYS LIKE THIS,
>MINUTES CAN MEAN DEATH INSIDE
>A SWELTERING VEHICLE. THE
>OWNER SAID HE WAS TAKING CARE
>OF SOME PAPERWORK AT THE
>BANK AND LOST TRACK OF TIME.
>
>((DOG OWNER SOT))
>THIS IS NOBODY'S BUSINESS BUT
>MY OWN. ALL YOU PEOPLE SHOULD
>JUST GO BACK TO YOUR OWN LIVES.
>
>((RILEY LIVE))
>THE OWNER—KEITH AVISE—WAS
>TICKETED FOR ANIMAL CRUELTY.

Then the director called for a split screen so Sophie could show viewers how much she also cared about animals by asking me questions.

((ANCHOR DOUBLE BOX))
RILEY, WHAT'S THE LATEST UPDATE
WITH BUDDY?

((RILEY DOUBLE BOX))
BUDDY HAS BEEN TAKEN TO THE
EMERGENCY ROOM AT THE U OF
M VETERINARY HOSPITAL AND
WE'RE AWAITING WORD ON HIS
CONDITION.

((ANCHOR DOUBLE BOX))
WELL, HERE'S HOPING BUDDY
WILL BE WELL ENOUGH TO JOIN US
LIVE HERE AT THE STATION FOR
TOMORROW'S NEWS.

When I returned to the newsroom an hour later, Noreen greeted me with a high five—a salute typically reserved if a story increases the network's lead in audience in the "overnight" ratings. We wouldn't know the actual numbers until morning, but Noreen clearly was optimistic the hot car story hooked viewers.

Right then I appreciated, rather than resented, the glass walls of her office. Usually the rest of the newsroom watched as she berated me for perceived blunders. But not tonight.

She was pleased not just because I nailed an exclusive on a piece with buzz, but because I helped save a dog, and she loved dogs. It had been a long time since Noreen had been this happy with me.

"Keep an eye on this one," she said. "Those shots of you holding the dog means we own this story."

That meant Channel 3 could air that video in prime-time promotions to suck in even more viewers for our late news. It was generally understood in the world of television news that animal stories meant ratings, and ratings meant money. Noreen championed coverage of new zoo baby bears and dolphins and heaped praise on photographers who captured video of duck families crossing the road in traffic.

"Riley, make sure our camera is there when Buddy's released from the hospital."

Just then, my cell phone vibrated. The number came from within the Minneapolis Police Department. Usually I had to hound them for information, but this call could be a response to a message I left regarding the crime scene of Kate's slaying.

"Just a minute, Noreen. This could be a break in that murder."

"We've done our job there, Riley. And I'm more than a little pissed at you for latching on to another murder, but am willing to overlook it because you enterprised this dog story."

I tilted my head, pretending I didn't know what she was talking about in regards to the homicide, but she continued to rant. "Unless there's an arrest in the killing, move on to something else. Maybe that gambling scandal with the youth sports association."

None of the newscast producers seemed eager for a homicide follow-up during the huddle that morning, but I thought they could be swayed to keep Kate's story alive if I landed a scoop. That's how I had bought time this afternoon to meet with the victim's sister at the crime scene. Unfortunately, Laura had nixed any interview idea, so I had tried reconnecting with the cops.

I answered my cell phone. "Riley Spartz here."

"Officer Paul Schultze." Instead of police homicide, the voice belonged to the street cop who responded to the dog-in-the-car call. By habit, I'd handed him my card at the scene.

"Just wanted to tell you the dog didn't make it." Somber. He sounded like he needed to share his disappointment with someone.

"Oh no, that's terrible." I tapped the side of Noreen's computer to get her attention as she checked her email. DOG DIED I mouthed while covering the phone with my hand.

"Yeah, the vet ended up having to euthanize him," the officer said. "Poor mutt."

Noreen mouthed back WHAT?

"Couldn't they do anything to help?" I scribbled DEAD DOG on the back of an envelope and handed it to Noreen.

"Apparently not. The vet says heatstroke took its toll."

"Can I do a camera interview with you about it? I know our viewers will care deeply." And so will my boss. And so did I . . . after all, I held that dying dog in my arms.

Bye Bye Buddy.

"That all has to be cleared with Chief Capacasa," he said.

"I understand."

I sure did. If anyone from the police department was going to be featured on the news, it was going to be The Chief. That is, unless the media was pushing for details concerning an excessive force allegation involving one of his officers versus an unarmed college student. The department's communications officer faced the spotlight in those types of cases.

"I appreciate the update, Officer Schultze. I'll be in touch."

"Are you talking about the dog in the car?" The words were out of Noreen's mouth before I even pressed the Off button on my phone. I nodded. "Buddy didn't make it." My stomach felt nauseous.

Noreen's lips curled. Her pride over Channel 3 playing a role in saving one of the earth's creatures had vanished. But she still had a means of revenge not available to most people.

She stuck her head out of her office. "Listen up, everyone. New lead story for ten."

CHAPTER 8

He stroked the jagged wood of the broken bat before wedging the shards against the matching half and putting it back in the trophy case.

The office wooden bat softball team had needed one more player that day, more than a year ago. They stuck him in right field and hoped no hits came anywhere near. He struck out each time at bat, never making contact with the ball.

Then came the cliché bottom of the ninth . . . tie game . . . two outs . . . a man on third . . . he was up. On the bench, he saw his teammates rolling their eyes and sighing in defeat, certain they were about to lose the game to the company marketing department.

He swung at the first pitch and heard a crack. He was more aware the bat had splintered than that the hit was fair. His colleagues screamed for him to run.

The blooping line drive bounced off the shortstop's glove and rolled to the second baseman, who also bobbled it. Even with the errors, he barely beat the throw to first, but by then the man on third had scored.

That's how he won the game. Or how his opponents lost it. And just as a winning pitcher is awarded the game ball, he was presented with the victory bat . . . or what was left of it. He didn't care it was broken, that flaw mirrored him. The bat was wounded on the outside like he was wounded on the inside. Both shattered. One physically, the other emotionally.

And each time he attacked a woman with the remains of it, his swing felt like a home run. If he concentrated, he could still make the cheers echo in his ears while they bled.

So far, he was playing four for four. He wished he could brag about his record like other men did in sports bars, but that would have to wait until he testified in court, impressing jurors and journalists with his brilliance. Then off to prison, where his swagger would be envied by other inmates who served their time as nobodies.

He had little doubt that, unless he stopped, his streak would end in arrest and he would spend the rest of his life behind bars.

But he did not want to stop, because for the first time in a long time, he was enjoying life.

CHAPTER 9

S uch a shame," muttered Dr. Howard Stang, the veterinarian who treated Buddy at the university's animal hospital emergency room. He wouldn't let me see the dog's body, but he did a camera interview, talking about how minutes in a hot car can put a pet through hell.

"Especially when you're talking about a black vehicle on black asphalt." He raised his hands helplessly, hunching up his shoulders. "Not a lot of leeway there with the science."

"When I last saw him," I said, "I thought I was covering a story about rescue and survival."

Dr. Stang shook his head. "Buddy's internal body temperature was still one hundred and eight degrees by the time he reached the ER. He was vomiting and clearly in distress. We inserted an IV into his bloodstream, but it soon became clear he was suffering a painful, lingering death."

"Nothing could be done?" I asked.

"I've autopsied dogs that died of heatstroke before. I know what I'll find. Buddy's organs will have turned to soup."

Every year pets, and even children, die in hot cars. That night Buddy became the poster dog for all of them in Minnesota. It wasn't the first time viewers were outraged over the death of an animal, but it was the first time Channel 3's website crashed because of all the angry audience comments.

THAT OWNER OUGHT TO BE FRIED.
NO WAY TO TREAT MAN'S BEST FRIEND.
DOG DAYS SHOULDN'T BE DYING DAYS.

I'd given Buddy's owner another chance to comment, but he'd declined. Officially, his home phone was unlisted, but I still had the number from Buddy's dog tag stored on my cell phone from that call attempt in the parking lot. When I finally reached Keith Avise, he'd already heard the news about his dog's demise.

"What's done's done," he said. "It was an accident. Don't call me again."

Then he hung up.

That cavalier response was only part of the reason neighbors toilet papered his house that night. They sent a photo of the deed to our weather center, hoping it would be used as a backdrop for the forecast. But the meteorologist passed, not wanting to get involved in controversy, and selected a photo of a birthday boy turning two, playing under a garden sprinkler.

When Malik and I spoke to Minneapolis police chief Vince Capacasa that night it became clear justice might not necessarily be served. Leaving a dog unattended in a parked car is only a petty misdemeanor in Minnesota, so under that law, the most Buddy's owner could receive was a twenty-five-dollar fine.

No jail time.

"You're kidding me, Chief."

"Check with the county attorney if you don't believe me."

"Viewers might have a hard time understanding such mild punishment."

"Then go to the county's top prosecutor and see what she says. Sure, prosecutors could force the issue and try to up it to felony animal cruelty, that could mean a fine of thousands of dollars, maybe even years in jail. But it also means less time for other legal cases. Law is about priorities."

The courthouse criminal backlog was well known. And I knew what the chief was really hinting at was that the lawyers were unlikely to use the F-word—felony—when the victim was an animal.

The public would certainly be split. Some would urge maximum justice for Buddy. But others might envision themselves in the same situation: What if they messed up and their pet died? Would they want the legal book thrown at them?

"Thanks, Chief. Anything else you'd like to add?"

"We here at the Minneapolis Police Department mourn the loss of Buddy, and regret there aren't more teeth in our law."

A really smooth sound bite. But I wasn't so naive that I didn't realize that the chief also understood the power of our video. He wanted to play good cop, and let the county attorney come off as the bad cop.

To be honest, Chief Capacasa and I have had a history of clashes over crime coverage. He even had me handcuffed once, later dismissing it as "just business." And while he doesn't realize I know it, the word on the street is that anybody in blue who tickets me gets a day off duty, off the books. So I always keep a close eye on my speedometer whenever I'm behind the wheel within city limits.

Because of our past, I probably should have simply thanked him for his insight and headed back to the station. After all, we both came out winners. I snagged a decent sound bite for the news and he got to show the taxpayers of Minneapolis that he cares about justice for dead dogs.

Instead, I brought up Kate's homicide because it seemed unlikely I'd get another chance with a camera rolling and because nobody from the department had returned my phone call. I knew the camera was still hot because Malik knew better than to turn it off until I specifically said "We're done here." We've worked together long enough to have a system to avoid interview regrets.

"So, Chief, while we're here, anything new on the Kate Warner investigation?"

"When there is, we'll let you know."

I sensed he wanted to snarl, but police work involves balancing politics as well as chasing criminals. The city was tracking more murders this year than anytime since 1995 when the *New York Times* dubbed the city "Murderapolis." Capacasa understood he better watch his mouth.

"Which of your homicide teams sketched the chalk fairy at the murder scene?" I asked.

His eyes narrowed at my audacity in implying a mistake might have been made in the investigation. More likely, he was angry because I knew about the mistake and he had no idea who my source was.

Moments like this always reminded me that his name sounded like a mafia cousin. Vinnie Capacasa. That name resonated mob muscle. I didn't actually expect an answer to my question; I just wanted him to know I was plugged into the case. Not surprisingly, he wanted to make it clear who was in charge.

"That homicide remains an active case which can't be commented on. Doing so could jeopardize the investigation."

"But Chief, couldn't the case already be jeopardized if the crime scene's been contaminated by your people? Have your guys given the defense a potential out?"

That's when he stood up and walked away with the station's high-priced wireless microphone still clipped handily to his lapel.

"Whoo, Chief," Malik yelled. "Need the mic back."

Chief Capacasa ripped it off, flinging the electronic device to the floor . . . as if he was throwing down a gauntlet. And even though he never looked back, we both knew he was.

CHAPTER 10

Lassie was the world's most famous collie.

Rin Tin Tin, the most celebrated German shepherd.

I'd always considered Old Yeller the most notable of dead dogs, until I cried my eyes out reading *Marley and Me*.

But then Buddy came along. And live, on the air, I lost it.

The anchors led the newscast with how journalists prefer to lead with good news and how unfortunate it is when good news turns bad.

Then they tossed to me to explain to viewers what they were talking about.

I'd scripted my story to read smoothly on the teleprompter. The narrow column of copy times out to a second a line to make it easy to gauge story length, and so the anchor's eyes don't shift back and forth. My piece should have been routine.

((RILEY LIVE))
EARLIER TONIGHT, I TOLD YOU
HOW A DOG NAMED BUDDY WAS
RESCUED FROM A HOT PICKUP
TRUCK. SO MANY OF YOU CALLED
THE STATION ROOTING FOR HIM . . .

Just then my throat got tight and I started choking up.

> ((RILEY LIVE))
> BUT NEWS STORIES DON'T ALWAYS
> END THE WAY WE WANT . . .

My voice got raspy. It wasn't a question of knowing what to say—I had a script—it was getting the words out. The harder I tried to enunciate the more constricted my speech became.

> ((RILEY LIVE))
> TONIGHT I HAVE TO REPORT
> THAT BUDDY . . . THAT BUDDY . . .
> BUDDY . . . BUDDY HAS DIED.

During the course of my news career, I must have reported a hundred grievous deaths of people—young and old, rich and poor. Most of them decent folks who didn't deserve their lives to end violently.

Never once did I break down on the air.

But unlike Buddy, I hadn't held any of those victims in my arms hours before their demise. The memory of his scratchy fur against my chin suddenly reminded me of Shep, a German shepherd who'd risked his life to save mine, and was now a star member of the police K-9 unit. And I couldn't help thinking, What if Shep had died?

By then I was crying too hard to talk.

In my earpiece, I heard the producer tell the director to kill my mic and cut back to the anchors. Sophie jumped in to finish reading my story about how Buddy's official cause of death was heatstroke.

CHAPTER 11

The next morning, all of Channel 3 gasped when they saw how many viewers had essentially watched Buddy's obituary and my meltdown the night before. The ratings resembled the days before cable TV and the Internet shrunk network audiences.

Television stations realize they can't be first every day. Their measure of success is how well they retain their network lead-in audience. If they build on that viewership, ad revenue increases and everyone keeps their jobs. But if the numbers reflect a significant drop-off, that means trouble. And Channel 3 had shown a pattern of problems lately.

So at the assignment meeting that morning, Noreen reveled in the numbers as concrete proof of her superior news instincts and management skill.

"Keep the Buddy story alive," she ordered. "Viewers will be expecting a follow-up report tonight. Don't disappoint them."

No one mentioned my blubbering on the set. All of Channel 3 seemed embarrassed by my behavior. My hope was that they had made a pact never to mention my on-air collapse again.

After the meeting, I followed Noreen back to her office to try to keep Kate's homicide on her radar. My hunch was we could have a more candid conversation behind closed doors.

"I'll check with the county attorney this morning, Noreen, and see if she anticipates any harsher charges against Buddy's owner."

Either way, we could pass that off as news.

"I'm not going to ask what happened last night," Noreen said, "You just need to assure me you're going to be able to hold it together on this story."

"I can't explain it either, but it won't happen again. Ever."

I suspected that because she was an animal lover, Noreen was going easier on me than she might have otherwise. I thanked her for being so understanding. It wasn't a line I ever expected to say to her, because she'd never been understanding before. Our track record regarding job evaluations was shaky.

She nodded in agreement and impatience, clearly wanting me to move along so she could begin her real boss business of running the newsroom.

"I'm getting the feeling there might be something unusual going on with the Kate Warner murder," I said. "I want to dig around a little more."

I didn't go into the specifics of the chalk fairy, because I generally don't like getting news directors all fired up over a specific story element unless I know it's reportable. Especially these days during media struggles. TV managers don't have much of an attention span. They want things NOW.

No time for hope; only time for results. And if I bring up an intriguing prospect, but don't deliver . . . that gets labeled failure fast.

So Noreen essentially reminded me of her long-held news theory that dead dogs often deliver more viewers than dead people.

"You show me how that murder will improve our household numbers or demographic ratings and I'm happy to revisit this discussion, but our research shows that viewers are tired of hearing about so much crime. If you find an obvious news development, such as an arrest, then we'll talk."

So I silently counted to three, as in Channel 3, thanked her for her time, and walked down to the Hennepin County Government Center to talk to the county attorney about options for prosecuting Buddy's owner.

After a few minutes of predictable chitchat about how the news was going downhill, it was clear that Melissa Kreimer, unlike my boss, definitely cared more about dead people than dead dogs. I didn't mention that voters and viewers might be more inclined to agree with Noreen, but it was clear the police chief had a better grasp on how to manipulate the media than did the county attorney.

"The key to the state's animal cruelty laws are the words 'intentionally violates,'" Kreimer said. "I don't think for a minute this man intended to kill his dog. That's why we have a separate law about leaving unattended pets in a motor vehicle. And that's the law most applicable in this case."

She agreed to meet me downstairs in the building atrium for a quick question-answer on camera. Most television interviews in the building were done there rather than having news crews taking all the equipment upstairs through security. Malik had already set up the tripod, and natural light from the overhead windows made artificial lighting unnecessary.

Kreimer gave me a usable sound bite of how fair laws balance priorities between society and Buddy's owner.

"While the monetary fine seems minimal in this case," she said, "let's keep in mind the owner also has to pay to repair his vehicle windows, and the cost for transportation and medical care for the animal. Plus, he no longer has a dog."

Maybe all that was enough suffering for Keith Avise, but my gut told me the county attorney might be in for a surprise when she heard from the general public. Kreimer didn't seem familiar with recent world outrage when a British woman dumped a cat in a garbage can explaining, "It's just a cat."

As much as I disagreed with Noreen about many of her news

decisions, they often proved canny. I imagined her anchor lead-in on my story.

> ((ANCHOR CU))
> AUTHORITIES SAY BUDDY WAS
> *JUST* A DOG AND HIS DEATH IS
> *ONLY* A PETTY MISDEMEANOR . . .
> BUT OUR PEOPLE-ON-THE-STREET
> INTERVIEWS SHOW A DIFFERENT
> PERSPECTIVE.

Because of staff cuts, the assignment desk was starting to keep closer tabs on those of us who work in the field. They constantly want to know *where* we are *when* and *who* we are doing *what* with while chasing stories. To be a good news trooper, I called to report that my interview was finished, my photographer clear. Ozzie immediately dispatched Malik to shoot a jackknifed semi that was clogging up traffic on the freeway.

Then he dropped a whammy and told me that someone had posted my Buddy blubbering episode on YouTube last night.

"You've got nearly 100,000 hits." He kept his voice neutral, but I couldn't imagine the station would be pleased. "I just wanted to warn you before you heard the news from someone else."

"Like Noreen?"

"Yeah."

"Is she looking for me?"

"Waiting for you."

"I'll grab an early lunch."

Ozzie gave me the go-ahead because even if breaking news was lacking, we were still allowed to break for lunch. I actually didn't feel like eating, but I couldn't face my station colleagues just then. Most of the staff would be constantly refreshing their computer screens to keep track of my YouTube hits. Getting the newscasts on the air might be as challenging as when MTV first came along and instead of writing scripts, the news producers were glued to Billy Joel and Michael Jackson.

I swung by Ed's liquor store to see if he was facing any fallout from his gun wielding antics in the parking lot as we tried to save Buddy.

"Nope, sweetie, most folks don't know me, and those that do, well, it's actually helping my reputation as a tough guy. Ain't none of them going to mess with me, though I don't ever expect to pull that trigger again."

If he'd seen my debacle covering Buddy's death, he didn't mention it, though he had heard that the dog didn't survive and shared some harsh words about his owner not suitable for television audiences.

"He had some similar things to say about me and the media when I tried to land an interview," I said.

Ed laughed. "Nothing you haven't heard before on the job." He reached under the counter. "Here's something to improve your spirits." He pulled out a case of Nordeast beer. "Found a few on the truck this morning."

I thanked Ed for watching out for me, and imagined how cheered Garnett would be to pop the cap off a cold bottle during his visit. Offhand, I couldn't think of any movie quotes concerning beer, but I was sure he could.

I still didn't want to head back to Channel 3, so I parked near Lake of the Isles and looked out over the water, forcing myself to concentrate on pleasant matters in life. But for those of us in the news business, disagreeable issues come more naturally to mind. Plenty of Canada geese hobbled and honked along the shore, and some even approached my vehicle to hiss. I felt lectured by angry birds.

My cell phone rang. It was Malik. "Turn on the radio."

Almost immediately, I wished I hadn't.

CHAPTER 12

The host of the top-rated radio talk show in the Twin Cities was inviting listeners to call in and vote on whether my sobbing live on the air was "human" or "unprofessional."

He was urging people to view it on YouTube if they hadn't been watching our news the night before, but for those without a computer handy, he gave a pretty vivid description and played the audio over the radio airwaves.

"Those of you familiar with the local media scene will recognize Channel 3's Riley Spartz as one tough news cookie. She can have bullets flying over her head and she won't cry. So what's up here? A couple days ago she covered a woman's murder. No tears there. But now, bawling like a baby."

He opened the phone lines, and took the first call.

"I was happy she showed some emotion," an older-sounding woman said. "Sometimes I get the feeling that those reporters, they don't really care about the stories they cover. For them, it's just a paycheck."

"Yes, but this particular reporter has covered a lot of crime stories," the host said. "And we haven't seen her show such passion for those victims. Does a dog deserve tears more than, say, a missing child? Or a murdered babysitter?"

"Well, you have a point there," she conceded.

He then took another call. "Very unprofessional," a man said. "She must have been faking it for ratings."

"Interesting theory," the host said. "Next caller."

"I wonder if she might have been on drugs," a younger woman said. "Lots of times addicts can't control their emotions. I hope the station has her drug tested before they put her on the air again."

Just then my cell phone rang and my parent's southern Minnesota phone number came up on my screen. That particular radio signal could be heard all the way down to the farm. So, certain that they were listening, I let their call roll to voice mail. Besides needing a break from my news cohorts, I couldn't face my family at that moment.

The host kept up more of the same, so I reached for the radio knob to find another station. Music, not talk. Suddenly I stopped because the next voice I heard sounded very familiar.

"You people have got nothing better to do than criticize other people who are doing the best they can. Well, I'm Riley Spartz's mother, and I want to tell you that she's the finest daughter any parents could ask for. And we are so proud of her. Why, when she was a little girl—"

I hit the radio Off button. Burying my face in a newspaper I found on the backseat of the car, I closed my eyes and tried to cry for Kate. But couldn't.

I honked my car horn twice and saw the geese scatter, but got no real satisfaction from their bewilderment. I had even more of a reason to avoid returning to work now, because if Malik knew of the radio broadcast, so did the rest of the newsroom.

I needed space, not hooting.

To kill time, I drove toward Kate's neighborhood—the opposite direction from Channel 3. I was hoping proximity might bring answers, but the street seemed quiet and ordinary except for the plywood still nailed across the front window of her house.

Then I played back events from the day of the murder and got an idea for a follow-up story. This would give me something to talk about when Noreen brought up the radio show.

"I've requested the 9-1-1 call from the homicide, Noreen. The transcript might yield something."

"Hardly," she snorted.

Broadcasting 911 tapes used to be routine for Minnesota news organizations and added drama to a story, be it a murder, tornado, or bridge collapse.

"If you'd checked with me first, Riley, I'd have told you not to even bother."

She was referring to a law change fifteen years earlier that made the actual audio portion of 911 calls private. The change was due to local news stations' repeated broadcasts of a father's distraught call after discovering his son had murdered their entire family. The audio was uncomfortable to hear. But that didn't stop radio or TV channels from playing it over and over.

Callers now need to sign media releases before their voices can be aired. Even if they say yes, by the time all the details are sorted out and permissions granted, the news value is usually nil.

"I'd still like to learn more about the circumstances of how her body was discovered, Noreen. The cops are keeping quiet about that."

As soon as I got back to my desk after being reamed on the radio, I had emailed a formal release application to the Minneapolis police public information officer. "Under the Minnesota Data Practices Law, I am requesting the 911 records regarding the murder of Kate Warner." To speed things up, I included the date, address, and approximate time the homicide was reported.

It was all I could think of to take my mind off Buddy. An hour later, I called the police PIO to make sure he'd seen the 911 request.

"Yeah, I have it right here, Ms. Spartz, but you know we have ten days to respond to any public records request."

His smart-aleck tone made me want to throw the phone against the floor, but I stayed cool. "That may be the letter of the law. But you and I both know it's not the spirit. The ten-day clause was designed for onerous demands seeking hundreds of pages of documents needing to be redacted. What I'm asking for is simple, and clearly public."

"Yes, but someone needs to listen to the call and transcribe it. That takes time on our end. And may well cost you money."

"Channel 3 is willing to pay all reasonable expenses, but my bet is that the homicide team has already processed the call. All you probably need to do is pull the page from the file."

"I suppose you expect it today." He spoke slow and heavy, like my request was a major burden.

"If it's not too much trouble." I reminded him a killer was running loose and media attention might help solve the case.

"I'll have to get back to you."

That meant he was going to check with the chief. While I prepared myself for a ten-day wait, I called the farm. My parents had also left a message on my office phone bewailing the radio show's exploitation of my live shot. If I didn't return their call, they'd visit me. Or worse, they'd visit the radio station and end up as talk-show guests.

After five rings, I was almost ready to give up when my mother picked up the phone. "Riley, we're so glad to hear from you. We've been worried."

"Worried? What do you have to worry about, Mom?"

She and Dad were retired. Church and lunch were the highlights of their day. For city folks, dinner might rank first, but living on a farm is all about the noon meal.

"Well, you of course, Riley. We watched your story last night. We know how disheartened you must be. We just want you to know we're here for you."

"Absolutely," I heard my dad pitch in. "And we know just the thing to cheer you up."

I hated even thinking what they might have in mind. "I'm fine," I insisted. "Everything I need I have. The only thing I'm ever lacking is a good story."

"A puppy!" they both yelled together. "Kloeckner's dog just had a litter."

I spent the next ten minutes reminding my parents that I worked full-time in a demanding job with unpredictable hours, and trying to convince them that if they drove two hours from the farm to surprise me with a puppy on my doorstep I would never forgive them.

They were the ones who needed canine company. Their old farm dog, Lucky, had gone to the big doghouse in the sky. But they claimed they missed him too much to replace him so soon.

But all farms need yard dogs to bark an alarm when a stranger drives in and to keep small animals like skunks and groundhogs away from the main house.

"You get yourselves a puppy," I said, "and I'll come visit. I promise."

CHAPTER 13

My email showed a message from the Minneapolis Police Department telling me they had complied with my data request. I was confused to find transcripts of not one, but two 911 calls.

The first came at 11:36 AM.

Caller: "Someone is breaking into my neighbor's house. He threw a chair through the window. Now he's climbing inside. Hurry."

Dispatcher: "You're saying an intruder is in your neighbor's house?"

Caller: "Yes. Please hurry."

Dispatcher: "Is anyone else home there?"

Caller: "Possibly. Her name is Kate. She works at home but lives alone. He's still inside."

The dispatcher then went on to check the address of the break-in, assure the caller that a squad was being dispatched, and get the neighbor's name. Until then, I hadn't even known if the caller was male or female.

Caller: "My name is Melinda Gordon. I'm very worried. I can't believe this is happening in broad daylight. Please hurry."

Dispatcher: "I'd like you to stay on the line with me until officers arrive. Let me know if you see the suspect leave."

Caller: "Do you want his license plate number?"

Dispatcher: "Can you see his vehicle?"

Caller: "Yes, it's a reddish-brown SUV, parked on the street in from of her house and has Minnesota plates."

The caller then recited a short series of numbers and letters.

The dispatcher repeated them for confirmation.

Caller: "I hear a siren. I see a police car."

Dispatcher: "Thank you for calling in your information. I'm going to disconnect now."

By the time Malik and I had arrived at the crime scene, the street was lined with various law enforcement vehicles and other media. I didn't recall seeing that particular SUV, but it might not have registered in my mind with all the commotion. I wondered why the police hadn't perp-walked a cuffed suspect out the door in front of all the cameras that day. That usually makes the public feel safer.

I turned to the next transcript and got some insight.

The second call came at 11:38 AM, two minutes after the first, obviously answered by another dispatcher.

Caller: "Help. I need an ambulance. My girlfriend needs help. I think she's dead."

The dispatcher confirmed that the emergency was happening at a specific address because 911 technology automatically pulls up metro street addresses on the screen along with homeowner information.

Caller: "I don't know the exact address. I just know it's near West Diamond Lake Road and Pillsbury Avenue South. You got to send an ambulance, but it might be too late already. I'm sure it's—"

Dispatcher: "What is your name, sir?"

Caller: "My name is— Wait, I hear someone outside. I wonder if the man who attacked her is still here—"

The transcript ended there, but if I ever got access to the actual audio, I'd expect to hear some background noise like "Police, freeze, hands in the air" before the phone was hung up.

• • •

I called up some file tape of the murder scene on my computer screen and the only vehicle in the driveway was the medical examiner van. No reddish-brown SUV parked anywhere along the street. By the time Malik and I had arrived, the male caller on the phone had apparently been released by police and left the scene or been hauled off to jail and had his vehicle towed.

"Can you pop a name and address for me?" I handed Lee Xiong, Channel 3's resident computer genius, a sheet of paper with the license plate number.

"I'm very busy."

He was always busy. As more news staff were cut, his duties increased. Computer-assisted reporting for my investigative stories was a small fraction of his job description; most of his time was now spent managing the station's website and figuring how to score online hits—an Internet version of ratings that could be used for a new source of ad revenue. The latest media trend was encouraging viewer participation with story comments via computer. Xiong was also responsible for monitoring those comments for slander and profanity. No wonder he was very busy.

"The guy could be a murderer." Women were often murdered by boyfriends. So it was worth a check. "Could be a new lead story for six."

Xiong preferred communicating by email or phone, not face-to-face. People made him uncomfortable. It wasn't often he mustered the nerve for a date, though I frequently reminded him that all he had to do to get women interested socially was to tell them he worked in TV news. His generation of Hmong, raised in the United States, was caught between courtship cultures.

"You don't have to be on the air yourself," I'd assure him. "They'll settle for you telling them what the rest of us are really like off camera. Hey, I trust your discretion."

I could have simply sent him an email with my instructions, but when I had time, I figured making Xiong talk to me directly was good training for him. As well as getting my request bumped to the top of the pile to speed my departure. But instead of looking grateful, he looked like he'd do anything to make me gone.

"Check back in five minutes," he said.

"Check by in five minutes, *Riley*," I said. "Women like it when you call them by name."

So he repeated himself for practice and I gave him space.

He had built a big-brotherish computer database of Minnesota license plate numbers, driver's licenses, hunting and fishing licenses, and all sorts of other public data on private citizens. If that didn't find me the boyfriend's name, I'd go back to the cops and push the issue. My sense was that names of 911 callers were public information unless they came from a confidential informant or a sexual assault victim.

Because I told Xiong I'd be out in the field, he texted me the name and address registered to the vehicle. Charles Heyden. But that wasn't my first stop. I drove to Kate's neighborhood to check out the house from where the first call to police came.

I remembered the stucco two-story with birch trees in the front yard from the murder day. Knocking, but getting no answer. Melinda Gordon must not have wanted to talk to the media then, but might have changed her mind since. I always give witnesses the benefit of the doubt.

This time, it might have helped that I didn't have a cameraman following me. A pretty woman about ten years younger than me was in the front yard raking leaves while a baby boy bounced in a springy chair.

I introduced myself with a media pass and explained I'd like to talk to her about her 911 call. "I have a copy of the transcript and know all about the man crashing the chair though the window. I'd like to compliment you on how composed you stayed on the line with police during the whole ordeal."

She seemed a little uneasy talking to me and looked back and forth down the block to see if anyone might be watching us. I suggested perhaps we move inside. To my surprise, she agreed.

Once in the kitchen, Melinda handed baby Johnny over to me and poured us each a cold drink from the refrigerator. Johnny held a sippy cup with chubby fingers and gummed a soda cracker. I made a goo-goo face at him to loosen things up with his mom.

"So, Melinda, what happened at Kate's after the police arrived?"

"Two squads arrived within seconds of each other. One blocked the man's car so he couldn't back out of the driveway. Both officers drew guns and crouched by the broken window. They jumped inside and I couldn't see anything else. It was very dramatic. Just like on TV. Oh sorry, I didn't mean anything by that."

I waved her off just as the phone rang. She checked the caller ID and rolled her eyes before saying, "Hello." After listening briefly, she replied, "Just company. I'll call you back later." Another pause, and I heard her say, "I understand. Thanks." Then she hung up.

"That was my mother-in-law," she explained. "She wanted to know who was visiting."

Mine was the only vehicle parked near their house. "How would she know you had a guest?"

"She lives next door," she said, without much enthusiasm.

"You moved next to your mother-in-law?" I asked.

She shook her head. "We lived here first. She moved next to us. Every time we have company, she calls to ask who."

"That could be annoying."

"Sometimes she wants to come over and meet them." She gave me a warning look.

I wrinkled my nose and shook my head. She'd probably bring a pan of bars, and want to hear about life in the world of television news. As much as I craved a warm brownie, that wasn't a conversation I enjoyed much these days. Especially not with amateurs.

"Every time the baby cries, she calls to say, 'I hear Johnny. What's wrong now?'"

Johnny seemed content in my arms. Any chance I had to hug a baby these days, I took. Now I felt pressure not to disturb him or grandma would show up demanding an explanation.

"Just now she used the excuse that she wanted to make sure I was safe. After what happened to Kate."

"Under the circumstances," I said, "her concern might be understandable." I decided to get back to business. "What about the man inside Kate's house? Did you see him leave?"

"Yes, about ten or fifteen minutes later the door opened and he came out."

"Was he handcuffed?"

"No, but one of the cops escorted him to his vehicle. The squad pulled away and the SUV followed him. Pretty soon more cops showed up, then the media."

"I was in that crowd that day." I didn't mention her not answering the door.

"My mother-in-law had been shopping and missed all the initial excitement. She was disappointed she didn't get to be the one to call 9-1-1."

"Let's hope she never has to."

Just then Johnny started squirming, then screaming. I handed him back to mom, who held him against her shoulder and patted his back.

"Hurry, Melinda, calm him before grandma surprises us."

She laughed. "You don't believe me, do you? Just watch."

"Did she surprise you when she moved in?"

"We had some warning. Our neighbor's house went into foreclosure soon after I became pregnant. My husband's mom insisted it was an omen. He convinced me she would make our life easier because he's an attorney and often works late hours and travels."

My parents lived a comfortable hundred-plus miles away. I tried to imagine us separated by only twenty yards and a couple of walls. Luckily they wouldn't ever consider moving from the farm. My folks were determined to die on that land. As for family meddling, all I had to endure was an occasional surprise visit because they didn't want to call ahead and be a "bother."

Now I had to worry about them bringing a dog along.

The doorbell rang. We could see an older woman standing outside holding a plate of cookies. "I hear Johnny."

She traded the plate for the baby, who quieted almost immediately. Then she sat down and made herself comfortable. Melinda introduced us and when Cheryl Gordon learned I worked in news, she wanted to know more. Especially about her neighbor's murder.

"So unsettling," she said. "I never dreamed such a horrible thing could happen when I moved onto this street. It's important we all stay vigilant." She looked at her daughter-in-law.

It occurred to me that, since Cheryl kept tabs on the block, she might have noticed anything unusual at Kate's house before the murder.

"You seem quite observant," I said. "You probably could have been a reporter yourself." She looked thrilled with the compliment. "How well did you know Kate?" I didn't share that I had a past connection with the family. That wasn't the kind of gossip I wanted spread around the neighborhood.

"We always said hello at the mailbox," she said. I nodded to keep encouraging her. "She was excited anytime she received a paycheck. And she'd just been out on a few dates with a young man named Chuck."

I checked the text message on my cell phone. CHARLES HEYDEN.

CHAPTER 14

Just as Kate's house didn't look like the kind of place a homicide would happen, her boyfriend's house didn't look like the kind of place a killer would live. It oozed ordinary rather than eerie.

My plan was to do a drive-by, not a door-knock, but the garage was open and sure enough, the vehicle inside had the correct license plate.

"Can you run a criminal background check, Xiong?"

I didn't want to waltz into the den of a possible killer without knowing whether he'd ever been charged with any violent crimes.

Journalists don't have the ability to search criminal records nationwide—you need a friendly cop for that kind of favor, real friendly, because running that kind of check leaves a trace and could get sources in trouble later as leaks if they can't justify the inquiry.

But statewide, Xiong assured me, the guy came up clean.

I parked one block down, so as not to look too obvious. Then I texted Malik the address with a message that I'd call him in an hour. This way, if I vanished, he'd know where to hunt first.

My knuckles were inches from the door when it opened. I stumbled to avoid hitting a tall man in the chest.

"What do you want?" He must have watched me walk up the driveway and seemed to think I was there to sell him something.

"Hello, Mr. Heyden, I've come to talk about your friend Kate and tell you how sorry I am about her death." I started to introduce myself as a reporter, but that wasn't necessary.

"I watch enough TV to know who you are." I gave a silent kudos to the Channel 3 promotion department when he continued with, "You're that reporter they thought killed the gossip guy."

Few people had the brazenness to bring up that episode straight to my face. "You're right. They did arrest me. Ends up, they were mistaken."

He shrugged like maybe he believed me or maybe not. "How'd you find me?" He seemed a little suspicious. "Did the cops tell you?"

"Police aren't talking much. I got your license plate from a witness, then your name came easy. I thought you might appreciate some company."

"I guess. You can call me Chuck." Chuck stuck his head out the door, like he was checking to make sure I was alone. He motioned for me to come inside. "Let's talk in here where the game's on."

My gut sensed he wanted information from me as much I did from him. So I followed him inside. That move might have been a bit reckless, but he seemed to think me capable of murder, so that might put us on par with each other because my first impression was he might be one of those killers the neighbors later describe as "quiet."

His living room resembled a north woods cabin except for the far wall, which had a big-screen television tuned to a Twins game at the team's new stadium. I hadn't been out to the field yet, so was more curious about the ballpark layout than the score.

Chuck moved a laptop computer from the couch to make room for me.

"So, Chuck, what do you do for work?" Usually a safe opening question.

"I'm a technical writer," he said. "I clarify jargon."

"So what kind of things do you write?"

He explained he worked at home writing annual reports and instruction manuals for several corporate and government clients.

"Some assembly required, huh?" I said. But he didn't react to the joke.

My plan was to let him speak next, but he was apparently busy watching baseball and pressing buttons on an unconventional remote control. So after a couple minutes of silence, I decided to try sympathizing to gain his attention.

"I hear you found Kate's body. That must have been rough."

"Wish I hadn't."

"Do you remember much?"

"I'm trying not to."

A man of few words. I nudged him toward conversation, so Chuck finally offered an explanation. "She didn't answer when I knocked, and I would have just left, except I glanced through the window along the top of the door."

Sure enough, he was tall enough to sneak a peak without looking like he was casing the place.

"She was lying on the floor."

I paused to see if he'd add anything, but he didn't. "Door unlocked?" I asked, not letting on I already knew where his story was headed.

"Nope." He shook his head. "I crashed through the front window with a patio chair. I wanted to check if she was still alive. But she wasn't, so I called the cops. And waited. Some of them think I did it."

"Really?" That allowed me to play a card that few other journalists could. "I know what that's like. I even spent a night behind bars, so I understand better than most folks that cops can make mistakes."

"Your case was all over the news," he said.

"So we sort of have something in common. Have they read you your rights yet? You know, you have the right to remain silent . . . all that stuff?"

"Nope."

"They're probably holding off as long as they can. Once they do that makes it harder for the police to question you without an attorney."

Chuck nodded again, like he was making mental notes. "You got an attorney yet?" I asked. "I know a pretty good one."

"Nope, I thought that would just make me look more guilty. They wanted to question me downtown, away from the scene. Mostly about where I was during the time Kate was killed."

"So where were you?"

"Watching TV."

"Here, at home?"

"Yeah."

"Anybody with you?"

"Nope."

That was a bummer of an alibi.

I helped myself to a bowl of pretzels on an end table to avoiding having to respond further. While I chewed, I thought.

I could see why investigators were looking at him as a suspect. He knew the victim. That's usually the case in homicides. And sometimes smart killers "find" the body. It's a convenient way to explain how their DNA wound up at the crime scene.

Chuck seemed like he might be one of those killers who are better thinkers than talkers, possibly shrewd enough to have thought this whole scenario through. Although his next statement changed my mind about his judgment.

"They also wanted my fingerprints and saliva. That way they could eliminate me as the killer."

That would also make it easier to convict him without having

to go through the bother of a subpoena, but I refrained from saying that out loud.

"What was Kate like?" I asked.

Chuck didn't answer right away. Maybe because the question
was complicated or maybe because the Twins and White Sox
were now tied.

"She was a nice enough girl," he said.

I was hoping for something a little more personal, but the
term "boyfriend" might have been an exaggeration regarding
him. He explained that they had met a few weeks earlier while
standing in line at the post office. He was buying stamps and
she was mailing a large padded envelope. They both worked at
home, so they had that in common.

"Usually nice girls don't pay much attention to me." He had a
receding hairline and a paunchy waistline. "But now that she's
dead, I kind of wish we hadn't met. Wasn't worth the trouble."

Just then Chuck reached over and pressed the remote again.
His action didn't affect the TV channel or volume, but gave me a
way to change the subject away from murder.

"What are you doing with that thing?" I asked.

"Oh, this? I forgot to ask how old you are."

"What's that got to do with anything?"

"You're a visitor. They want to know how old you are. I already punched in that you're female."

A few seconds passed before I understood that I was staring
at one of the most powerful tools of modern television: a people
meter.

I'd never actually seen one before, and it was all I could do
to refrain from grabbing it and switching it to Channel 3. Then
I realized the remote only confirmed *who* was watching; the
small black box hooked directly to the television confirmed *what*
was being watched. Networks, TV stations, and advertisers paid
dearly for that combination of ratings data.

In the Twin Cities, barely six hundred people meters repre-
sented the viewing habits of 3.5 million people. How Chuck
Heyden landed in this secret society of Nielsen families, I didn't
know; but for a TV reporter, meeting him was like winning the
ratings lottery.

So to keep tight, I told him my age. Then casually asked if we
could see what else was on TV, maybe even check Channel 3.

"No, I want the game."

Chuck explained that when he watched television, every fifteen minutes he had to press an OK button to verify he was still
watching.

If more than forty minutes passed without him confirming,
red lights flashed rapidly.

He signed a two-year contract last fall to divulge his male TV
viewing habits, and for such privileged information, Nielsen paid
him twenty-five bucks a month.

"Don't tell them I told you any of this," he said. "We're supposed to keep quiet."

"I know. I know. Believe me, they'll never hear from me."

So I conspired against Nielsen, and promised to keep in touch
about Kate's murder. Whether he was guilty or not, meeting him
was going to make Channel 3 an overnight news sensation. Just
as soon as I got back to the station and told Noreen.

"You what?" she screamed. "You met with a Nielsen family?"

"He was more like a Nielsen individual," I explained.

She was more upset about that part of the encounter than she
was about me sitting on a couch all cozy with a possible killer.
"You could get us flagged."

"Flagged" was slang for when Nielsen put an asterisk after the
station's ratings; this indicated to advertisers that the sample
might have been tampered with or otherwise tainted.

"I didn't find out about it right away," I said. "Suddenly I realize he's holding a people meter."

Noreen radiated fury, but she was also quite curious about the device and its functions.

"Don't you understand?" I said. "This means we can report that Chuck may have a better alibi than the cops think. The Nielsen data could actually corroborate that he was home watching TV during the murder."

Noreen now looked puzzled.

"If the tracking shows that he pressed all the right buttons every fifteen minutes, he couldn't have killed Kate. Geographically, they live too far apart."

"Riley, you're not thinking of reporting that he's a Nielsen household?"

I could see worry lines furrowing her brow. And rather than a reassuring smile, like those flashed by anchors, Noreen's was frightening. The rest of the newsroom staff was probably watching from their desks, through the glass wall, imagining what news jam I'd landed in now.

"Well, yeah," I answered. "It's a story no one has ever done before. We'll be first. We'll also either help clear a guy or convict him. Those are both noble goals for our profession."

I could see she wasn't impressed by my journalism principles, so I changed tactics from ethics to enterprise. "Either way, Noreen, it's a fabulous story."

"Do you think Nielsen will see it that way?"

I explained that we can't just quietly hand the information to the cops. "We can't be agents for the police. But if we report it on the air, they can subpoena the documents from Nielsen as part of their investigation."

"Right now, there's no rush," Noreen said. "The guy hasn't actually been arrested. He might never need an alibi."

"It doesn't exactly work that way." I told her how the cops like to build an easy case if they see one. "Once they've put in the work, they resent having to throw it out and start over on a new suspect."

Her body language—eyes narrowed, arms across chest, body leaning back—told me her mind was set. The only thing that kept her from being the scariest news director in television was that she was also the most beautiful. In most industries, those two traits clashed, but in ours, she somehow made it work.

But her being boss didn't stop me from being pissed.

"You haven't wanted me to put any energy into that murder story all along. You just keep saying there's nothing newsworthy. It's just another murder. Well, now there is something newsworthy, and you still don't want to cover it."

"Oh, I've changed my mind about the murder," Noreen said. "I want continuous coverage. I just don't want to report that one of the suspects is a Nielsen household."

"Well, what else is there to report?"

"I don't care what. Find something. Or rehash what we've already broadcast. And then call your new source and tell him to tune in to Channel 3 for the latest."

OMG. Suddenly I understood Noreen's plan.

Deep in their business souls, all news directors want to be general managers. That corporate ladder used to be easier to climb when the news department ruled the building. But now sales is the dominate force, and most of the GMs these days come from the second floor, not the first.

If she could show dramatic ratings momentum, that would keep her in the promotion radar of our network owners.

"So we decide to own coverage of the Kate Warner murder and use that to get her boyfriend and his people meter locked on our newscasts," I said. "Is one household even enough to shift viewing patterns?"

"We'll find out," Noreen said. "We both will."

So I packaged a story that night about why Buddy's death

didn't rate as a felony. Not taking any chances, the newscast producer had me tape the segment rather than go live. By then, my YouTube video had nearly half a million hits. But I couldn't bear to watch it.

I finished up and drove home, but my head was a mess. Needing a distraction, I reached to my bookcases for something to read. I decided against crime fiction, because I was living that genre. I wanted some escapist fantasy that didn't require much thought.

Beckoning from the lowest shelf were my school yearbooks. I grabbed one from college and looked up Laura's picture. Mine was on the back side of the page, she and I both being at the tail end of the alphabet. I flipped back and forth between us, marveling again that, minus haircuts, we really hadn't changed much.

Inside the front cover, amid all the good wishes from classmates, I found her message. "From Laura to Riley, best friends forever." Ah, I thought, that's how we've changed.

I spent the rest of the evening trying to brainstorm a fresh angle on her sister's homicide for tomorrow's news. To my surprise, by the time I got to downtown Minneapolis the next morning, one was waiting for me and had Kate's name written all over it.

CHAPTER 15

The crowd gathered outside the Hennepin County Government Center, waving signs reading "Justice for Buddy" and "Dogs Are People, Too."

They probably would have demonstrated inside the building, except several of them brought their pets along on leash, and only service animals are allowed indoors.

I heard about the protest from county attorney Kreimer, who called to express her irritation. "I suppose I have you to thank for this mess."

"I just put it on the air," I explained. "I can't predict what's going to set them off."

Hers wasn't the only Buddy call I'd received, but it was the only one I'd returned. A dozen messages, even one from the owner's ex-wife, were stacked up next to my phone. But listening to them bellyache wasn't going to advance my story, while listening to the county's top prosecutor just might.

"Well, Ms. Spartz, why don't you examine what's wrong with a world that cares more about the accidental death of an animal than the intentional homicides of our citizens?" Kreimer said. "Where are the protesters against murder?"

I suddenly realized she was right and saw a way to please Noreen and still do an intriguing story about what motivates people to picket for a cause.

((ANCHOR CU))
MINNEAPOLIS IS HEADED FOR A
RECORD YEAR OF HOMICIDES, YET
TODAY PROTESTERS DECRIED THE
DEATH OF A DOG WE FIRST TOLD
YOU ABOUT LAST NIGHT.
RILEY SPARTZ EXAMINES THE
PHENOMENON.

I had been worried I might simply have to report that authorities continued to seek tips in the Kate Warner homicide. A Crime Stopper version of the case. That would be lame, so soon after the crime, and our competitors would hoot in derision at such an uninspired follow-up.

Both 911 callers, the neighbor and the boyfriend, had signed consent forms for me to get the audio recordings, but that sound wasn't worth an entire story. Mostly that would add color if Chuck was ultimately charged with the crime. And right now, I didn't want the other media to meet either caller. Especially not Chuck.

Going public with the chalk fairy business could be a story, but would upset Laura and launch a war with the cops. I wasn't prepared to do either just yet, thought I hadn't ruled out reporting it eventually.

"I'll pitch the animal-human sociology story if you speak on that issue," I told the county attorney.

So I collected a sound bite from Kreimer decrying the rationale of the demonstrators outside, another from a university expert analyzing human behavior, but the most interesting feedback came from the marchers themselves. I felt like I was talking to clones of my old animal rights activist source, Toby Elness; except he was behind bars.

> ((PROTESTER SOT))
> WE SPEAK FOR BUDDY BECAUSE
> HE CAN'T.
> ((PROTESTER SOT))
> ANIMALS ARE THE TRULY
> INNOCENT.
> ((PROTESTER SOT))
> PETS DESERVE EQUAL LAW.

Wrapped in the same story, Kate Warner became the Channel 3 poster girl for Minneapolis murders. Her face appeared next to Buddy's in a nicely produced split screen effect. I spoke about Kate being the girl next door, and Buddy being every dog.

I tagged the piece out with the traditional call to action.

> ((RILEY LIVE))
> AUTHORITIES WANT JUSTICE FOR
> ALL THE CITY'S HOMICIDE VICTIMS,
> IF YOU HAVE INFORMATION ABOUT
> KATE'S DEATH OR ANY OF THE
> OTHER CASES CALL MINNEAPOLIS
> POLICE.

Once the piece was ready to air, Noreen watched as I dialed Chuck's number from a special cell phone registered to a post office box we kept for our investigative unit. This way, phone calls or mail couldn't be immediately connected to the station. If Nielsen ever scanned Chuck's bills, my call wouldn't attract attention.

When he answered my call, I assured him that even though there hadn't been a break in the case, Channel 3 was keeping Kate's murder in the news.

"This way, if anyone out there knows anything, Chuck, it might take the heat off you." Or might land him in jail, though I was careful not to share that thought.

As he thanked me, I reminded him that if the time came when it made sense for him to do a camera interview, we'd be there to tell his story.

Then I repeated the information about that night's newscast: "Remember, Chuck, the story about Kate will be on Channel 3 at ten o'clock." Ends up, he was in the backyard and didn't have a pen handy. "Don't worry, Chuck, I'll call a few minutes before airtime and remind you."

My boss winked.

And the next morning, the overnight ratings had us leading our competitors by a point. Usually we trailed by three points. We'd hoped to tighten the viewer gap, or at least keep our lead-in audience from eroding, but a swing this size was unexpected. And I knew the other network affiliates would be trying to analyze what happened, before dismissing it as a statistical fluke.

Some of the gain undoubtably came from dog lovers, because the Buddy angle had been heavily promoted during the network prime-time shows. And there was still some curiosity from viewers eager to see if I could hold myself together during a live shot.

But Noreen and I both knew Chuck Heyden's finger on the trigger of his invaluable remote was what fired the shot heard around the viewing area.

Noreen praised the entire newsroom staff during the assignment meeting, never once mentioning the name Kate Warner. Then she hauled me into her office and made it clear this hush-

hush scheme was going to be a continuing strategy "for however long it lasts."

"Riley, we need to find another reason to mention Kate Warner's name in the news tonight. So start looking."

I didn't have to look long before a story landed on my lap, or rather, my laptop.

CHAPTER 16

Laura didn't say anything, just opened the door a crack to the house where her sister died. Her face was as white as if she'd just heard the word "homicide." For a second, I thought she'd changed her mind and wasn't going to let me in.

No answer when I called last night to give her a head's up about the Kate follow-up, and also to check whether the biohazard clean-up had been completed. But today I got a frantic call that she needed me immediately. Because I was under orders to keep alive the story of Kate's death, I had no problem leaving the station.

Laura handed me an envelope with Kate's name. "Look what I found in the mail."

The postmark and return address indicated it had been sent from New York City. Inside was a sizable check dated a few days earlier. Bigger than my paycheck. Even bigger than the number on my W-2 tax form at the end of last year.

Piles of cash in the back of a closet or under a bed often mean trouble. Trouble with drugs. Or sex. Certainly trouble with the IRS. But checks are generally good clean income, though Laura's face showed no glow of having won a lottery.

"I don't know my sister anymore."

I took my eyes off the dollar sign with all the numbers. I didn't recognize the company issuing the check, but noticed the words "Desiree Fleur" typed on the memo line.

"What do you think it means?" I tried to keep my question neutral. I didn't volunteer that my first thought was the name sounded like a porn star. But Laura was way ahead of me down that path.

"It means my sister was a smut peddler."

My eyes widened. I hadn't expected her to use such harsh language. And she talked like she meant it.

I mumbled something about being sure there was a good explanation—just the kind of thing I've learned over the years to say on the job when there really *isn't* a good explanation.

"Follow me." Laura grabbed my arm and led me past the murder scene and down the hall into a home office. Messy, like mine. A laptop computer sat on a desk near the window. A bookcase dominated the room. I looked closely because I believe you can tell a lot about a person by their books.

Laura pointed to the bottom shelf, and immediately I saw why she was so agitated. About a dozen paperbacks bragged "Desiree Fleur" on the spine. I pulled them out and saw sensual covers with sweaty couples in erotic embraces. I set them on a table in the office, and noticed another one titled *Black Angel Lace*.

"Tramp," Laura said.

"Calm down. So your sister wrote novels. Sure the covers are a little racy. But authors don't get to pick their covers. That's a publisher—"

"But nothing, read inside. Raunchy."

I opened the book randomly and started reading a graphic depiction of a boy and girl having sex in a cemetery. I flipped through the pages and noticed the plot seemed to move from one steamy scene to another.

I understood Laura's point. While *Black Angel Lace* wouldn't legally qualify as pornography, it was a long shot from a Harlequin romance or even *Lady Chatterley's Lover*.

"Whore." Laura was going overboard with the name-calling.

"It's not as bad as you think. Your sister was not a prostitute. If she was a whore, she was a whore of words. You could say the same thing about lots of lawyers or politicians."

Laura wasn't buying the comparison. "She knew what she was doing was shameful. That's why she kept it hidden."

The sisters came from a strict Catholic family who probably believed reading *The Da Vinci Code* to be sinful. Clearly Kate was able to shake that philosophy.

"Possibly she wanted to shield you from embarrassment or just avoid a family fight," I said. "She wrote for the money, she certainly wasn't writing for fame."

I reminded Laura that her sister used a pen name. And her book jacket bore no author photo. The bio on the inside cover vaguely stated only that she lived in the Midwest.

Those points seemed to calm Laura. "You're right, Riley. I just have to hope no one else finds out."

Here's where journalism gets tricky. And why it's best not to get involved in stories with friends or relatives. Discovering that the deceased was a secret and successful author of erotica suddenly made her murder more interesting than it was an hour ago, when she was merely a dead medical transcriptionist.

I wouldn't be so cruel as to debate the rule of on the record versus off the record with Laura. But this bit of information about her sister was more than just a news scoop for me. It could be a clue to finding her killer.

"Laura, you have to take this to the police."

She shook her head, sat in the office chair, and put her hands over her face. "Absolutely not. Clearly my sister felt guilt or she'd not have kept this hidden."

"I know you'd like to keep this hush-hush. But it's not the kind of thing that can stay quiet. For one thing, you have to tell Kate's publisher that she's dead."

"No way. I'm not talking to those freaks."

She grabbed *Black Angel Lace* from my hands and threw it against the office wall. As the book hit the floor, the binding appeared to tear. She repeated the exercise with three more paperbacks before calming down.

I picked a book called *Beyond Passion* off the stack and held it in her face to make my point.

"Laura, this information about Kate could be vital to the homicide case. What if this ends up being an important clue to finding her killer?"

"How could that happen?"

"You can't ever tell where an investigation might lead," I said. "But not letting the cops in on this development could hold back justice for your sister."

Laura was quiet. She seemed to brood over my words. Then, without looking up, she mumbled, "Fine."

Years of interviewing people has taught me that saying something and meaning it are very different. And avoiding eye contact with me was evidence that Laura was still not completely swayed.

"What are you going to tell the police?" she asked.

"Me? No, I think it best if you're the one who goes to the cops first. Show them the check and the books. They can take it from there."

That's when she told me that she'd had enough of the police. She'd already talked to them plenty about her sister's murder. This would just lead to more questions she couldn't answer.

"You don't understand, Riley. She was more than my sister. She was my closest friend. It's hurtful she deceived me like this. I don't want to have to discuss it with them."

She flung two more "Desiree Fleur" books against the wall. Because of the tears on her cheeks, I resisted the temptation to remind Laura that I once considered her *my* closest friend.

"Laura, those are feelings you're going to have to come to terms with eventually. In the meantime, if her publisher confirms Kate Warner and Desiree Fleur to be the same person, that's not something I can sit on. I'm breaking it as a news story."

She glared. "Well, I'm not going to do any media interviews—not even with you, Riley."

That didn't matter. I could tell this story without interviewing Laura. The script would be simple, and I warned her the police would probably contact her after it ran.

> ((ANCHOR LEAD))
> NOW WITH AN EXCLUSIVE UPDATE
> ABOUT THE LATEST MINNEAPOLIS
> MURDER IS CHANNEL 3
> INVESTIGATIVE REPORTER RILEY
> SPARTZ.
>
> ((RILEY STANDUP))
> MURDER VICTIM KATE WARNER . . .
> WHO LIVE AND DIED IN THIS
> HOUSE LAST WEEK . . . LED A
> SECRET LIFE.

The word "secret" is always an attention getter. The newscast producer would probably fight me to let the anchor read that line, but I was determined to hold firm. After all, it was my story.

> ((RILEY VICTIM PIX))
> SHE HAD AN IDENTITY NOT KNOWN
> TO THE POLICE, HER NEIGHBORS,
> OR EVEN HER FAMILY.

I suspected if the cops had known such a juicy tidbit, it would have leaked out already. Or they would have released it publicly, in hopes of tips.

((BOOK COVER PIX))
KATE WARNER WAS A BESTSELLING
AUTHOR OF EROTIC FICTION
UNDER THE PEN NAME "DESIREE
FLEUR."

Then the director would probably cut to a double box shot of me and Sophie and Sophie would ask what erotica was and I would essentially explain the facts of life to her—and all of Channel 3's audience. Sophie would blush. And the producer would order news control to go black. Then Noreen would storm onto the set.

I shook that scenario out of my mind, admonishing myself to concentrate on the problem in front of me: Laura.

"I have to report this anyway, Laura."

"I'm not surprised, Riley. All you care about is news."

I ignored the dig on how our relationship ended, reminding myself that our discord was her fault, not mine. I also reminded myself to be skeptical of what she told me because she had proved capable of lying before.

Then I walked over to the books scattered on the floor, picked one up for an on-set prop, and left. But not before admiring what a nice job the biohazard team had done cleaning and repairing the living room. If I didn't know it, I never would have guessed a woman had bled to death days earlier where I now stood.

CHAPTER 17

I drove straight to the station because I wanted to make the call from a land line. Not wanting to risk losing a cell tower signal just when the interview became important.

I entered through the back alley door by the Dumpsters. Security buzzed me in. This way I wouldn't bump into Noreen and be grilled about what progress I'd made on whatever Kate Warner story she'd slated for that night.

Online, I found numerous references to Desiree Fleur—a bestselling and award-winning author of erotica. Much of her popularity seemed to come from her anonymity. Speculation ranged widely as to her identity—some fans certain she was a reclusive Hollywood actress, others thought her a conservative politician with a wild streak.

No one guessed her a mousy writer named Kate Warner.

"Every man and woman craves the satisfaction my characters discover," Desiree wrote once in an early blog. "A few might chance upon it in real life. But most will have to find it in my writing."

I dialed her publisher, Lascivious Press, and asked to speak to the editor of Desiree Fleur.

"Who's calling?" The switchboard operator sounded more annoyed than helpful.

I identified myself as a member of the news media and was immediately transferred to the publicity department. There it was explained to me that Desiree Fleur never did broadcast interviews to avoid being identified by face or voice.

"Sorry, but we can't even put your name on a waiting list," I was told.

"It would be a long wait," I responded.

That's when I told them she was dead.

Her editor, Mary Kay Berarducci, would not confirm that Kate Warner's pen name was Desiree Fleur. She seemed to think my claim that Kate was dead was a tacky media ruse to learn the author's true identity.

"Your strategy won't work," Berarducci said. "We've had experience dealing with your kind. As long as she is one of my authors, Desiree Fleur will remain incognito."

"Well, tonight on our late newscast," I said, "I'm going to report that Kate Warner and Desiree Fleur are the same person. And the word 'murdered' is going to appear multiple times in that story."

She gasped. "I will have to call you back." Berarducci's breathing seemed forced. Rather than a powerful wham, even her telephone hang-up click sounded feeble.

At my desk, I opened the cover to *Black Angel Lace*. It was Desiree's most recent book, and the title page contained an inscription followed by an illegible signature. "Taunting Teresa is tempting death."

I had no idea what the words meant. Or whether it was even Kate's handwriting. So I shrugged and read on.

Chapter one introduced a young woman yearning for something, just unsure what. Chapter two told us, in graphic detail, how her ardor was fulfilled. The story then introduced an element of danger amid sex as she begins to feel haunted by a deadly angel, whose existence is dismissed by those around her. I jumped to the end where she dies mysteriously and becomes part of a legend.

Just then the phone rang. Lascivious Press was back on the line to confirm that Kate Warner aka Desiree Fleur had been their top-selling author.

"Her prose captured the silent fantasies of readers around the world," Berarducci said. "Writing sex is much more difficult than having sex."

She explained how the ebook publishing phenomenon made Kate's work, translated into eleven languages, an Internet sensation on electronic readers for fans too shy to flash hard copies of her book covers on the bus or beach. "Her prose brought desire into their lives."

Meanwhile, I texted Malik that if he was in the building to bring a camera to my office ASAP.

"While Desiree Fleur is not a household name like Danielle Steel, and doesn't top traditional bestseller lists, her success is much envied across the industry," Berarducci said.

"Why did she keep her identity secret?" I figured the answer was obvious—that kind of art might attract weirdos—but wanted to hear it for myself.

Her editor wasn't that overt. "Kate wanted her professional life separate from her personal life. That's not uncommon in erotica. Many of her readers also keep their hobby private. Hers weren't the kind of novels book clubs tended to discuss or the *Today* show liked to feature. So there was no real advantage to going public for her."

Malik stuck his head in my office and I pointed at my computer and motioned him to set up the camera.

"Could she have been killed because she *was* Desiree Fleur?" I asked. So far, I hadn't found a motive for anyone to murder Kate

Warner, but her alter ego might hold a whole different set of enemies. Crazed fans or competitors, perhaps. "How many people knew her beyond her pen name?"

"I don't know those answers. In the publishing industry, some pseudonyms are widely known. For instance, Nora Roberts also writes as J. D. Robb. But I assure you, Desiree Fleur's true identity was shielded, and anyone seeking to locate her would encounter difficulty."

She expressed regret at having lost such a creative writer; I gave her my condolences and asked if she'd mind doing an online video interview.

"Mary Kay, I'd like to include someone who recognized Kate's talent in my story."

"As her editor, I would feel honored."

I started to explain the mechanics of how we'd see each other by camera on our computer screens, but she was familiar with the technology. So Malik rolled video and within a few minutes we had our choice of sound bites eulogizing Kate's life and promoting Desiree's writing.

After we wrapped, Kate's editor told me they'd be going back to press for more print runs of her books. "People are going to want them for souvenirs. I only wish she could have signed them."

Now it was time to pull Noreen into the story.

I carried *Black Angel Lace* to my boss's office, handing it to her while she was on the phone. One glance at the racy cover—not fit for television audiences—and she pushed it away. She told the caller she'd get back to them and hung up.

"Why are you bothering me with this garbage, Riley?"

"It's tonight's lead story," I said.

And when I spelled out the specifics, her eyes got bright and shiny as she sensed a blockbuster.

We debated whether I should seek police reaction before or after the news aired, because it would be too easy for our competitors to get a piece of the story from their own cop sources. We decided law enforcement response would be an excellent day-after report.

"But there is *one* person you are going to tell, right?" Noreen asked. "Don't forget."

And I knew who she was talking about.

Chuck Heyden seemed clueless as to why I was waving a paperback of naked people in his face and ranting about his girlfriend's writing career.

He insisted Kate worked at home as a medical transcriptionist. "She called it boring but stable work. It was something we had in common. What are you talking about?"

I kept our conversation outside, telling him I had to hurry back to the station to finish the story, but I wanted him to understand that I would be reporting Kate was also Desiree.

"Unless you already knew?" I asked, watching his face carefully as he answered.

Again he denied knowing anything about Kate having a covert career. "You're wrong."

I warned him that with this new lead, other media might come looking for him. And he shouldn't be so friendly.

"It might be best for you, Chuck, not to answer the door for the next couple days."

Malik was in the back of the van, shooting us through tinted glass, in case Chuck became important to the story. And because I didn't want to talk about erotica with a possible murder suspect out of eyeshot of anyone else.

As our chat became more explicit, Chuck became more agitated. Especially when I blundered, asking about Kate and kinky sex.

"She was a nice girl!" he shouted, before slamming the door.

Remembering Noreen's priority, I pounded and called his name. "Chuck, FYI the story is running tonight at ten. Channel 3."

He didn't answer, but I was sure he'd be watching the newscast. Malik assured me Chuck's eyes were following me from between the window blinds as I drove away in the van.

And that's how Channel 3 went from having to make up news about Kate Warner to having to beat the competition off with microphones for the story.

CHAPTER 18

He forsook the couch to sit mesmerized on the floor in front of the television screen, hanging on the nuances of audio and video.

((RILEY DOUBLE BOX))
NO, SOPHIE, THERE'S NO
INDICATION YET WHETHER
THE BOOKS THE VICTIM WROTE
HAD ANYTHING TO DO WITH
HER MURDER . . . BUT THAT'S
CERTAINLY AN AVENUE FOR THE
POLICE TO INVESTIGATE.

He turned off the television immediately after the reporter finished speaking. The story couldn't have lasted more than a couple minutes, but the words felt like infinity.

Killing Kate might have been a mistake. Because unlike the other women, he and she could be connected.

He'd felt no jeopardy from the early news reports on her homicide, or frankly from any of the media reports on any of the previous slayings. Frustration was a better word. His role of messenger had gone unnoticed by the police and the public.

Some days that made him angry. Why didn't they try harder? Other times, he reveled in his superiority over their mindless- ness . . . reminding himself that eventually acclaim would come.

Just thinking of all this conflict made him feel unclean. The man stepped under hot water and let it shower over him, wash- ing away the smell of sweat and the tightness in his shoulders. As an adult, he'd felt guilt over his private yearnings. But last year, his discovery that he was not a servant of Satan, but rather a de- scendant of Teresa, freed him to act without remorse.

So with her blessing, he did.

He closed his eyes and imagined her angelic rapture at fi- nally receiving the recognition she deserved, rather than mere superstition. But the water turned cold, ending the fantasy. He grabbed a towel and dried himself, but before slumber, he had a routine.

He posed naked in front of the mirror in his special stance—a salute to his brutal bloodline. The pose always calmed him. Yet he still slept poorly that night.

CHAPTER 19

I was still at home, breakfasting on peanut butter toast while I checked my voice mail messages.

One came from Ed, my pal down at the liquor store. I expected he might have a case of Nordeast tucked away for me, but instead, his recording said he had a story idea.

"Just had a visit from the cops, dearie. And they took a hundred bucks out of my cash register."

I'd heard rumblings over the years that certain cops might be on the take, hitting up businesses, usually bars, for protection money to either patrol more or patrol less. I was very anxious to hear what Ed was promised for his one hundred dollars.

"I thought that message might bring you around," he said as I walked through the door of the liquor store on my way to the station.

"Who were they? Did the surveillance cameras catch them?"

I looked up toward the ceiling, doubting an investigation could be nailed so easy. But I felt I was due for a break soon after such a bad run of news.

"Sure," Ed said, "but that's not going to do either of us any good."

"Why not?"

"I called you about counterfeiting, not bribery."

"Counterfeiting?"

"Bad bills being passed around town. The cops took the hundred and the camera tape of the customer as evidence."

Ed's bank had called yesterday, rejecting a twenty-dollar bill from his deposit bag.

"They said it was phony. So I'm out the money. But today a guy comes in and buys a bottle of Shakers Vodka. His hundred seemed a little off to me. So after he left, I called the cops."

"Why'd you take the bill, Ed? You should have told the guy to take a hike."

He explained his philosophy that counterfeiting was part of the cost of doing business.

"If I tell someone their money's no good, I could be wrong, or could risk pissing off a customer who might have gotten it passed to them unknowingly. If the shopper is a crook, I risk getting punched or worse."

Seemed to me Ed was overlooking the obvious. "But you have a gun."

He crunched his lips together and shook his head. "Unless your life is at stake, you generally don't want them to know you have a gun. Criminals can always use another gun, especially one that's not registered to them. They might come back to get yours."

So Ed simply reported the crime, hoping that if the cops busted a counterfeit ring, he might be eligible for a reward.

CHAPTER 20

I had to sideline my research on counterfeit cash, because to show the citizens of Minneapolis that the Kate Warner homicide case was under control, the police arrested Chuck.

Channel 3 didn't get perp parade video because our first word about the news was a phone call from him, in jail, asking me for the name of that attorney I had mentioned.

"I'll send him down," I promised. Neither of us brought up how our previous encounter had ended.

Benny Walsh was one of the top criminal lawyers in town. His dark suits and black stares were legendary in the courthouse. I wasn't sure Chuck could afford him, but Benny was willing to head down to the slammer to find out. Sometimes, if he thought the case had enormous potential for publicity, Benny could be flexible about money. But most times if a defendant couldn't cough up a hefty retainer, he turned him over to the public defender's office.

Suspects can be held in Minnesota jails for thirty-six hours before being charged. That gives the cops time to make their case. So Chuck's best hope of not spending the rest of his life in prison was not to be charged with murder in the first place.

I told Benny about the people meter alibi, figuring if I attributed the information to him, Channel 3 could report it without fear of retribution from the ratings giant.

Benny had a hard time following my account of how the ratings system worked. "So if I subpoena these records from Nielsen, they'll show that he couldn't have committed the crime?"

"If what he says is true, the data will show that somebody was watching TV in Chuck's house during the time of the murder. It's up to you to convince the cops or jury that it was Chuck."

"Interesting," he said.

"Remember, Benny, you have to learn about this from him and keep me out of it."

"Yeah, I got it. But you keep this straight, Riley, if I take him as a client, my allegiance is to him, not you. His secrets are my secrets. You get nothing unless I determine it to be in his best interest."

I didn't need Benny to tell me that. I'd been a criminal defendant myself.

I handed Noreen a copy of Chuck's mug shot. He looked dazed, like he'd been pulled out of bed and hauled off to jail.

She was pissed on a couple of matters. First, that Chuck was behind bars and couldn't turn his people meter remote to Channel 3 for the news. Second, that Benny knew about the ratings device from me.

"Riley, you've put us in quite a quandary."

I disagreed. "Nielsen will never know we knew about it first. We're merely reporting the news via his lawyer. And privately, as journalists, we'll know we did the right thing to get the truth out. If the ratings data clears him, fair's fair."

That interpretation did not reassure her. "It's entirely possible he's lying about being home and was actually out committing murder."

That was true. When it comes to homicide, more often than not, the suspect is the killer. "If that's how this plays out," I acknowledged, "we'll report it."

Then Noreen warned me in her familiar boss voice that I'd be held accountable if this predicament got messy for the station.

"Being held accountable" was a businesslike way of saying being punished. I tried looking somber as I left her office so she'd know I took her rebuke seriously.

Then I went to work on the arrest story. This wouldn't be any exclusive. Because of the erotica author angle the other media now wanted a piece of Kate's death.

> ((ANCHOR CU))
> A BREAK IN THE MURDER CASE OF
> THE EROTICA AUTHOR . . . RILEY
> SPARTZ JOINS US LIVE OUTSIDE
> HENNEPIN COUNTY JAIL WITH THE
> NEWS.
>
> ((RILEY LIVE))
> MINNEAPOLIS POLICE MADE AN
> ARREST IN THE KILLING OF KATE
> WARNER, ALSO KNOWN BY HER
> PEN NAME OF DESIREE FLEUR.
> THEY HAVE A FRIEND OF THE
> VICTIM IN CUSTODY BUT SO FAR
> HAVE NOT CHARGED HIM WITH
> THE CRIME.

I deliberately left Chuck's name out of the script because our broadcast policy was not to name suspects unless charged. The exceptions were public figures such as politicians or celebrities or suspects who were an immediate threat to society. Chuck didn't fit either criteria.

Benny spent an hour in jail with Chuck and came out representing the guy. He even called to thank me for the referral. I didn't bother quizzing him about whether he thought his client was guilty, because I knew Benny didn't care. More important to him was whether he'd make air that night on the news.

I saw a way to make my story different from the competition. So I asked whether he had confirmed the stuff about the people meter.

"Yeah, Riley, the guy says he was home watching TV. Alone. Took a bit of pulling to get him to explain how he's one of those ratings households you were talking about. But then even he could see this might firm up his alibi."

"So you calling Nielsen for the data?"

"Absolutely."

"They won't hand it over," I warned. "They'll consider it proprietary—trade secrets."

"I'll get a court order. A man's freedom is at stake."

Benny swung by the station to do a quick on-camera interview with me. "It'll rattle the cops because it's something they won't have expected. They might even kick my guy loose to avoid looking like idiots."

I started reworking the story.

((ANCHOR BOX))

CHANNEL 3 HAS LEARNED THAT
THE SUSPECT BEING HELD IN THE
EROTICA AUTHOR MURDER MAY
HAVE AN UNUSUAL ALIBI. RILEY
SPARTZ JOINS US LIVE FROM THE
HENNEPIN COUNTY JAIL.

((RILEY LIVE))

THE HOMICIDE SUSPECT CLAIMS
HE WAS HOME ALONE WATCHING

TELEVISION . . . AND BECAUSE
OF A NEW FORM OF RATINGS
TECHNOLOGY, HIS ATTORNEY SAYS
HE JUST MIGHT BE ABLE TO PROVE
IT.

((BENNY SOT))
IN A FIRST OF ITS KIND
SUBPOENA . . . I'LL BE CHECKING
HIS ALIBI AGAINST COMPUTERIZED
RECORDS OF HIS TELEVISION
VIEWING . . . IT'LL BE LIKE RATINGS
FORENSICS.

I explained to viewers how Nielsen measures audience size with people meters and that the suspect's TV viewing habits were monitored by the ratings company.

Noreen grimaced as she read the news script.

I tried reassuring her. "Now that he's under arrest, the fact that he's a Nielsen household is going to come out as part of his defense. So we might as well be the ones breaking it."

"Don't you forget." She waved her finger at me. "This goes bad, I'm holding *you* accountable."

Just then, neither of us had any idea how bad it could go.

CHAPTER 21

This time, watching the news on television upset him.

He could live without glory. He had proved that over the last several months. What he couldn't bear was seeing fame go to someone else. That needed to stop. He realized his reaction sounded vain and knew he should make his dissatisfaction about maintaining accuracy, not taking credit.

That was more admirable than egotistic.

Errors must be corrected.

He wrote down the reporter's name. Riley Spartz.

CHAPTER 22

I didn't feel his eyes watching me the next morning when I walked to the station after parking my car. My mind was on Garnett flying home and his arms around my body. I didn't know anything was amiss until the blow to the back of my head.

My bag fell to the sidewalk. My knees buckled and my hands reached upward; my hair wet and sticky. But when I held my fingers to my face, instead of seeing red, they looked . . . yellowish.

I turned toward my attacker and another egg hit me, this time in the chest.

"See how you like it." The man appeared familiar but it still took me about ten seconds to recognize Keith Avise, Buddy's owner. "Doesn't feel so good, does it?"

I dodged the next egg, and the yolk hit the station's yellow limestone wall, blending nicely. But the succeeding one struck me across the chin. The edges of the shell sharp against my skin.

"Stop it," I yelled, finally able to speak.

"No," he said. "You deserve it."

By now a crowd had gathered, at a safe distance, to watch the confrontation. Some looked puzzled. One sniggered and pointed.

"How'd you like to wake up every morning and find your truck egged?" He pointed to his black pickup, parked illegally, and I saw yolk and eggshell dried on the side. "They keep punishing me for that damn dog. It wasn't my fault; it was an accident. You made it worse."

He lifted his arm to throw another one, but a well-dressed young man stepped between us. "Beat it or I will call the cops." He held up a cell phone to show he'd already punched 911 on the screen. All he had to do was hit Send.

My attacker hesitated.

"Do you want the police?" the man asked me.

As tempting as assault charges sounded, I knew the resulting police report would be emailed immediately to all the other media. I could only imagine the headline: *Reporter Gets Egg on Face.* The radio talk shows would be even worse, using words like "scrambled," "cracked," and "rotten" to describe me. Being called a crybaby after Buddy's death was starting to look like a compliment.

"No," I said. "Just let him go."

Keith looked infuriated at being interrupted. His hand trembled and he seemed to contemplate striking my protector.

"Don't try it," the man said. "Or I will call the police."

The crowd cheered at his bravado and started chanting, "Nine one one . . . Nine one one . . ."

Keith's fist closed tight upon his fragile weapon. The mood was so quiet we could hear the shell crunch. Disgusting liquid oozed down his arm, dripping onto the sidewalk at his feet.

He shook the goo from his hand and everyone stepped back to avoid being spattered with yolk. Keith swore before driving away in his pickup truck. I noticed the shattered window glass, through which Buddy had been rescued, had been replaced. Other than the egg scars, the vehicle looked new.

I glanced around, trying to thank the man who aided me, but

he was gone. The incident was such a blur, I couldn't remember what he looked like, other than his face was pallid.

When I entered the sanctuary of Channel 3, the first person to see me was Noreen.

"What happened to you?" she said. "You're a mess. You're not thinking of going on the air looking like that?"

CHAPTER 23

On the walk to his office, he played back in his mind the scene of coming to the reporter's aid. Such a gallant deed was out of character, but he was surprised how bold and strong playing hero made him feel. Where that confidence came from, to speak so cockily in front of onlookers, he didn't know.

Acting the villain did not make him feel this powerful even when he lorded over their bodies. He attributed the rush of vigor to the witnesses, and pondered whether public credit for the killings would have the same impact.

Her vehicle plate and driver's license were registered to the station address rather than her home. That's why Channel 3 was the starting point. He had been waiting on that street corner to observe, not participate. To learn her pattern: when she came to work, where she parked, what door she entered. At the end of the day, he'd reverse the process. Then repeat. Such was research. The easy part about tracking this target was that geography made his time investment minutes, not hours.

All that talk of calling the police on her attacker was a bluff. He didn't want 911 to have his cell phone number. And he sure didn't want his name listed as a bystander in any police report tied to the TV reporter.

As it was, if anything happened to her, someone would probably mention the man armed with eggs. And police would waste time investigating that lead. He wasn't sure about the nature of her attacker's complaint, but was horrified at how little finesse the man demonstrated.

"Good morning, Mr. Dolezal."

The receptionist at the law firm greeted him cheerily, but he knew she was just doing her job. If their paths crossed else-where, he had no doubt, she would look right past him. Nor-mally he just nodded, but this morning, feeling empowered, he hailed her by name, and asked if she had plans for the weekend.

What Karl Dolezal lacked in morals, he made up for in work ethic. And he had plenty of legal duties ahead today. Certificates to file. Documents to notarize. Clients to reassure. The best part of working in a law firm's tax and probate division was that his kind were seldom considered suspects in violent crimes. Paper-work malfeasance, sure. But nothing gruesome.

Certainly, his colleagues, if pressed, would concede he had the necessary intellect for murder. Their surprise would be that he had the passion.

The year following his father's atrocity, he shuffled between a couple of foster homes before a maternal grandmother, long es-tranged from his family, came forward to raise him to study long and work hard. She told him his surname, Dolezal, was Czech for "lazy man," and he must constantly fight that label.

Always, she kept him busy. Constantly warning: "Idle hands are the devil's workshop."

But as he recently discovered, busy hands can also do the devil's bidding.

Dolezal finished his billing hours. Not wanting to risk another face-to-face encounter with the TV reporter, he avoided tracking her the rest of the day. Only five blocks separated their work-places, so there would be plenty of other opportunities.

Besides, he didn't have permission to take her. No tortured deadline, yet, to anticipate.

So after work, he drove south . . . for hours . . . without stopping. The familiar road trip comforted him. It didn't matter that it would be dark before he reached his destination. He preferred the obscurity of nightfall anyway. Just him and the stars before his altar.

For added company, he conjured up Kate's face. Still vivid. Because his motivation for her was more personal than the others, her ambush was also more gratifying. He was tempted to close his eyes to savor the experience again, but he needed to watch the pavement before him.

"Taunting Teresa is tempting death." Weeks earlier, that line had been Kate's first hint of trouble. Now it was her last memory of life. From her eyes, he discerned that, unlike the others, she knew why he had come and that no escape was possible.

Again he uttered the words, alone on the road, under the moon. "Taunting Teresa is tempting death."

Keeping both hands fixed on the wheel, he imagined the heft of the club. Then smiled and kept driving as he repeated his anthem over and over.

CHAPTER 24

Vali-Hi was one of the few drive-in theaters left in Minnesota, much less the rest of the country. The screen stood high off the ground on one end. Cars lined up in the dark waiting for the film to roll.

Earlier, the scene was a tailgating party of coolers, grills, and lawn chairs. Nick Garnett and I had missed most of that pre-movie action. I'd picked him up at the airport and we'd made a spontaneous decision to catch a flick outdoors instead of dining fine.

This was our weekend to catch up on each other's lives. He'd been immersed in government security issues and didn't know about the egg man humiliating me on a public street.

The van next to us had a couple of kids on a campy air mattress on the roof. The car on the other side had a young couple in the backseat not paying attention to the show.

Their moves reminded me of Desiree Fleur's narrative. And since the movie wasn't all that captivating anyway, I started filling Garnett in on my murder victim's hidden author life.

"So you say her books are R-rated . . . *R* for erotica?" He made the lingo match our setting.

"X-rated would probably be more accurate," I conceded.

"Maybe we should explore the difference. Cinematically, I believe they are classified by full-frontal nudity. Wherein lies the literary line between *R* and *X*?"

He reached under my sweater, and I squirmed to shrug him away. Even though it was dark, and we had the car doors closed, I didn't need any eagle-eyed news viewers blogging or tweeting about seeing me making out at the drive-in. Or even worse, nabbing an X-rated cell phone photo to post on my Facebook page.

"I have a morals clause in my television contract," I reminded my date.

"I'm just trying to help research your story. The more I understand about the victim's life, the more I can help."

"Why don't I just read some of her work to you," I said. "Then you'll get the true flavor of her writing."

I keep a flashlight in the glove compartment for emergencies, and this seemed like one of them. Garnett blinked as the glaring beam caught his face while I scanned *Black Angel Lace* for an appropriate passage.

In a whisper, I read: *"Her lips trembled as his tongue navigated the terrain of her breast and his fingers caressed her thighs. Her entire bosom heaved with desire for his—"*

"Does yours?" Garnett interrupted me.

"Does what?" I asked.

"Does your bosom heave with desire?"

"My bosom has nothing to do with this."

Even in the dim light, his eye held a gleam. "I'm not sure that's entirely true, Riley."

I realized he might have a point, but knowing an off-duty cop patrolled the rows of cars at the drive-in made me feel more like discussing the murder investigation than exploring our physical relationship. Feeling that way made me wonder if I was using Garnett for his mind and if he might be using me for my body. And if that were the case, could we find happiness together if our goals were incongruous.

"Maybe reading wasn't such a good idea." I shut the book and turned off the flashlight.

"Maybe we could save it for later, for a bedtime story." He leaned over and kissed my ear. "We could take turns reading to each other under the covers. One of us could narrate; the other, demonstrate. We could have our own private book club."

To change the mood, I fumbled for my cell phone to distract him with the aftermath of Kate's crime scene. True, once a detective, always a detective, but I underestimated his interest in the picture.

"Look at this." I held the screen up to him. Even in the dark, the white outline where her body once lay was vivid. "Surprise . . . a chalk fairy."

"What?" He reached for my phone and stared at the photo. "How did *you* get *this*?" His voice suddenly tense, all romance gone.

"I shot it."

"That's not possible." He shook his head. "Come on, who gave it to you?"

"I shot it a few days ago. It's the murder scene from the case I've been telling you about. Remember, my old roommate's sister? I asked you for a biohazard company to handle the cleanup."

"Hold off calling them."

"It's too late. They already finished the job."

Even in the dark, his face looked pale. "Damn."

"What's going on, Nick? Was the crime scene contaminated?" If the case against her sister's murderer was jeopardized because of an amateurish police screwup, Laura would be furious. She might even be willing to go on camera and fume.

Garnett stared at the photo as if he stood over the chalk fairy. Touching the screen, he traced around the shadowy figure.

"Minneapolis homicide processed the scene," I told him. "They're sure to have better photos."

He still didn't answer.

I tried to understand why he was so intrigued. I didn't want to sound tacky, but the detective squad wasn't acting like Kate's was an especially important murder. Mostly the cops were sniggering about her day job now. Then it occurred to me that if one of their own had endangered the investigation, they might want to purposely downplay the crime and keep it out of the news.

I tried to imagine the headline possibilities if the truth were reported.

Cops Chalk Homicide Mess Up to Inexperience

Body Outline Kills Murder Case

No Happily-Ever-After for This Chalk Fairy

Publicity like this could do more damage to the police homicide department than when a college student went missing years ago after a Halloween party in a local bar and his murder was mistakenly called a suicide. On a certain level, the public expects occasional police misconduct. They're even willing to overlook an unjustified shooting if the victim has a violent criminal record and might be deserving of a bullet in the back.

What they won't tolerate is police incompetence. That's the kind of thing that gets cops fired.

"The chief isn't acting half as curious about this case as you are," I said. "And I think I know why."

"No, you don't." His words came without hesitation, and he seemed to have no interest in hearing my hypothesis.

"So what aren't you telling me, Nick?"

He turned my phone off and looked me in the eye with the same intensity I recognized from his homicide detective days.

"Riley, the cops didn't draw the chalk outline around the victim. The killer did."

CHAPTER 25

I worried that parking outside Kate's house, especially so late at night, might get my car noticed by the neighborhood's ever curious mother-in-law. When we last spoke, she told me she was going to keep an extra close watch on the block because of a "feeling" she had that the killer might return.

"We can sort that all out later," Garnett said. "I need a look/see now. A brief drive-by might even be enough."

"Okay, we're close, that's it." I pointed to the brick rambler—now tainted with a deadly past. All dark.

But sure enough, across the street a couple doors down, a light was burning. I noted to Garnett that it might be best if we remained inside the vehicle.

"They already arrested a guy she was dating." I started to fill him in on Chuck, but he cut me off. "Not him."

"How do know?"

But he didn't answer. "Think back. What do you recall from inside the house? Beyond the specific crime scene. What about the peripheral details?"

"I didn't really get the sense that she surprised a burglar," I said. "No cut screens. And her TV and computer seemed untouched. A knife lay on the kitchen counter where she'd been chopping vegetables. So she didn't feel startled, like she had to defend herself."

"This wasn't a burglary." Garnett spoke with a sense of assurance. "He came after her. A stalker. Otherwise he could have grabbed a random victim in a city park. The question is: Why her?"

We talked about how some murderers often kill in the victim's home for privacy and to avoid leaving her DNA in their own house or car. Of course, they have to be careful about what forensic clues they may inadvertently leave behind or take away. DNA testing is now so sophisticated that a single cell is enough to confirm an identity.

"Homicide toward the front of the house?" he asked.

"Yes, we almost stepped on the crime scene when we came in the door." I remembered Laura's revulsion that day.

"Might mean the victim let her killer inside, right through the front door," Garnett said. "Or it might mean she was trying to escape."

"Either way, he whacked her," I replied.

"You're sure about the cause of death?" he asked.

"Blunt trauma, according to the M.E. But the cops wouldn't be more specific."

Garnett nodded like that made sense. "Saving the weapon details as something only the killer would know."

That ingenuity helps police sort out false confessions.

Garnett was being coy about why he thought Kate's killer drew her body outline. I shouldn't have been surprised, detectives prefer gathering information to sharing it. The opposite of journalists who like to shout news to anyone who will listen.

He was also reverting from his current security priority in *preventing* crimes back a couple of jobs to *solving* crimes. I'd put money down that he missed his days as a homicide investigator.

"Was the outline paint or chalk?" he asked.

"It was powdery, just like chalk." I recalled fingering the white dust on Kate's floor.

"I hope the forensics team took a sample."

Just then headlights came around the corner, and a vehicle pulled up behind us. Red flashing lights.

"Just wait," Garnett said. "Let him come to us. I'll do the talking."

Nearly a minute passed before a uniformed officer carrying a flashlight approached my side of the car.

I rolled down the window and waited for further instructions. I hoped he'd be content to glance at my driver's license and not order me to step outside the vehicle for a pat-down. Although it couldn't be any worse than going through airport security these days.

From her front porch, the mother-in-law watched.

"May I see some identification, Ms. Spartz?" The cop must have run my plates, and he probably recognized me from TV.

Part of me wanted to say, If you know who I am, why do you need identification? He seemed almost gleeful to find me . . . unaware I was aware that the Minneapolis police chief had a price on my head. I was pretty sure the day-off bonus only counted for moving violations, and that parking on a dark street was not breaking any law.

But before I could get all smart-alecky, Garnett spoke up.

"You don't care about her." He flashed a homeland security badge at the officer.

Gold. Shiny. An eagle across the top. I vowed to get a closer look at the impressive design. Maybe if he waved it at me later on, in the privacy of my own home, I'd even let him frisk me.

The cop shined the light from the badge to Garnett's face. I heard an intake of breath as he recognized my companion.

"Nick Garnett. What brings you back to town?"

"Well, an hour ago I would have told you pleasure." He smiled at me. "But now I'm afraid it's turned into work."

"Anything we locals can assist you feds with?"

"Actually, it's going to be the other way around. I'm going to be assisting your office . . . with a murder investigation."

He tilted his head in the direction of the homicide house. The officer didn't react. He'd clearly been briefed about the address's recent history when he received the call about a suspicious vehicle.

Garnett opened the car door and stepped out. "See you later, Riley." His farewell held a hint of regret as he slammed the vehicle shut.

Then he turned to the cop. "Why don't I catch a ride downtown with you." He said it like he was giving an order, not asking a favor. After all, he used to be one of them. One of their best. And the officer didn't disagree.

"Hey, what are you doing, Nick?" I said. "We're on a date."

"You're right. Sorry." He walked over, leaned through the window, and planted a quick kiss on my mouth. "Duty calls."

And the two of them left me parked alone on a dark street reeking of murder.

I was mad about a couple of things—personal and professional. First, being cut out of the case after giving him an important clue . . . even though I still wasn't sure what the photo meant, it clearly held significance. Second, even though we were sort of, almost, maybe engaged . . . I was pissed to be kissed like some kind of trophy. It was like he was showing off to that other cop that he had me in his pocket.

I wanted to follow the squad car, but I knew they'd ditch me by driving down the underground entrance to the cop shop.

I also wanted to go up to Cheryl Gordon's house and yell at her for calling the police in the first place, but I was afraid she'd just flex her telephone muscles and redial 911.

So I knocked softly on her door, and she answered all excited when she turned on the outside light and saw me.

"Did you see that car over there? I called the police and they took a man off to jail."

I explained the man was a law enforcement officer and friend of mine and that I was pointing out the crime scene when the flashing lights arrived. Handing her another of my business cards, I reminded her, besides calling the police, to phone me if she noticed anything.

"Oh heavens," she said. "You're so busy, I'd hate to bother you."

"No trouble. I'll make time."

CHAPTER 26

I didn't want to wait up for Nick because that might make him think I cared about him. But I didn't want to go to sleep either. That would make it easier for him to sneak under the covers next to me, hoping I wouldn't notice and might have calmed down by morning.

I threw a pillow and blanket on the couch for him, determined he wasn't getting within an arm's length of me unless I got a straight answer about what he thought he knew about Kate Warner's murder.

But over the next couple of hours, I figured it out myself.

When Garnett looked at my chalk fairy photo, he acted like he recognized something. He must have seen a similar picture before—or a similar crime scene.

I turned my phone back on, emailing the picture to my computer. Then I printed out a larger version and propped it against the wall by my bed. The quality was much better than I expected. And again, I was struck that the outline around Kate's body wasn't the traditional kind you see in police dramas or old crime scene photographs.

Her arms were distorted. Like her killer had been in a hurry to finish. But that also made the fatal artwork unique. A murderer's signature. And Garnett had clearly seen it before. Which meant Kate's killer had killed before.

A signature is a ritualistic crime scene behavior that goes beyond what is necessary to kill that person. Often, it becomes a clue left behind when slaughter alone is not enough for psychosexual gratification. But sometimes the conduct is designed to mock law enforcement—catch me if you can.

Garnett had explained the concept of signature in homicide to me once before when I was covering a serial killer story. I didn't think I'd cross paths with another such madman the rest of my career in news.

A mass murderer, sure. Their kind snap, killing multiple victims at the same time and place. Spree killing is the law enforcement term; going postal is the slang. Such a rampage murder can happen anywhere people gather. A school. Workplace. Political rally. Church. Family home. The crimes are obvious, nothing subtle about them. And often, the killers add themselves to the death toll, making the cases easy to solve.

But serial killers are hard to detect . . . and much harder to apprehend.

I must have drifted off to nightmare land when I heard the door open. I jerked awake in a panic before remembering that Garnett had a key and now stood next to my bed.

"So tell me what's going on," I mumbled before remembering I wasn't speaking to him.

"I can't right now." He sounded committed, not tired.

"Then the wedding is off." I tried to sound like I meant it.

"Stop talking like that. Neither of us is supposed to tell the other how to do our jobs. That's always been our understanding."

I explained that investigating Kate's murder was *my* job, not *his*. "You're supposed to be protecting our national security. So unless you can prove a terrorist connection to Kate's death and that of the other women, you're out of your game . . . and out of my bedroom."

I pulled a blanket over my head to show I meant business.

He grabbed the covers back so he could see my face or maybe so I could see his. Either way, he wanted to know what other women I was referring to.

I continued my bluff and he bought it. "The other ones Kate's killer drew chalk fairies around."

"How do you know about them?"

"I'm a reporter. It's my job."

"I think you're just guessing."

"Well, it looks like I guessed right." In retrospect, I probably sounded a little too smug. "Because you just confirmed that there *are* others. And I'm going on the air to report that Kate Warner was the victim of a serial killer."

"I'm not sure you have enough to support that story."

I conceded to myself he could be right, but didn't want to say that out loud. "Yeah, well, I have a hot photograph that's sure to go viral. You just wait and see what I end up broadcasting."

That's when he noticed the picture of Kate's outline now lying on my nightstand, and realized I was determined to break the story.

"How about if we both just put this disagreement aside till morning," he said, "and go back to that book you were reading from earlier at the drive-in?"

I couldn't believe he still thought our weekend together would end in a fit of passion. A fit of rage, more likely. "Sure, Nick." I pulled *Black Angel Lace* out of my bag and threw it through the bedroom door toward the couch. "Read yourself to sleep out there."

Mumbling something about waiting for an apology, he grabbed one of the blankets and disappeared into the hall.

I almost called out, "Love means never having to say you're sorry." But then he'd crawl under the covers with me and whisper, "*Love Story*, 1970. Ali MacGraw and Ryan O'Neal." He might mess up on the actors. Few people remember that both stars spoke the trademark line; she in the middle of the film, he at the end.

I could use that flub as an excuse to kick him out of bed, but if he nailed the answer correctly, I'd have to let him stay. And he'd certainly want to reenact their dorm room sex scene.

But part of me still wanted to go to bed mad. So I simply lay there, yearning. Nothing but silence. I could outlast him for sleep because I hadn't been traveling all day. Then a faint, familiar snore sounded from down the hall.

I closed my eyes and craved black. Even at night, I never seemed to see total blackness. It's more like the inside of my eyelids are painted near black with thin fingerprint etchings that sometimes look red and other times look gray.

Black would be such a relief.

CHAPTER 27

He reached Iowa City amid thunder and lightning. Summer storms had flooded the state's farmland that season, but this latest torrential rain did not deter him.

He drove through the metal gate, following a narrow road up a hill and around a curve. And there she stood.

The Black Angel.

Her wings reached down as if to embrace him. Magnificent among the other grave markers; her blood was his blood.

He turned off his headlights to avoid attracting attention to his visit. The cemetery had closed hours earlier, and trespassers were discouraged. But a streetlight overhead illuminated the larger-than-life statue.

The tombstone was the legacy of Teresa Dolezal Feldevert. Local lore had the sculpture, once golden bronze, turning black as evidence of her malevolence.

Karl knelt on the cement slab at her hem, raising his blurry eyes to the monument's immortal ones.

"I have come for your blessing, cousin," he said.

A crack of lightning lit up the sky. Then, as if on cue, the rain slowed to a drizzle.

Carvings on the base showed Teresa to have been born in 1836; her date of death was left blank. The curious take that as proof that she isn't actually dead, but continues to prey on those who disrespect the Angel. But Karl knew, from his genealogy studies, that she had died on November 18, 1924, at the age of eighty-eight, and that her ashes were buried here under the sculpture.

When his research found a family connection between the two of them, his life took on a new directive. His cravings now endorsed, he felt free to act. No matter their relationship was distant. He had few living relatives, she had no direct descendants; he might as well be mentored by her ghost.

Each visit to Oakland Cemetery made him more certain of his path. Proud to claim Teresa as kin, he had established a routine of obtaining her benediction before proceeding on his next calling.

He stood before the Angel, his arms spread wide, mirroring the distinctive slope of her wings and pose of her body. Her silhouette dwarfed him; head to ground more than twelve feet tall, towering twice his height. But he was ready to vow another sacrifice at the foot of his master.

He whispered the next name.

"Riley Spartz."

Deep in his soul, Karl Dolezal knew he had permission.

CHAPTER 28

I woke up too scared to scream.

Seconds passed before I understood I was home in bed. Blankets tangled. Pillows scattered. Somewhere outside, a police siren confused me. My nightmare had something to do with the angel of death.

I reached for a lamp switch. The picture of the chalk fairy outline was the first thing I saw. And suddenly, I realized the drawing wasn't a fairy after all, but an angel.

An angel of death.

Funny how our minds work while we sleep. Sometimes the answer we're searching for finds us instead. At that moment, I sensed I had learned something important about Kate's killer.

Her murderer fancied himself the Angel of Death.

I caught myself just then and realized I shouldn't necessarily assume the murderer was a man. A woman could also be capable of inflicting blunt force trauma.

All killers leave evidence behind, usually not by choice: fingerprints, DNA, tire marks, witnesses. But this murderer—male or female—deliberately left a clue. A clue that might suggest the killer had an affinity for religion.

Was the angel wing outline simply a way of showing off? Or

was the slayer marking victims like an artist signing a painting? Or an author signing a book?

Then I remembered Kate's book, *Black Angel Lace*, and wondered if its pages held an inkling. Looking around, I realized Garnett had the paperback. Daybreak was still a couple of hours away, so I didn't want to sneak in and risk waking him. I also wasn't sure I wanted to share my death angel theory. You have to give to get. I'd already given him a hell of a photo and gotten zip.

And hours earlier, we had discussed marriage. Could there be a happily-ever-after in our future if we never seemed to be on the same team? We both liked chasing things, but for different outcomes. Him for justice; me for news. Our professions both needed each other's, but did *we* actually need each other? Our personalities clashed so much that, deep down, I wondered if I'd be better off married to a shoe salesmen.

For the next hour, I lay with a cover over my head, debating what to say to Garnett in the morning. Imagining possible conversations wasn't particularly helpful, but at least it kept my mind off the Angel of Death.

I slept late, and when I awoke, my man was gone.

Garnett left an empty bottle of Nordeast beer on the counter along with a note. I expected to read something about him being sorry or stupid. But he mentioned nothing about me going to bed mad, instead that he was off to the Mall of America to meet with a security colleague and would connect with me later.

His suitcase lay in the other room, so he clearly intended to return to the scene of our fight. How things unfolded next would have to wait, but I was actually glad to postpone any showdown.

My Angel of Death nightmare was still vivid in my mind and I was eager to pursue the hunch. More research was needed. While I was no expert on angels, I knew where to go.

CHAPTER 29

S o you're interested in angels, my dear?"

Father Mountain clasped my hands in a warm greeting after the mass crowd had left. His bright green vestments made him look every inch a man of God.

"I thought you might be here to discuss matrimonial vows, but I don't see your gentleman friend along." He winked, pretending to look behind me.

Last time I'd stopped by church was with Garnett, because he wanted to meet significant people in my life. I figured my childhood priest was a safe place to start. At least he'd be unlikely to spill embarrassing secrets from my past. But Father Mountain sounded eager for a wedding. He'd gotten cheated out of marrying me to my first husband, Hugh Boyer, when we eloped. But he'd been there to offer comfort when I lost my love to a terrorist.

"No wedding today, Father," I said. "This is a work visit. I need a crash course on angels. What can you tell me?"

"Well, Riley, angels appear as messengers in many cultures and religions dating back thousands of years," he said. "In the Bible, you'll see angels play important roles in communication between God and man."

He led me back inside the church and pointed to a familiar gilded frame hanging near the baptismal fountain.

"Here you see the angel Gabriel telling Mary that she is to be the mother of the Messiah. Keep in mind the Annunciation is among the most popular of all biblical scenes with artists."

He rattled off a list of great masters including Da Vinci, El Greco, Botticelli, and Rubens who have all painted their versions of that famous conversation between Virgin and angel.

I knew the winged figures were a staple of art in the Renaissance, Medieval, and even Greek periods. Looking around the church, I saw that affirmed in stained glass, marble, and even wood. Their shape ranged from cherub to warrior.

"Angels are everywhere in the Bible, from beginning to end," Father Mountain continued. "From the Book of Genesis to the Book of Revelation. And they're not just pretty faces either. They have jobs to do."

"Yes, as messengers," I said to show I was paying attention.

"Right. Who reassured Joseph to take Mary as his wife? An angel. Who announced the birth of Christ to the shepherds? An angel. Who led Moses and the Israelites to the promised land?" He paused, like a theology teacher calling on a student. "Riley?"

"An angel?" I answered.

"Absolutely. And who saved Daniel in the lion's den?"

"An angel." I replied with more confidence this time.

"So there you have it, a quick overview on angels." He smiled, as if tickled to be of help.

"Aren't you forgetting one?" I asked.

He looked puzzled. "Do you have a special one in mind?

"The angel of death."

Father Mountain's eyes widened, then he shook his head. "That's a complicated question, debated even by religious scholars."

I needed a more satisfying answer than that. "I'm a smart person, Father. Try me."

"Well, the angel of death is thought to come to a person at the moment of death. Here's the disagreement: Is the angel there to cause the actual passing? Or simply observe it?"

My gut told me the angel I was tracking was there to cause death, but I didn't want to interrupt Father Mountain.

"Then the angel transports the deceased's soul to their next world, heaven or hell, all per the order of God," he continued.

"Does the same angel have access to both places?" I asked.

"Nobody really knows. The angel of death concept is not taught in the Bible. Nor is it a core belief of the Catholic Church. Much of the theory about the angel of death has meshed in popular culture with that of the grim reaper."

I tried to imagine what kind of person would be drawn to play such a dreaded role. They would have to be mad. And I mean insane rather than angry.

"Why don't you tell me what's going on, Riley? What are you really hoping to learn?"

So I told him about my hunch: a killer drawing angel figures around corpses.

"Perhaps giving them wings is the murderer's way of allowing their souls to fly to their journey's end," I speculated. "Any ideas?"

"It all seems far-fetched," Father Mountain said. "What do the police think?"

"I haven't actually run it by the cops yet. Me and the cops are a bit at odds this go-round."

"Well, I just hope your imagination hasn't run too wild."

His skepticism wasn't what I expected. So I showed him the chalk outline photo, still on my cell phone. "Does this look like my imagination?"

He stared at the picture, then blinked. Taking my phone from my hand, he held it up closer to his face, then looked back at me. It was like Garnett's reaction the night before. They both recognized something in the photo.

"I'm sure it's nothing," he said.

"What is?"

"Probably just a coincidence."

After a career in investigative reporting, I'd stopped believing in coincidences. "Tell me."

"I'm afraid it's going to sound nonsensical."

"Let me decide."

"This reminds me of the Black Angel."

Father Mountain couldn't believe I had never heard the legend of the Black Angel, but assured me the drawing on my phone matched the distinctive shape of a historic cemetery marker in Iowa City, where he'd grown up.

"It's very old," he said. "Has to be close to a hundred years by now. And it's considered the most haunted site in Iowa. When I was a boy, we were always daring each other to visit it."

He couldn't remember the name of the woman buried at the foot of the statue, but told me townsfolk believe the angel, once golden, turned black as a sign of her evil.

"Children are raised to beware her wrath. Touching the angel on Halloween is supposed to lead to death in seven years. Any girl kissed at the grave in the moonlight will die within six months. And kissing the angel itself is believed to cause a person's heart to stop beating."

"Now you're scaring me," I said.

"Everyone for miles around calls the sculpture the Angel of Death. Disrespecting the angel is believed to lead to fatal retribution."

And suddenly, Kate's book title and the drawing all fell together. If kissing under the angel tempted death, certainly a cemetery sex scene, even a fictional one, making the angel an unwilling witness to fornication, might be deemed an insult that merited lethal retaliation.

I certainly didn't blame Kate's murder on a ghost. But could her killer be taking inspiration from the supernatural tale? And demanding revenge?

I was concentrating so hard on that possibility, I didn't realize Father Mountain was still talking, until he nudged me.

"Riley! Riley!"

"Yes, Father? What?" I answered, startled.

"You seemed to be focused on another world. I hope it's not the hereafter." He looked concerned. But that's a look priests routinely practice, so I couldn't be sure his worry was genuine, or a ruse to get me to abandon my interest in death angels.

"Maybe I was." And I told him about my nightmare jarring me awake.

"Tonight, say a prayer to your guardian angel," he advised.

My guardian angel. "I've forgotten all about guardian angels."

"We all have one watching over us," he said, "guiding us in good deeds and protecting us from evil."

"With my luck, my angel probably still needs to earn his wings, like Clarence in *It's a Wonderful Life.*"

Father Mountain made an exasperated face. "I'll never understand how Hollywood's version of a guardian angel gets top billing over the Bible's."

"You have to admit, Father, as far as storytelling goes, the Bible is complicated and dark. People like happy endings."

"For the righteous, the Good Book ends happily," he said, "for the wicked, maybe not so much."

Knowing I couldn't win an argument about religion with a priest, I decided to head home.

As always, he offered to take my confession. I passed, but he left me with the counsel not to underestimate my guardian angel.

"Such angels are thought to manifest themselves as mysterious strangers who appear abruptly to help mortals in distress. When the trouble has passed, they disappear just as suddenly. You may have been aided by an angel, Riley, and never even realized it."

In the car, I reflected back on some close calls I'd had recently with danger. But I never really thought to credit my survival to a guardian angel. Occasionally, during some tough scrapes, I had felt like someone *was* watching over me, but I always thought it must be my dead husband.

Do people become angels after they die? That seemed the type of role Hugh might embrace in an afterlife, because as a cop, he protected and served while here on earth.

I remembered my despair upon learning he was killed in the line of duty. So where was his guardian angel?

CHAPTER 30

An online photo from a website about Iowa history showed that Father Mountain was correct. The Black Angel's winged silhouette was remarkably similar to the outline the killer drew around Kate's body.

I hit print for a copy of Iowa's angel when I heard Garnett's key in the door. I hit stop on the printer because I didn't want him to see where my investigation was headed. I quickly clicked away from the Black Angel web picture and back to my Internet home page of Channel 3.

"Are you working?" He looked over my shoulder at the computer screen, but because it was a weekend, the day's news was lame.

"I'm always working." I rebuffed an approaching kiss, so he changed tactics to a different kind of hunger.

"Let's grab something to eat."

He took the car keys off my desk. I expected we'd end up at the Uptown Diner or some greasy spoon that cops favor, but instead he drove across the river to the Muffaletta, a romantic restaurant in St. Paul. That choice seemed like he was apologizing without saying the words out loud.

Now it was up to me to decide, over chablis and salmon,

whether to forgive him for caring more about being a cop than a boyfriend.

"You've helped me on other murders, Nick," I said. "What's changed?"

He shook his head. "These aren't cold cases. They're still warm. The last one is even hot."

He had a point. Media generally got turned loose on old cold homicides that the public had forgotten, and where law enforcement took whatever exposure they could get in hopes of a fresh tip. In current cases, police tried to control media coverage—all the better to not jeopardize the investigation. Sometimes cops wanted help from the public; other times they wanted the public left in the dark.

I tried a playful approach. "Kate's murder was assigned to me, not you. My story, not your case. You're just butting in." Although I tried to keep my tone light, I meant that last line.

"Who is it who likes to say, 'I'm always working?' Well, I'm always working, too."

I couldn't dispute that. It's one thing news and law enforcement have in common: our eyes are always open for the next big break. One difference: their mouths are usually shut.

Just for a change, I kept my mouth shut on the drive home. My silence seemed to rattle him, making him talk more than usual. But most of his remarks were about politics, airports, and terror—nothing I wanted to hear just then. I wanted his insight about my angel photo, but I was careful not to call it by that name.

"How about my chalk fairy photo?"

"Let's just say I saw something in your picture I needed to act on immediately. I felt it was my duty as a law enforcement officer." He kept his eyes focused on the road to avoid eye contact with me.

My cell phone buzzed and one of my few girlfriends texted me an FYI that she had seen a guy who looked like my boyfriend in a jewelry store at the Mall of America earlier today. She posted a :) symbol at the end, but I couldn't bring myself to smile.

At that moment, Garnett pulling a ring out of his pocket seemed as far-fetched as me letting him slip it on my finger. But I had to admit, when times were dire, he had my back. And lately, dire seemed normal. That's why we had developed what folks of my parents' generation called "an understanding."

Right now, "misunderstanding" felt more accurate.

We arrived at my rental house near Lake Nokomis in south Minneapolis. Real estate was bargain priced—the house next door was for sale, foreclosure priced—and I had enough cash in the bank for a down payment. But I'd held off buying a place of my own because I wasn't sure where my personal life was headed.

Some nights, I wanted to be part of a couple again, curled up together, looking at carpet samples and talking about how our days had gone. Other times, Greta Garbo's classic line "I want to be alone" resonated and the idea of trading privacy for companionship had as much appeal as Minnesota's Metrodome during a snowstorm.

So far I hadn't come up with a tactful way of telling Garnett that, much of the time, I actually enjoyed living a thousand miles apart—me in the Midwest, him on the East Coast. The distance kept our relationship vibrant. Or so that's what I told myself.

He pulled into the garage and took my hand as we walked across the yard to the front door. Fumbling for my house keys gave me the excuse to untwine my fingers from his before we stepped inside. The decor didn't reflect me; it came with the rent check. I'd sold or given away most of my furniture and other belongings when I'd sold my house, craving a fresh start with no troubling memories. The problem with that approach was I never felt I was home when I was home.

I hung my coat in the closet, tossed my bag on the counter,

and continued our debate. "Nick, can we talk about our disagreement over the serial killer story?"

He looked exasperated that I wouldn't drop the subject. A fancy lunch was supposed to buy peace. And love. "What are you saying, Riley? No story, no sex? I thought we already established that last night. What's new?"

"I wasn't going to be so crude. I was going to propose a deal rather than an ultimatum."

"So what's the deal?"

"Off the record. Tell me what my photo means off the record." I held up my cell phone and clicked the crime scene so there'd be no doubt what picture was at stake.

"Do you mean off the record, you won't report the story? Or off the record, you won't attribute it to me?"

It was a good question. More sources should think to establish the parameters before offering information.

"How about I quote 'a law enforcement source,' and leave you out of it?"

"No, you can't broadcast the story, period. It's not about shielding me, it's about protecting the investigation. That's got to be the deal."

"But this is a local investigation, you're a fed now. Why are you so concerned?"

"The feds will be running it sooner rather than later." He spoke cryptically, but I knew exactly what his hint meant.

"So the murders cross state lines. Our killer likes to travel."

He didn't answer.

"Okay, I won't report the serial-killer angel . . . angle now." I said angel by mistake, luckily he didn't notice. "But you have to fill me in on what's going on with the case and keep me up to speed as best you can. But if I can confirm anything with other sources, or it leaks out, then I'm free to run with it."

Maybe he was tired of fighting, or maybe he just wanted us to feel close again. And I wanted both of those things, too. So when he pulled me tight and kissed me deep, I led him to my bedroom and we crawled under the covers together.

As we undid buttons and zippers, he told me about the similar chalk pictures he'd seen a couple of months earlier at a briefing in Quantico at the National Center for the Analysis of Violent Crime.

"Is that part of VICAP?" I asked. VICAP—the Violent Criminal Apprehension Program—helped far-flung jurisdictions find clues for investigations of serial killings, missing children, and unidentified human remains.

"Actually VICAP is part of us," he said. "Much of my agency's work also involves behavioral analysis of terrorism threats. That was my primary mission, but I stuck around for another discussion involving two Midwest murders."

"Once a homicide detective, always a homicide detective." And not just with Garnett either; I'd seen that pattern in cop after cop. Unable to leave the beat. As he nuzzled my neck with his beard stubble, my fingernails dug into his back.

"When I saw your chalk fairy, déjà vu hit," he said. "Those other murders had been tagged because the victims had chalk outlines around their bodies. All the officers on the scene swore they didn't mark them. Yet there they were. Speculation came that the outlines might have been made by the killer. Seeing your photo makes me certain."

"Where did the other cases happen?"

"Ames, Iowa, and Madison, Wisconsin."

"Both victims young women?"

"Yeah, but I don't want to talk about crime anymore. I just want to concentrate on you."

So he did. And ten minutes later the bed was a mess and we lay breathless in each other's arms.

I teased him. "Not bad for an old guy like you."

"It's not the years, honey, it's the mileage."

"Harrison Ford, *Raiders of the Lost Ark*, 1981." The film

opened the same day Major League Baseball went on strike. I remembered having tickets to the Minnesota Twins and having to settle for a movie instead.

I drifted off to sleep—no nightmares—reminded of the advantages of not being a thousand miles apart from a man who loves you.

CHAPTER 31

The next morning, I cracked a couple of eggs to make an omelet for Garnett. The yolks stared at me from the bottom of the bowl like a pair of jaundiced eyes, and I thought back to my pelting in front of the station and the man who rescued me while the crowd gawked.

A mysterious stranger, coming to my aid, then vanishing. His face suddenly became clearer to me. Could he have been my guardian angel?

While Garnett and I shared breakfast, I broached the subject.

"Do you believe in guardian angels?"

"In what? Where's this coming from?"

I told him about my encounter with the egg man and he couldn't believe I hadn't filed assault charges.

"I didn't feel like being ridiculed by every radio talk-show host every time I go on the air. It's like I attract crazies. It seemed best to just forget the blitz."

"But you haven't forgotten it, have you, Riley? I bet you're looking over your shoulder all day."

He had a point, but he switched direction. "So you think this other man was your guardian angel?"

"I don't know what to think, Nick, but something about him felt different from regular guys."

"Well, my philosophy concerning protection is a little more straightforward than yours. You want to meet my guardian angel?" He opened his jacket and slammed a handgun on the table. He pushed the weapon toward me. "Meet Saint Glock."

Rush hour was especially heavy while I drove Garnett to the airport for his flight back to our nation's capital. All the stop-and-go traffic gave us additional time to talk that I hadn't counted on. To avoid intimate dialogue, I complained about gridlock, the news biz, and how best to nail the supposed serial killer.

"Think how more relaxed things would be if we were married," Garnett said.

"For me or you, Nick?" I decided his comment wasn't specific enough to count as a proposal, mere discussion.

"With me, you could live the life of Riley." He said the words teasingly.

"What do you mean? Aren't I already doing that?"

He explained that "living the life of Riley" was an idiom meaning living an easy and pleasant life. "You don't seem to have either. I'd like to change that."

I hadn't heard the expression before, even though I wore the name. Easy and pleasant had a tempting ring, but I told him that goal might be something I had to learn to do for myself and not depend on others to deliver.

Because of the road delay, all we had time for at the airport was a quick kiss and promise to talk later.

Noreen seemed irritated that I was late, and waved me into her office, pointing to her computer. "You remember Fitz Opheim?"

The station consultant—my recent nemesis—stared at me from the screen in that computer application that allowed people in two locations to watch each other as they spoke. Cyber meetings at the click of a mouse.

"Certainly, I remember you, Fitz." Knowing he was watching, I kept my face and voice neutral. An easy task for a television reporter.

Consultants make their living telling TV newsrooms what they're doing wrong. The last time I'd seen him face to face, Fitz read a long list of Channel 3's flaws. Immediately, Noreen had implemented his changes: from painting the green room to symbolize a fresh start to commanding the staff to join social networks such as Facebook and Twitter.

I hadn't noticed any long-term shift in the ratings, but since our general manager had signed a two-year contract with Fitz, those of us in the news trenches were stuck with his advice.

One of the producers had mentioned recently that Fitz was proposing "modernizing" our newscasts by having our anchor team read the news standing up instead of sitting behind a traditional desk. No more talent wearing jeans on the job.

The hope was that change might bring in younger viewers— those twenty-five to fifty-four years old—coveted by advertisers. Channel 3 had a loyal but older audience. We liked bragging that we don't lose our viewers to the competition, we lose them to death or dementia. Deafness also used to take some until close-captioned television came along.

Budget cuts had slashed the number of times the station could fly Fitz in from California to lecture us in person. That was one of the few good situations to come out of the media meltdown, so the last thing I wanted to do was talk one-on-one with him through cyberspace.

"Fitz has some interesting observations on the Buddy story," Noreen said. "He'd like to discuss them with you."

She motioned me to sit in *her* chair so Fitz could see me better. Uncomfortable. Her watching him watching me.

I knew why I was in the hot seat. By now the YouTube video of me crying over a dead dog had more than 750,000 hits. I braced myself to be labeled an idiot in front of my boss.

Instead, Fitz was calling me a genius.

"I don't know what instinct kicked in and made you tear up on camera like that, Riley," he said, "but we need to see more of the same."

"More?" I said. "You got to be kidding, I'm a laughingstock around town and in newsrooms across the country."

"They're all jealous. We tested you in front of focus groups and we're getting a very positive reaction."

And the ratings had spiked . . . it could be curiosity over me, but it could also have been our insider-trading strategy with Chuck Heyden's people meter. I glanced at Noreen, but she volunteered nothing. Because Fitz couldn't see her, she put a finger to her lips to signal me to hush.

"So we need to figure out what other stories might best lend themselves to this type of coverage," Fitz continued. "And then assign them to you."

"Wait a minute," I interrupted. "I didn't mean to fall apart that day on camera, and I sure don't want to ever have it happen again."

"Sure, Riley, I understand how thinking about it might make you uncomfortable. That's why I'm here to practice with you, until an emotional outburst seems natural. I'll count to three, then you start crying. One . . . Two . . ."

"No." I shook my head.

"What do you mean, no?"

"I'm not going to stage crying on the air."

"I'm not asking you to pinch your wrist or poke your thigh with a pin." He sounded like I was being unreasonable. "Simply try mustering the saddest thought you can, and let nature take over."

My life was full of enough misery, I didn't need Fitz Opheim coaching me into tears. So I reached over to press the Escape button on the computer.

"Riley!" Noreen perceived my intent too late. By then the

screen was dark, with nary a good-bye on either end. "You can't believe that was the best way to handle this. He'll be livid."

"Why did you just sit there all quiet?" I asked. "He works for you."

"Actually, he works for the GM. And so do we. You could have handled that a bit more diplomatically."

"There are lines I believe can't or at least shouldn't be crossed, Noreen. Almost everything out of that man's mouth falls into that category."

I understood the importance of branding in this business. Some reporters develop a reputation for humor. Others for landing exclusive interviews. I couldn't be the Twin Cities' star investigative reporter if I was also the crybaby reporter.

"What am I supposed to tell Fitz when he calls back?" she asked.

"Tell him I'm in the field, covering news. That's my job. Tell him there's been a school bus crash."

"It would have much easier if you'd pretended you were trying to cry, but were unable."

"Easier for who? I'm the one the viewers see."

"For both of us," she insisted. "I'm the one who answers to the man upstairs."

She wasn't talking about God either. The general manager had the top-floor corner office, and because Channel 3's ratings were shaky, a consultant like Fitz probably had more job security than a news director like Noreen—sort of like a coach for the Minnesota Vikings. Whether talking fans or viewers, it's all about winning.

"We need to finish sweeps higher or he'll bring in staff he thinks can move the ratings needle. It's not about the news, it's all about the numbers."

"Well, I am partial to being first," I said.

"Not first with the story, Riley, first in the overnights."

She and I hadn't had such an animated conversation in some

time. If she had a sense of humor, we could have laughed together about Fitz. But I doubted she'd smiled much since her recent divorce from Toby Elness, her fellow animal lover and my animal activist source. I wondered whether to tell her I'd visited her ex in prison, but decided better to wait.

"Fitz now has input in all personal services contracts." Noreen looked unhappy about sacrificing some of her clout. "Including yours."

"Then it's a good thing my contract isn't up for another year." I grinned like I was joking, but down inside I knew that growing shift in news priorities could spell trouble for me at renegotiation time.

Before my boss could admonish me further, my phone buzzed with a text from attorney Benny Walsh telling me the jail was kicking loose his client, Chuck Heyden.

I showed Noreen the text just as her phone rang with a number from California. Suspecting Fitz on the other end, I hurried to slide out from behind her desk and give her chair back.

"Tell him news called, and I answered."

She waved me back from her door, so to prove I was serious, I called out a lead for her to take to the news huddle.

((ANCHOR CU))
MINNEAPOLIS POLICE TODAY
RELEASED A MAN THEY'D BEEN
HOLDING AS A SUSPECT IN THE
MURDER OF A BESTSELLING
AUTHOR OF EROTICA.

Then I left to go after the story.

CHAPTER 32

The jail was less than a mile from the station, downtown parking was always a chore, and no photographer was immediately available . . . so I ran.

The assignment desk was trying to muster a camera for video of the release, but jail processing was unpredictable and I had no guarantee a photographer would make it in time or might not have to leave for another shoot before Chuck was freed.

I took the skyway to avoid the rain now falling and having to wait for traffic lights. As I cut through the crowd, I thought I passed the man who saved me from the egg attack. I turned around, but he was lost in the horde of people. Nothing unusual, I told myself. Less likely that he's my guardian angel than he simply works downtown.

Benny was shutting the door to a cab when I arrived outside the jail. Chuck sat in the backseat. I grabbed the door handle on the street side and climbed in next to him. Benny opened his door again and scrambled in too. Harder for him because he held an umbrella.

So him, Chuck, and me. All scrunched in a row.

"Where you want to go?" the cabbie asked.

"Hey, Riley," Benny said. "No media interviews. Get out."

"One quick question, Chuck," I said. "Don't even need it on

camera. When you discovered Kate's body, was there a chalk outline around it?"

"What kind of question is that?" Benny asked.

"I have a reason."

"I'm sure you do, but I'm not sure I'm going to let my client answer."

"It could help your case," I insisted. If Chuck could definitively say the chalk outline was there when he found the body, that might tie this murder to the others Garnett mentioned, and could clear him. Unless he was the killer.

Chuck paused like he was thinking. "I can't remember."

"Where do you want to go?" the cabbie asked again.

"You got your answer," Benny said. "Now you and I are getting out and he's going home."

"You sure, Chuck?" I asked one more time. "This might be important."

"I don't want to remember her body. It's something I'd like to forget."

"Give address or get out," the cabbie said.

I thanked Chuck, climbed out of the cab, and assured him Channel 3 would report the news of his release. The cab pulled away. Benny opened his umbrella and I ducked underneath.

"So what happened with the cops?" I asked.

"Their thirty-six hours to make their case came and went," Benny said. "Clearly they don't have enough evidence on my guy. I told them to put up or shut up. They declined charges . . . for now."

I wondered if this development had anything to do with Garnett talking to the homicide team this weekend about the chalk outline.

"So Chuck's back to being a witness, not a suspect?" I asked.

"Unclear. But I warned him to keep his mouth shut. I hope he understands that means you, too."

I explained to Benny that I was trying to connect this murder to others in the Midwest. "It might come down to whether a chalk outline of the body was made by the killer, or an overeager cop."

"Good luck getting the police to own up to that one."

"Chuck was the first on the scene. He knows."

"But you heard him, he can't remember. So drop it."

Then I mentioned a case that happened years ago in Denver in which the witness who found the body couldn't remember a key fact. The police brought in a hypnotist and all became clear. The cause of death changed from suicide to murder.

"You're not suggesting I let the cops hypnotize my client? That's insane. They'll just try to trick a confession out of him."

I saw Benny's point. So I dropped the idea.

Just then a station van pulled up alongside us and honked. I waved the photographer off. "Too late, he's gone."

"What do you mean too late?" Benny said. "You got me, don't you?"

So I called the camera back and we taped a sound bite on the street of Benny in his lawyer suit and voice talking about how the police had obviously recognized they had the wrong man.

No one from the cop shop wanted to be on TV answering questions about whether an innocent man had spent the weekend in jail. Even off-camera they wouldn't say whether they were spooked by Chuck's supposed people meter alibi or whether something else—possibly Garnett's serial killer theory, though I couldn't bring it up—played into their decision to release their suspect.

I caught up with homicide detective Delmonico in the basement of city hall, but all he would pony up in regard to Chuck Heyden's discharge was a statement that the investigation was continuing, and he couldn't comment further.

"Have the feds showed any interest in the case?" I followed

him as he proceeded down the hall toward the safety of the homicide department—off limits to the media unless invited.

I could tell that my question surprised him, but he stuck to his single talking point. "I am unable to comment on the investigation."

"If the feds had reason to move in, how might that affect your case, Detective?"

When jurisdiction overlaps, the FBI and local police almost always clash because the feds like to come in and play bigfoot, and the locals fight to protect their turf. I knew it; Delmonico knew it. Why I continued down that path of inquiry troubled him. So he ignored me.

"I'm hoping maybe we can chat off the record." I winked just to keep the mood casual. "I was talking to the chief the other day about the chalk fairy outline and thought you might have something to add."

As part of the homicide team, I knew Delmonico had Garnett's information. I could also see my use of the term "chalk fairy" disturbed him.

"Excuse me, but I need to get back to the job." Delmonico escaped through the homicide door, shutting it in my face.

"As a matter of fact, so do I." I pounded my fist, then called after him ominously. "Got to write a story for tonight."

CHAPTER 33

This was his day to visit her.

Dolezal bought flowers from the farmer's market during his lunch hour so she could brag to her friends about him being "such a good boy." Folks living in her senior housing gained standing among their peers if they had regular company. Especially if the visitors remembered the names of other residents like Doris or Otto.

"Hello, Nanna." He put the bouquet in a vase she kept on the kitchen counter and held it to her face to smell.

"My boy, my boy." She paused to catch her breath, and he wondered if these blooms were too pungent. "You are so good to me."

"Nanna, you deserve it."

When she battled cancer, he remained at her side, pretending he couldn't tell she wore wigs or no longer had breasts.

Now twice each month he held a free genealogy class in the dining hall of her building to teach residents how to track their family trees with birth, death, and marriage records.

"Leave this be your legacy," he told them as he checked their progress. "Because when you are gone, so will be the knowledge. Write names on the back of photographs. Record memories of special happenings in your life."

None of his students had been able to trace their roots to anything important like the *Mayflower*, but one insisted at each lesson, with no documentation, that the blood of Charlemagne flowed through his veins.

Dolezal always congratulated the man on his ancestry, but privately doubted the lineage.

All this made Nanna important among the residents and staff. Occasionally some of the seniors needed legal work and a few had even become clients of the firm because of the ease of Dolezal handling their paperwork.

He enjoyed taking Nanna for a drive in her older model Ford Taurus just to make sure the car didn't sit too long between trips. Other times, if she didn't feel like riding the road, she encouraged him to take the car by himself and bring it back serviced.

"You like driving for me, don't you, Karl?"

"Very much, Nanna."

"You must care for my car because one day it will be yours."

The Taurus was nothing special, but Karl Dolezal had reason to appreciate driving a vehicle registered to an eighty-two-year-old woman.

"I raised you well, Karl." She squeezed his hand in contentment. "You make me proud."

He only hoped she died before ever learning the truth.

CHAPTER 34

((ANCHOR SOT))
POLICE ARE KEEPING QUIET
ABOUT WHETHER THE MAN
RELEASED FROM JAIL IN THE
MURDER OF THE EROTIC AUTHOR
REMAINS A SUSPECT OR IF THEIR
INVESTIGATION HAS TAKEN A NEW
DIRECTION.

Back at my desk, I started cranking out the story while sixteen email messages waited for attention. I opened one labeled BUDDY'S REAL FAMILY. It was a note from Barbara Avise, a woman claiming to be Keith Avise's ex-wife and Buddy's true owner.

Please call me and I will tell you the bona fide story.

The last thing I wanted was to hear any more about the egg man's personal life. Not hard to understand him having an ex; I figured whatever her story was, she was better off alone. Parties in nasty divorces sometimes try to get the media involved for revenge. I always strived to steer clear of such motives and not let one spouse use me to bad-mouth the other on our air.

Barbara had included two attachments she described as a photo of her and Buddy, plus legal documents supporting her claim. Declining to look at either, I sent a polite reply expressing sorrow for her loss and explaining that station staff aren't allowed to open attachments from unknown sources. *As you know, Barb, Buddy's death affected me deeply, but I feel Channel 3 has told his story.* Wishing her the best, I hit Send and finished my script for that night's newscast.

> ((ANCHOR TWOSHOT))
> CHANNEL 3'S INVESTIGATIVE
> REPORTER . . . RILEY SPARTZ . . .
> JOINS US NOW WITH THE STORY.

I'd phoned Laura on my way back from the jail to let her know about the police not filing murder charges against Chuck.

She sounded upset. "Does this mean my sister's killer is going free?"

"I don't know what it means, Laura. I'm not sure the cops even know. I just didn't want you to hear it cold on TV."

I kept my word to Garnett not to mention any possibility of a serial killer. But I did put my photo of Kate's crime scene outline in the story, because after all, that belonged to me.

> ((RILEY SOT/PIX))
> CHANNEL 3 HAS LEARNED THAT
> POLICE ARE PUZZLED ABOUT THIS
> CHALK OUTLINE DRAWN AROUND
> THE VICTIM'S BODY AND ARE
> TRYING TO DETERMINE WHETHER
> IT WAS MADE BY AN OFFICER AT
> THE SCENE . . . OR PERHAPS LEFT
> BY THE KILLER.

I recorded my voice track and went back to work, this time concentrating on my Angel of Death theory. While I'd promised Garnett I wouldn't broadcast the other cases, we had no agreement that I wouldn't investigate them.

I taped a map of the Midwest on the wall of my office and starred Ames, Iowa, and Madison, Wisconsin, with a red marker. Because I had a time line and because both cities were small enough that homicides were infrequent, I was confident I could identify the correct homicides even without the victims' names.

I did a computer search of the local newspapers in Ames for murders in the past year. Two popped. I disregarded an elderly man who died in an arson fire and concentrated on a young woman beaten to death in her garage a couple of months ago. I wrote her name—Kathy Loecher—and her date of death on a Post-it and stuck it on the map.

I repeated the search for Madison and found only one murder. Maggie Agnes killed in her home a few months earlier. I added those details to the map, then printed the news accounts of both cases and put them in a file folder.

I also marked a red star on Minneapolis—the freshest lead. The feds would be converging soon, if only to discount the conjecture. I printed out a photo of Kate and taped it to the map.

I thought back on my last question to Garnett as he unloaded his suitcase from my car trunk outside the airport terminal. I was trying to understand the killer's motivation.

"What do you think this chalk outline business is about, Nick? Do you think the murderer might have always wanted to be a cop?"

All he would offer up was that anything's possible. Then he turned back and whispered in my ear, "It's also possible he is a cop. But whatever he does for his day job, when he's not out killing, he's smarter than most serials. So leave this one to the pros."

I chose that moment to plant a big kiss on his lips, as a means of saying good-bye and ending the conversation.

The television monitor on my desk was tuned to the station's in-house feed, which showed what the news control booth could see in the studio. Sophie sat at the anchor desk in the newsroom recording brief promos of the most interesting, but not necessarily important, reports. The purpose of promotion was to alert viewers to stories they might not expect to see on the news and convince them to tune in for the details.

A floor director walked into the shot to tweak Sophie's microphone and point out which camera she'd be reading. I noticed Chuck's release was included in the day's lineup, and the facts were essentially correct, so I turned off the monitor to concentrate on my homicide cases.

The next hour was spent on the phone offering my condolences to the families of the two murdered women in Wisconsin and Iowa and arranging for them to email me photographs of the victims.

"What did she do for a living?" I asked in each case.

The only things the women appeared to have in common, besides their deaths, were their age and occupation—both were waitresses in their early twenties.

"Do you know if the police have any suspects?"

Neither family seemed to have a grasp on the status of the investigation, nor were they media savvy enough to question why a television station was calling about a homicide so far outside its viewing area.

The police departments of Ames and Madison weren't quite so dense.

"What station are you with again?" and "Why are you calling about this case?" were the first words out of their mouths. It was like they were channeling each other.

I tried taking an academic approach. "Channel 3 is conducting a study about homicides in the Midwest during the last six months. I'd like to confirm whether your case is still open."

Yes from both jurisdictions.

"Have there been any arrests?"

No to either.

"Do you have any suspects whose descriptions you'd like us to broadcast?"

No witness saw anyone leaving the scene in either case. As with most homicides, their leads involved investigating people who knew the victims.

"Did anything strike you unusual about the crime scene?"

Neither detective offered up any details about the chalk outline, so they may not have realized three cases could be connected, or they might have been keeping that clue quiet as something only the killer would know.

The investigator in Madison mentioned that blunt force trauma was not typical.

"When it comes to homicide, the leading cause of death is gunshots, followed by stabbing, strangulation, then blunt objects. The fact that the assailant chose to beat his victim isn't the norm according to murder stats."

I thanked him for his perspective. And asked if either body appeared to be posed.

Both departments declined to answer.

"Did there appear to be any markings on or around the body?"

Neither investigator responded. One told me he had to get back to work soon. The other asked how much longer my survey was going to take. I wrapped up the interviews with a final question.

"If our station decides to feature this case in our story, would you or someone within your department be available for a camera interview?"

Both answered maybe, typical when it came to cops. So far, no breaks in the cases, but at least they were now familiar with me, and didn't hang up.

I stuck a photo of the Black Angel next to Iowa City because the statue added intrigue to my murder map. To keep honest, I added a big question mark to the picture and tried to think of what other connections the area might have to any of the homicides.

While I'd never heard of the cemetery before, the University of Iowa, besides being a sports rival of the University of Minnesota, was internationally known for its prestigious writers' workshop.

Because Kate turned out to be an author and had used a Black Angel as a character in one of her books, I was guessing she might have attended the university, its campus less than two miles from the graveyard. If so, that might be further evidence of a link.

I called the university records department and asked to verify attendance on a former student. I had her date of birth from the police report of her murder.

"No degree was conferred," the office voice said.

"Excuse me?" I asked.

"She never graduated."

"I realize that," I bluffed. "I'd just like details of when she attended, and what classes she took."

The voice said Kate Warner attended two semesters, four years earlier. "That's all the information I'm allowed to release." Then she hung up.

Kate might have recognized her style of writing did not fit the university's literary bent. Or the university might have recognized this for her.

CHAPTER 35

The station's front-door receptionist paged me on the overhead speaker while I was on the phone with the Secret Service learning about the crime of counterfeiting. Besides protecting our president, the agency is also in charge of protecting the physical integrity of U.S. currency.

"When it comes to bad bills, we're more interested in the printer than the passer," I'd just been told. "Sometimes they're the same, but often the passer can lead us to the money ring."

Now I had a visitor in the lobby.

My news experience told me that seldom did any good story ever walk in cold through the front door. Usually just nut jobs who thought that was how best to get on TV. Or outraged viewers who wanted to complain in your face about why you kept mispronouncing a particular surname or city.

I told the Secret Service agent I'd like to call them back to arrange an on-camera interview.

"Did you get a name for this visitor?" I asked the receptionist.

"Yes, Barbara Avise. She has a package she wants to give you."

I closed my eyes and thought, damn. For this I cut a source short. She must have printed out the attachments I didn't want to open. Either that or she wanted to throw an egg at me, just like her ex-husband.

"Can you tell her I'm in a meeting and just take the package?"

I heard her repeat that line and another voice answer that she didn't mind waiting. They were the worst. She'd figure her wait had earned her a lengthy one-on-one, and would probably want to pitch the story by reading the documents out loud to me. If I left her sitting there and ducked out through the back alley, she'd lambast me on my Facebook page. Then Fitz would add one more transgression to my file. "I'll be out when I can."

I sorted through my emails and saw both families had sent photos of the murder victims. I sent replies thanking them and promising to stay in touch. Then I hit Print, adding the pictures to my wall map of murder.

Finally I gave up and went out to make Barbara go away. I walked by the assignment desk and asked Ozzie to rescue me if I wasn't back in ten minutes.

"Make it sound like I'm in big trouble if I don't come with you, okay?"

He nodded without much enthusiasm.

A middle-aged woman clutched a manila envelope as she watched a network soap opera in the lobby. Her face lit with optimism when she saw me walk through the door.

"Hello, you must be Barbara Avise. I'm Riley Spartz."

As much as I wanted to snarl at her for being pushy, I also wanted to spend the least amount of time necessary with her. So I sat down on the couch across from her and started in with business.

"Again, I want to tell you how sorry I am about Buddy's death. I'll look through your materials, but I'm not sure there's much more Channel 3 can do."

I reached for the envelope, but she held tight. "Let me just review a few things for you."

She pulled out a holiday card of her and Buddy, in front of a Christmas tree, wearing matching Santa hats. "I know how important pictures are in TV news. And I want you to have a nice one of Buddy, from happier times."

She was right about visuals, but seasonal backdrops are never popular with newsrooms. We much prefer neutral photos, but sometimes our graphics designers can fix things.

"I loved that dog." She choked up a bit. Then she handed over a pile of legal documents. "Now here are my divorce papers."

I saw it coming—marital wars. "I can understand how you and your ex-husband may not be on the best of terms, but most of our viewers already hate his guts. And frankly, I don't want to get any further involved in his life."

"I loved that dog." She was starting to repeat herself.

I glanced at my watch, a couple more minutes before I could expect Ozzie. "I'm sure you cared for him deeply, Barb. I didn't know him long, but even I thought he was special."

"I raised Buddy from a pup. I was the one who fed him and filled his water dish. I was the one who walked him each morning and night. I should have had sole custody."

"What do you mean?"

"When Keith and I split up, he vowed to take my dog from me. He didn't want guardianship because he loved Buddy; he did it to hurt me. And rather than deciding what was in Buddy's best interest, the judge treated him like a piece of furniture."

She pointed to one of the divorce papers that resembled a calendar. "Our negotiation became contentious. Here's a copy of our doggie visitation agreement. We had to share custody, and alternate weeks with a dog swap."

She teared up as she talked about how glad Buddy always was to see her, and how he never wanted to get in the car with her ex-husband. "I just knew he wasn't being treated well. If Buddy could have talked . . ."

I didn't interrupt as she wiped her eyes, but I worried her tears might be contagious. The last thing I wanted was the two of us crying in the lobby over her dead dog. She pulled a gold chain from under her blouse, hanging from it I recognized Buddy's dog tag.

"I tried going back to court," she continued, "but was told to stop wasting the judge's time. If the court had only listened to me, Buddy would be alive today."

Her face welled up with cheesy emotion just as Ozzie came out to tell me they needed me to go chase a school bus crash in Anoka. I figured Noreen must have fed him the line.

"I'm in the middle of something, Ozzie. Can you get someone else this one time?"

"No, everybody else is already assigned."

I motioned toward Barb with my head. "I really need to finish up here."

He shook his head. "You'll have to handle it later."

I guessed he was playing bad cop, thinking I wanted to come across as the good cop. What he didn't know was, I really did have a few more questions for my visitor. What I didn't know was, there really was a school bus crash.

A minute later, Ozzie made me understand I needed to head to the crash scene with a photographer now. I promised Barb I would look over her file, discuss it with my boss, but I couldn't guarantee anything would end up on the air.

"I'll call you later." I handed her a business card.

"I understand all that, but you need to understand this." She dropped her voice low, and surprised me with her next words. "Buddy's death was no accident. Buddy was murdered."

CHAPTER 36

On the drive north, I filled Malik in about the latest on Buddy's dysfunctional family life.

"She sounds a little nuts to me," he said. "But so did the other guy."

"You and me both. But I better keep Noreen in the loop or I'm headed for trouble. She has a soft spot for this story."

I told him how I'd been impudent with our consultant who wanted me to shed tears on a regular basis as I covered the news.

"Maybe this crash will be worth crying over, Riley."

"No way. I'm a professional journalist, and I intend to act that way."

Suddenly we saw traffic backed up ahead. Police were on the scene; so was an ambulance. Plenty of flashing lights to shoot.

Any time a school bus is involved in a crash, a crew needs to be dispatched. Often the accident becomes the day's lead—if children are killed, if the driver is drunk, if the bus wasn't properly maintained and its brakes failed. Lots of factors can make for a compelling story.

But not this time. An SUV rear-ended the bus, but it ended up being one of those accidents that looked worse than it was. No serious injuries, although a couple students were being transported to Unity Hospital to be checked.

I didn't blame Ozzie for the chase. No news organization can wait for all the answers before heading out to cover breaking news. We'd be beat every time. Malik and I taped some interviews, crash video, a standup, and headed back to the station with a story that might merit a minute in the second section of the newscast unless something better came along. Then it would be busted down to twenty seconds flat.

My voice mail message light flashed at my desk. Barb had more to add about her deceased pet.

"I watched your stories about Buddy," she said. "Only one thing stood in the way of authorities charging him with a felony. One word. *Intentional.* I don't think Keith lacked intent at all. I think he left Buddy in that hot truck on purpose to kill him and break my heart.

"That prosecutor you interviewed said the dog's owner had suffered enough. I disagree. Keith needs to suffer much more."

Barb delivered the words with plenty of punch, and would probably be an excellent sound bite . . . if any of what she said was true. I reached for her divorce folder and began to read.

After the news, Noreen poked her head through my office door. She seemed to want to sit, so I cleared papers from a chair to make room for her. Any time she sought me out, I always knew there was a good chance she was going to fire me. I figured this must not be the day, because if she was going to sack me, she'd do it in her own office so the rest of the newsroom could watch and fear.

She started out with girl chat. Like did I have plans for the coming weekend? This kind of question never bodes well from a boss. She was probably setting me up to cover a Saturday news shift.

I was about to make up some prior social commitment when she got to the point. She needed a house sitter. Or rather, a dog sitter. She was going out of town for a news directors' conference and hoped I might watch her menagerie. When she and Toby split up, she assumed responsibility for her dalmatian, plus a consortium of cats, dogs, fish, and birds that Toby raised in a country house just outside the western suburbs.

"The only ones that really need supervision are the dogs," she said. "So if you'd rather, I could drop them off at your place."

She must have been desperate if she was asking me for this favor. I was the only friend she and Toby had in common. I guess I shared some of the credit for their marriage as well as blame for their divorce. They fell in love because of me and a story, and broke up because of me and a story.

"So we're talking Speckles, Blackie, and Husky?"

Husky was quiet and always seemed fond of me, and I liked those traits in a dog. As for the others, Blackie was a little more aggressive and Speckles a little high-strung. But if it was only a weekend . . .

She nodded.

"Okay, Noreen, I'll do it."

"Really?"

I told her I'd let her know later if I wanted to sit at her place or mine. "In the meantime, let's talk about pet custody."

"What's to discuss? Obviously I kept the animals. Prisoners aren't allowed pets."

Toby's longtime concern for animal rights had got him in trouble with the law, and I had reported the crime for which he was now serving a five-year sentence. Surprisingly, that didn't mean we weren't still friends. And I knew that hearing I took care of his animals would please him.

"I'm not talking about your pets, I'm talking about Buddy."

She looked perplexed, so I showed her the holiday photo of Barbara Avise and her bowwow.

"Who's this?"

"She claims *she's* Buddy's owner." I told her about the accusations Barb was making. And that so far, the divorce documents seemed to corroborate a nasty custody battle over their dog.

"Whether her ex meant to kill Buddy or not gets tricky," I said. "I'm not sure her allegation is reportable unless we come up with some actual evidence, or criminal charges are filed against him. Otherwise we're just letting one spouse bad-mouth the other."

Noreen had mixed feelings about that assessment, probably because of her unwavering conviction that viewers care deeply about animal stories. "I don't see us as picking one spouse over the other. A dog died and there are unanswered questions. We have a responsibility to the public and to Buddy to follow up."

I reminded her of my clash with Keith Avise outside the station. "I'm not sure I should be the one interviewing him. Maybe it's better if we hand the story off to someone else."

"But it's an extremely promotable story, Riley. And viewers associate you with it because of the video of you holding Buddy. Putting another reporter on it could confuse them about which channel to watch."

Then she explained that while the network was winning prime-time ratings, Channel 3 was failing to hold those viewers for its late newscast. "We're losing our lead-in audience. That means my job is on the line. Which means your job is on the line."

My job was always on the line, so talk like that didn't scare me. But clearly this unease was a new feeling for Noreen.

"Well, we can do an interesting story about who gets custody of a beloved pet during a divorce," I said. "We can examine how the courts work. We can interview the attorneys, maybe even the judge in this case."

"Does this woman have any home video of Buddy?"

"I'll certainly ask. She gave me the impression he was the child she never had. No doubt, she'll go on camera. And we can let her make the claim that had Buddy been placed in her care, he'd still be alive today."

Noreen nodded. "We might even do an online poll asking viewers what they think regarding pet custody."

I didn't answer because I question the accuracy of that method of surveying, since the respondents select themselves rather than being randomly chosen. But the polls had proven popular with viewers, so I had no hope of changing Noreen's mind.

Then my boss stood up, like she was getting ready to leave. Instead, she walked over to my murder map.

"What's this?"

I tried to think of a convincing lie, but because Noreen and I were getting along so well, I told her the truth about the significance of the chalk outline around Kate's body. And the other murders. And even my hunch that the killer was turning the dead into angels.

"Maybe he thinks he's giving them an afterlife," I said.

"How long have you been working on this?"

"About twenty-four hours, Noreen. But all my info is off the record, so we can't air anything, except for tonight's piece where I showed the crime scene photo. That should make the homicide cops play ball with me."

She didn't answer.

"Noreen, I made a deal."

"When do you think we can break this story?"

"I'm working on it. I'll let you know as soon as it's a go. The best about this one is there's bound to be follow-ups."

"We better not get beat."

I assured her we were the only media anywhere close, and that balancing strong journalism with Chuck's people meter, we had a reasonable chance of winning the household ratings.

"What about the demos?" she asked.

I shrugged. The demos were the only numbers news directors cared about these days. But no one had a ratings crystal ball.

CHAPTER 37

K arl Dolezal felt certain the TV reporter had noticed him, that their eyes had connected intimately as they passed each other in the downtown skyway. When he watched the news that night, he had no doubt.

Broadcasting the outline of his Black Angel on the news was a dare for him to come after her. And he would. On his terms.

He vowed that very soon he would know what car she drove, where she parked, and, most important, where she lived. But since she was aware of him, he must remain cautious.

His agenda made him restless. He turned off the television, climbed out of bed, and paced back and forth. He took the broken bat from the display case and kissed it.

Then he printed a picture of Riley Spartz from his computer. He wrapped it tight around the bat, imagining the wood against her skin and bone . . . but decided keeping the paper prop was unnecessary and unwise. Instead, he ran her photo through a shredder, then stuck the colored confetti inside his pillowcase.

Dolezal crawled back under the covers.

He reached for the stack of Desiree Fleur books he kept on the floor by his bed—not *Black Angel Lace*, he'd banned that one from his living quarters—and reread favorite passages about characters who cajole, caress, and chase their companions until all are satisfied.

He remembered how fate introduced him to Kate Warner. Upon learning that a legal client was an author, he had no idea that he would connect with her writing in such a powerful way, becoming her biggest fan. Until she disrespected his Black Angel. That was like a kiss from Judas.

CHAPTER 38

I went to sleep dreaming of scooping the other media in town on the serial killer case, but woke up discovering I'd been robbed.

The sky was still dark when Noreen called, screaming at me to turn my television to Channel 8 and keep my phone line open.

Chief Capacasa, in a rare live television interview, was giving my story to our morning competitor under a gaudy EXCLUSIVE banner.

"We believe this latest Minneapolis murder is connected to two others in the Midwest." He spoke with authority. "Ames, Iowa, and Madison, Wisconsin, are the other locations."

"What ties them together?" Channel 8's morning anchor, Jenny Turrentine, asked.

I never liked her. Not just because she was beating me on my own case, or because she looked stunning in the wee hours of the morning, but because whenever our paths crossed she made a point of telling me how much she had enjoyed watching my stories when she was growing up.

She and I both knew her remarks weren't meant to cheer me, but to remind me that she was young and—at thirty-six—I was old.

And television was a young person's game.

Meanwhile, the chief kept talking. "The victims were all women, and their manner of death, blunt force trauma, was similar."

"But there must be something more specific, Chief." Jenny leaned forward in anticipation. "Do you have DNA from the killer?"

DNA is a magic word that makes viewers look up from their breakfast. They forget they're watching a morning newscast and think they're tuned to a prime-time crime drama. DNA makes the cops sound smart and an arrest sound imminent.

"We have evidence linking the three cases, but don't want to release too much just now," the chief said. "We'll hold a news conference later today and keep the public updated as best we can." He essentially wrapped up his own interview, leaving the anchor to thank him and toss to the commercial break.

"You and your off-the-record deal. How come he's on their air and not on ours?" Noreen asked.

"I'm not sure." But I had deep suspicions that it might have something to do with the chief showing me who's boss. "But I'll find out."

"It's too late now. Channel 8 is stealing our story. I pay you to find news before it ends up on our competitor's air. You better come up with something good or I'm going to hand the case off to someone who can."

No sense in reminding Noreen that she didn't even care about this murder last week. That was irrelevant now because, in the world of news, timing is everything. Today's lame-duck report can be tomorrow's golden goose story. So I limped into the station to try to salvage my investigation.

"May I speak to the chief, please? This is Riley Spartz from Channel 3."

I didn't expect to be patched through, and I wasn't. But I went through the motions because journalists can't simply assume people don't want to talk to us. We make the call and make them shoot us down.

"Could you please ask him to call me?"

Chief Capacasa's secretary explained that her boss would be happy to answer my questions at the news conference along with the rest of the media, but until then I should expect no comment on their murder investigation.

Garnett apologized for the story getting away.

"Sorry doesn't help me with my boss," I said. "And it doesn't help you with me."

I couldn't decide whether I was sad or angry, so opted for both. Our relationship seemed to swing from extremes. Living under the same roof seemed less and less likely as long as we both held jobs with conflicting goals.

"I'll see what I can find out, Riley, but it doesn't make much sense that the chief would go public with word of a serial killer. His administration prefers shouting good news and ignoring bad."

"I'll certainly ask him about that philosophy at the news conference," I said. "But I'm not sure how forthcoming he'll be."

"That's also strange," Garnett answered. "The chief hates the mechanics of news conferences. Oh, he enjoys being on television, but under his own conditions. He hates a crowd of lights and cameras and questions."

"So do I. I much prefer one-on-one interviews. I should have landed this one. He hosed me."

"I'll see what I can find out," Garnett repeated.

There was a silence on his end. Like he was lingering. Maybe even contemplating signing off with a reassurance of amour, but I feared such a good-bye would only ignite a lover's quarrel. So I quickly thanked him and hung up.

• • •

Xiong sensed my anxiety and tried to cheer me with some humorous perspective sent in an email link. My YouTube video, crying over a dead dog, seemed to have peaked just short of a million hits.

But now the online TV news insider buzz was all about a Las Vegas morning news anchor team standing by for a live casino implosion during their newscast. They droned on about how exciting this event was going to be . . . when the control booth suddenly cut away from the view of the casino to a shot of their meteorologist in the weather center.

Just then the casino blew, and they missed it.

The pair's mortified meltdown, which showed them ripping script paper and slamming the news desk, trumped any memory of my tears. My fault was showing emotion; theirs was showing incompetence.

I replied "thnks" to Xiong, and started scripting what I knew of the serial killer story. I'd sent an order for graphic maps and photos of the victims so the women's faces could pop onto the screen as I read their names. Sounded slick, but by the end of the day, our competition would look the same.

Because the chief was holding the news conference at noon, and because Channel 3 had a noon newscast, Noreen's plan was to carry part of the event live.

As Malik and I drove over to the police station to set up, my cell phone rang. Garnett on the other end.

"I think I know what happened, Riley."

"I'm on my way over to the news conference. Talk fast."

"That's what I'm calling about. The FBI is moving in. They're taking over the murder investigation. The chief's trying to bigfoot the feds to show the citizens of Minneapolis how tough he is."

"Will the FBI be at the news conference?"

"Uncertain, they dislike the media more than the chief does. Behind the scenes, there'll be some pushing and shoving going on for control."

That scenario could be newsworthy on its own. "Before you became a fed, Nick, you'd have been pushing them too." I bid him good-bye as we pulled up outside city hall.

The local TV and radio stations, along with both area newspapers, gathered as well. A few were carrying the video on their websites, but we were the only ones actually broadcasting the feed live because no one else had a newscast scheduled at that time. TV news directors know that if they cut into afternoon soaps their message better be to take cover for weather or war.

I was scheduled for the lead story, but that wasn't saying much since it wasn't quite noon and most news of the day hadn't happened yet.

The hope in the control booth was that by the time I'd given the story background for the viewers and we'd rolled some file tape of the crime scene, Chief Capacasa would be standing at attention by a podium decorated with mic flags advertising each station in attendance. So I turned off my cell phone and started to fill air.

((RILEY LIVE))
I'M RILEY SPARTZ LIVE HERE AT
THE MINNEAPOLIS POLICE STATION
WHERE WE'RE WAITING FOR
THE LATEST ON A MURDER CITY
OFFICIALS SAY MAY BE THE WORK
OF A SERIAL KILLER.

Two minutes stretched after the hour, but still no chief. In my ear, the noon producer finally gave me a wrap. I went with our live event contingency plan.

((RILEY LIVE))
WE'LL CONTINUE TO STAND BY
HERE AND BRING YOU THAT NEWS
CONFERENCE WHEN IT BEGINS . . .
TILL THEN . . . I'M RILEY SPARTZ
AT THE MINNEAPOLIS POLICE
STATION.

More orders came barking through my earpiece from the newscast producer. "I'm checking, I'm checking," I said. Channel 3 then ran through the first section of stories and went black to the commercial break.

Just then the police chief arrived to make good his promise to make news. Because none of the other stations were carrying the news conference live, they didn't particularly care when he started talking, and even had reason to delay it past the end of our newscast. Jenny Turrentine, who had scored that morning's exclusive for Channel 8, tried to stall the chief during his march to the front of the room by confirming how to spell his last name. C-a-p-a-c-a-s-a.

I didn't panic because Channel 3 was still in commercial anyway, but I gave news control a thirty-second time cue to keep them sharp. I heard them scrambling as the chief stepped behind the podium. Usually he wore a suit and tie, but today he was in full dress blue uniform to impress the citizens of Minneapolis and look more like a law enforcement agent than a politician.

"Standby," I told news control, signaling Malik to keep his camera off me and on the chief. The anchor desk would have to introduce him in a double box as the station took the news conference live out of the break.

The chief began to speak. "Minneapolis police believe a recent local homicide is connected to two others in the Midwest."

Commercial just ended in my ear, so I knew we'd missed the chief's opening remark. I could hear our anchor scrambling.

((ANCHOR LIVE))
THAT NEWS CONFERENCE WE
TOLD YOU ABOUT EARLIER IS
JUST GETTING UNDER WAY NOW.
HERE'S THE MINNEAPOLIS CHIEF
OF POLICE.

"Does this mean a serial killer?" the Channel 8 anchor blurted out the question, wanting to get her voice on a competitor's air.

"Yes," the chief answered. "But we want to assure our citizens that these cases are widely scattered, and we believe the killer has moved on and poses no immediate threat here."

A wall of reporter questions moved across the room.

"What links the cases?"

"Do you have DNA from the killer?"

"Did the women know each other?"

The chief took his pick. "We don't believe the victims knew each other personally. They lived hundreds of miles apart, but the cases are connected forensically."

"How?" At least three reporters shouted the same question.

"That's not something we're prepared to reveal at this time. We don't want to facilitate copy cats."

That meant the forensic nugget was the scoop everyone would be trying to land.

I decided I needed to get in play with a question; Channel 3 was probably only going to carry the news conference for another minute or so. Because this type of question-answer format—all for one, one for all—doesn't allow for scoops, I didn't want to draw attention to the chalk outlines by asking whether the killer had left any marks at the crime scenes.

Then in the back corner of the room, I recognized a local FBI guy who I'd tangled with on previous stories. He was dressed in a dark gray suit and tie with his arms crossed over his chest and a frown across his face. I could never remember his name, but he always gave his cases Latin monikers to make them sound important. I wondered what the Latin word for angel might be, but knew better than to ask.

I spoke up with another question. "Because this investigation seems to cross state lines, will the feds be taking over?"

The chief glowered. He'd likely also noticed the FBI guy who, from the back of the room, looked most interested in his answer.

But then a woman rushed in, panting. People turned to look, but I was the only one who recognized Laura.

She didn't seem to notice me, instead sticking her head between the cameras and yelling a question of her own at the chief. "What do you mean, my sister and a serial killer?"

When crime strikes a family, whether it be homicide or a missing person case, relatives sometimes keep the case in the news by granting interviews or handing out photos of the victims. Laura hadn't done any of this groundwork, not even with me. As a fresh angle, the media abandoned the chief and mobbed her with questions of their own to deliver a new face to viewers.

"Did your sister get any threats?"

"Are you afraid for your own life?"

"Do you think the police are doing a good job?"

Laura's eyes and mouth opened wide like the Lowry Tunnel near downtown Minneapolis. More likely, she'd been looking for the chief, rather than publicity, not realizing that in this case they went hand in hand. I tried shouting her name and grabbing her arm, but Mr. FBI Guy beat me to her elbow and whisked her out the door and down the hall past security.

That's when I noticed Malik's camera pointed at me, and remembered we were broadcasting live.

"You made a mess of the Noon Report," Noreen said when I got back to the station.

My cell phone showed a missed call from Laura while the news conference was under way. When I tried dialing her back, all I got was voice mail. My guess was the police were giving her a civics lesson in keeping her mouth shut.

"I thought you were tight with the victim's family," my boss continued. "Didn't you claim to have some inside track with the sister?"

"Yep."

When Laura and I first reconnected, I'd stressed that if she wanted help telling her sister's story, I'd be happy to do so.

"Actually, Riley, I'd prefer to keep work out of our relationship" was her reply.

"You certainly don't have to do any interview with me," I said. "But you can't do one with my competition and still expect to stay friends."

I was no longer sure our friendship held any bearing with her.

Now all the media had video of Laura and would be plastering her face across the airwaves. Tonight Channel 3 would look like Channel 6, which would look like Channel 8 which would look like Channel 10.

I saw only one way to set our coverage apart on this serial killer hunt.

CHAPTER 39

Three hundred miles separated Minneapolis from Iowa City and me from the Black Angel.

I sold Noreen on the trip with the promise our investigation would be first exploring any connection between the outline of the statue and the chalk body shape. Because I needed both daytime and nighttime shots, the assignment meant either an overnight stay and/or massive overtime. Time and money. Two things Channel 3 lacked.

But I reminded Noreen the death of Buddy and our inside track with a Nielsen family had put the station on a ratings roll.

"A heavily promoted story about a death angel amok on a Sunday night might deliver an enormous audience."

So she agreed to let me take Malik, and we hit the road south.

"So you think this Black Angel is cursed?" he asked.

"Well, over the years it's developed a reputation. Folks say it turns a shade darker each Halloween to symbolize all the new blood it's spilled."

I filled him in on the research I'd done on Teresa Dolezal Feldevert, the woman who commissioned the monument and was now buried under it next to her husband and son.

"Legend calls her Iowa's patron saint for evil," I said.

"*Sounds* like an angel of death," he replied.

"That's certainly one theory."

"But I'm not sure your sculpture *looks* imposing enough for the title." He shook his head at a Black Angel photograph I'd taped to the dashboard. "In Islamic theology, the angel of death has four faces and four thousand wings," Malik said. "Your picture seems tame for a death angel."

"I can't speak for Muslim culture, but as far as Christianity goes . . . black as night, staring down toward hell . . . makes for one scary angel."

Malik was Muslim, and enjoyed sharing information about his faith when it meshed with his job. Sometimes his religious views helped us land interviews, other times it cost us them. The assignment desk had learned the hard way to stop sending him to photograph government building exteriors. Even shooting on a public street, security staff always surrounded him and demanded identification.

Malik continued with his theology lesson. "Islam calls our angel of death Azrael, though the Koran uses the name Malak al-Maut, which means 'angel of death,' literally."

"That's interesting because Father Mountain says the Bible teaches nothing of a specific angel of death."

"Well, there certainly is in the Muslim world . . . Malak al-Maut . . . angel of death." He lowered his voice to make the words sound exotic and sinister.

"Malak sounds a little like Malik," I observed, thinking that probably explained his interest.

He shook his head. "Malak means angel; Malik means master."

"Don't get any ideas." I was driving the station van because Malik had learned to nap almost anytime anywhere from his days in the United States army. He called it sleep efficiency. "You get to siesta only because I'm Minnesota Nice, not because you're my master."

"I work better behind the camera," he said. "You work better behind the wheel. Wake me when we get there."

He didn't seem to remember that I already had a job—behind the microphone. But I let him doze, figuring we'd both try to stay up late driving back rather than spending the night in Iowa City. This allowed Malik to rack up scarce overtime money toward a new stove with a convection oven for his wife, Missy, rather than having the station pay for hotel rooms.

While he slept, I drove past flooded fields of corn and soybeans, pondering the mysteries of heaven and angels.

More than four hours later, we stood face-to-face with the Black Angel. She was jarring. And magnificent. I'd worried it might be hard to find the famed figure, but the monument was the centerpiece of death in the massive forty-acre cemetery.

Even Malik was impressed. "Malak al-Maut." He said the words with respect.

I stepped back to give him room while he shot the statue from all directions—every zoom and pan imaginable. I let him play artist, but made sure he recorded the angle that matched the chalk outline I'd taken on my cell phone. That wasn't difficult. It was our first view of the angel as we drove along the cemetery road. And as Father Mountain had mentioned, it was distinctive.

Nearby, on the ground behind the sculpture, I found a long, black feather.

Chills along my back. I bent to pick it up, but changed my mind.

"Malik, get a shot of this."

He saw where I was pointing in the grass and noted the irony. "'Blackbird singing in the dead of night'?"

"I was thinking less Beatles and more Poe. 'Quoth the Raven, nevermore.'"

"Maybe our angel simply sheds at night, returning to her concrete perch after a journey of horror." He looked wistful to capture video of such a diabolical scene.

"You could camp here and find out firsthand," I suggested. "After all, you like to brag you can sleep anywhere. Then you'd earn even more overtime."

Just then I noticed a middle-aged man in a blue uniform driving a green cart toward us on the cemetery road. The maintenance building just outside the main gate had been empty when we drove by, but I figured him to be one of the groundskeepers.

"I'm hoping you're the local lore," I said, introducing Malik and myself as a Minnesota news crew. "We've come to learn about your famed Black Angel."

"What do you want to know?" Ends up, we were speaking to the head groundskeeper, Bob Wachal. "The history or the mystery?"

"We're journalists, so let's start with the history."

"I can give you that," he said, "but nobody is ever content with the truth. The truth is the color change is the result of the natural oxidation of the metal. When outdoors, bronze turns from gold to black. End of story."

"We drove hundreds of miles." I handed him a business card that he pocketed. "I need to bring back more than that for my boss or my next assignment will be six feet under."

Wachal chuckled at my graveyard humor. "People would rather believe in spirits than science. I have a hard time selling what I don't believe." He pulled out a cell phone and asked for my number, then texted me a name and phone number. "But I do accept that the angel is a piece of the town's past, so I'm going to point you in the direction of a better storyteller."

He assured us that Carole Schram, a long-retired schoolteacher, would be worth an interview. "She knows more about the Black Angel rumors than anybody."

I called the number and she agreed to share her expertise.

"When would you like to come over?" she asked.

I explained that we'd rather interview her in the cemetery, next to the statue. "Is there any chance you could meet us here? Or we could come get you."

Carole agreed to be there in about an hour, but cautioned the sun would be setting. Even better, I thought. "That's fine, we need day and night video."

Meanwhile, Malik shot cover of the groundskeeper trimming some shrubs, the Black Angel observing him in the background. Some interesting clouds moved across the sky, forming a wall of white and gray. Tombstones lined the horizon in all directions. I felt outnumbered; more people lay buried in this cemetery than had ever lived in the farm town where I grew up.

"I'm surprised you drove all the way down from Minneapolis." Wachal seemed a little suspicious of our purpose. "The only bronze statue around here that Twin Cities media has ever cared about is a pig, not an angel."

"You mean Floyd of Rosedale?" Malik asked.

Floyd is a rival trophy in college football between the Universities of Minnesota and Iowa. The tradition dates back to 1935 when the governors of the two states bet a live hog over whether the Gophers or Hawkeyes would win the big game. The practicality of exchanging livestock annually gave way to a pig-shaped traveling trophy.

"You head on over to the campus and you'll see Floyd's bronze has turned black, too," Wachal said. "You going to report it's because he's an evil pig?"

"Well, I'm pretty sure I've seen football players kiss Floyd and not die," I said, "but if we can find people who believe he's jinxed, sure, we might be able to make it into a story."

"I think it's the Gophers who are jinxed," said Malik, like most U of M alumni, discouraged by the team's dismal performance.

"But if we're going to talk sports and the Black Angel," I said, "shouldn't we be talking baseball?"

I'd done my homework, and learned that Desiree Fleur's book wasn't the angel's only literary fame. About twenty-four years earlier, W. P. Kinsella, author of *Shoeless Joe*, wrote another novel, *The Iowa Baseball Confederacy*, in which the Black Angel came to life and played right field in a game erased from the memory of those who witnessed it.

"I hear she can catch fly balls with her wings," I said. "No telling what else she's capable of doing."

Wachal shook his head the way people often do when they are tiring of bothersome company. "My yard work is done." Then he pointed us in the direction of some other angel markers—white ones—before heading back toward the main gate.

"Say, Bob," I called out after him, "before you go, have you seen any strange people hanging around here lately?"

"You mean ghosts? Folks are always reporting seeing glowing lights and shadowy figures in the cemetery."

"No, I mean real-life guys who give you the creeps. Like a Black Angel fan club."

"Their kind lurk around here, too. I try to size up whether they're trouble, figuring that's a job the cops are paid to handle." He glanced at his watch, saying he really needed to get home. And so Malik and I stood alone, the dark landmark our only company amid the dead.

We were daring each other to touch the Black Angel when our next interviewee drove up. Her car was old, but Carole Schram was older. A frail lady wearing a dress style popular at least a decade earlier. Compared to the monument, she was tiny. I apologized for dragging her all the way out here.

"Nonsense," our new guide said. "This is my hobby. And it appears you've come a long ways for our legend."

"Absolutely. So what can you tell us about Teresa Dolezal Feldevert?" I asked.

"Where would you like me to begin?"

"Assume we know nothing," I said.

Malik snickered behind me, but I shut him up with a well-practiced glare.

"The Black Angel has stood in this spot for ninety-nine years," she said. "Almost a century of intrigue."

I nodded to show I was paying attention. "How old are you by the way, Carole?"

"I'm eighty-one," she said, proudly. "Plenty old enough to know what I'm talking about."

"That's what we like to hear," Malik said as he clipped a microphone to her neckline. "You're my kind of expert."

"But the angel outranks you," I joked. "So give us the basics."

"The statue stands watch over three sets of human remains." She held up three fingers, then did a countdown. "The first is Teresa's husband." She explained that she had commissioned the statue following his death, for five thousand dollars. "That would cost well over a hundred grand today, but her husband left her a wealthy woman."

Malik whistled in admiration. "Angels don't come cheap."

"The second remains are those of her son." According to Carole, seventeen-year-old Eddie Dolezal had died from meningitis twenty years before the angel's arrival, and was buried in the cemetery under a custom-made tree-stump monument; Teresa moved his body and concrete marker next to the angel so her family would be together after death.

I'd wondered about the significance of the tree stump at the foot of the statue. "It symbolizes a life cut short," she explained.

The final line of Eddie's inscription read, *Do not weep for me, dear mother. I am at peace in my cool grave.*

"And finally, Teresa makes three." Carole's most interesting insight was that while Teresa's year of birth—1836—appears on the Black Angel's platform, her year of death is blank.

Malik crouched to shoot a close-up of the strange enigma.

"So is she dead or not dead?" I asked.

"She died in 1924, but the real debate is not over her death, but the mystery concerning the angel's sinister color metamorphosis."

"What are the leading theories?"

"You mean besides oxidation?"

"Well, yeah. But we're most curious about the supernatural secrets."

"One view has the angel turning black after being struck by lightning the night of Teresa's funeral," she said. "But most of the conjecture centers around a curse of evil—and rumors of infidelity or murder. Legend speculates that Teresa cheated on the memory of her husband, or perhaps that her son died by her hand; thus the blackness serves as a reminder of her sins and a warning to stay clear of her grave."

"Wide-ranging gossip," I said. "I understand she moved to Iowa as a widow, and didn't marry the man buried here until years after Eddie passed away. How did she support herself and son?"

"That's an interesting question," Carole said, "and leads to another reason some townsfolk back then may have felt the angel's hue change as evidence of her own malevolence."

"She was a prostitute?" I asked.

She shook her head. "No, Teresa was a midwife. She built a thriving practice."

I didn't understand what she was implying. "So she helped women give birth. What's so bad about that? Were doctors jealous of her business?"

Carole paused before answering. "At that time, many midwives also performed abortions, of course illegal back then."

Now I understood why Teresa Dolezal Feldevert might have seemed controversial to certain neighbors.

"While that's not one of the romantic rumors cited in current superstition, decades ago it no doubt caused tongue-wagging and promoted fear that pregnant women who walked beneath the angel's wings would miscarry."

Malik looked at me, with apparent misgivings over our earlier jesting. He lowered his camera. "How about us? Would she consider us intruders?"

"Only if you show disrespect," she answered.

"We promise to behave," I said. "But what happens to visitors who don't?"

"Finis. Tales abound of people who kiss under the angel and die inexplicable deaths. Generations have believed that only virgins will be spared from the angel's wrath. Kissing the statue itself is considered a fatal breach of etiquette."

Malik motioned upward, toward the right hand of the angel. "What happened here?" The statue's hand appeared scarred—fingers missing. Malik showed me a close-up through his view-finder.

"Over the years, the monument has been desecrated by souvenir hunters. That's upset the community, thus the police and neighbors try to keep a closer watch on the cemetery, especially Halloween nights."

"So what do you think, Carole? Does the Black Angel evoke evil?"

"Enough baffling anecdotes persist that I don't know what to believe, and I don't think anyone else does either. Some narratives recollect that in her final years, Teresa Dolezal Feldevert felt such shame over the color transformation of her family symbol that she would come to the cemetery in a wheelchair and try to scrape the blackness off the statue."

The image was pathetic. And visual. As a television reporter I regretted not being able to capture her futile action.

"But it didn't work," I said.

"No, it didn't."

The blackness remained obvious.

CHAPTER 40

Dolezal froze while watching Channel 3 unfold the history of Teresa Dolezal Feldevert and the Black Angel.

> ((RILEY STANDUP))
> NO ONE KNOWS WHETHER THE
> DESIGN OF THE STATUE AND
> THE DRAWING LEFT BEHIND
> AT THE MURDER SCENES
> ARE HAPPENSTANCE . . . OR A
> MESSAGE FROM A KILLER. . . .
> BUT TOWNSFOLK HAVE LONG
> BEEN IN AGREEMENT THAT
> THE BLACK ANGEL IS AMONG
> THE MOST HAUNTED SITES IN
> THE MIDWEST . . . RILEY SPARTZ
> REPORTING, FROM IOWA CITY.

He thought the reporter's delivery irreverent and was determined to put her on notice for her sins. Riley Spartz couldn't claim he didn't warn her.

· · ·

To please Noreen and stack the numbers our way, I'd called Chuck ahead of time so he could tune in and stay up to date on any development involving Kate's death. Channel 3 had promoted the Black Angel story throughout the network's prime-time crime dramas.

It proved a good fit. From my news desk the next morning, I called up the overnight numbers and saw a twelve rating—a high Nielsen score in these days of shrinking commercial television audiences.

On my bulletin board, I'd pinned the black feather that I'd picked up from the Iowa cemetery. It oozed mystery, reminding me the case remained unsolved.

Then I clicked to the station's website and admired a picture of the Black Angel statue dominating the page next to the Channel 3 logo. I looked for Internet feedback and already saw more than a dozen comments from viewers. That would also please Noreen. Two of the commenters discussed plans to visit Iowa City as tourists and wanted to know if Oakland Cemetery was open to the public. Others complimented me for an intriguing tale. A couple thought it was a big waste of time since ghosts don't exist.

One comment gave me chills and a flashback: "Taunting Teresa is tempting death."

I mashed through piles of junk on my desk, looking for the *Black Angel Lace* book that I'd taken from Kate's house. I finally found the steamy tale hidden under a stack of files on the floor by my feet. I guess I hadn't wanted the racy cover visible.

Just as I recalled, the title page bore the same line now up on my computer screen. *Taunting Teresa is tempting death*.

For research, I looked up the origin of the name "Teresa" and discovered it Greek for "reaper." And I found myself thinking grim reaper.

• • •

"Can you tell where the comment came from?" I asked Xiong. "An email account or, even better, a physical street address?"

"I will work on it. I will contact you."

That was his way of telling me to move along. So I left him undisturbed, but eager for a cyber chase.

I checked the newsroom refrigerator to see if there might be any abandoned leftovers that wouldn't give me food poisoning. Everything looked risky. My cell phone vibrated, showing Chuck Heyden on the other end. Even though I'd given him that number on our first visit, he'd never called me, I'd always called him.

"My alibi is no good," he said.

"What do you mean?" I headed back to my office in case I needed to take notes.

He explained that Benny, his attorney, had just received the people meter records from Nielsen. "I didn't push the buttons when I was supposed to."

"You mean you didn't register your viewing every fifteen minutes?"

"I guess not."

This was bad for Chuck. Not only was the device not a witness to his whereabouts, it was evidence against him. Once again I had the feeling I might be talking to Kate's killer.

"You still believe me, don't you?" he asked.

"Sure, Chuck."

I didn't know what else to say, but apparently it wasn't convincing enough.

"You don't really sound like you do."

"Well, let's think about this a moment," I said. "The first thing the cops are going to wonder is, Why didn't you push the buttons?"

Chuck paused, and I found myself wishing I could read his face, not just his voice. "I must have fallen asleep."

"Well, that clears up that confusion, Chuck." Claiming to be asleep during a homicide is a poor defense for a suspect, but I figured I'd let Benny explain that nuance to Chuck. "Keep me posted if you hear anything new, and I'll do the same."

"Nielsen wants the equipment back."

He meant the people meter. That didn't surprise me; secrecy is part of the Nielsen family contract. I just hoped Chuck hadn't mentioned me by name.

"Do whatever your attorney tells you to do," I advised him.

As soon as we said good-bye, I hit speed dial for Benny.

His opening line was contemptuous. "Thanks for that murder referral, Riley."

"Chuck just called me."

"So you know your pal's high-tech alibi isn't holding up."

"It seemed worth a try," I said. "If the records had confirmed he was sitting in front of his TV at the time of the murder, that would have been an interesting, and newsworthy, argument."

"Yep, but now I represent a client who's likely guilty."

"That's never bothered you before."

"I cut him a deal on my fee that now I wish I hadn't. This case could end up being a lot of work. Especially if he is a serial killer."

"But the cops don't have even one homicide case yet, Benny. Before they can charge Chuck, they'd have to link him to these other murders as well."

"Being he works at home, and lives alone, there's not a lot of eyewitnesses to corroborate his statements. When I asked him where he was on the dates of those murders, he couldn't give me much beyond 'home watching TV.' And we've seen how well that can be proved. Oh except one of the nights he thought he was at his now dead girlfriend's house."

And so it all comes back to Kate.

• • •

As for my "Taunting Teresa," Xiong replied by email with a jargon of IP addresses and host names, but his bottom line: the message was sent around half past ten that morning from the downtown Minneapolis branch of the Hennepin County Library system, about three quarters of a mile from the station. He also included the email address from where it was dispatched, but his note warned me not to be hopeful.

"Often patrons of public computers forget to sign off, and their accounts are temporarily hijacked by others. That is quite possible in the case of your communication."

I knew what he said was true, but I needed some kind of break on this story and so wanted the email to match the sender. I don't appreciate smart killers who hide their tracks. Give me the dumb ones who leave fingerprints, DNA, or even a signed confession behind. I'd learned on the job.

I sent a "thanks" email to the viewer (keeping it gender neutral) for commenting on my Black Angel story and asking if they'd like to discuss the idea more.

These days, journalists don't have to do much on-site library research, except for very old newspaper archives. So rather than get into a debate with the assignment desk, I simply called out that I was grabbing lunch. Ozzie waved me off.

I didn't bother taking the skyway—it didn't hook to either the station or the library—instead I just marched down the mall like downtown belonged to me. In a way, it did. I'd worked at the station longer than I'd lived anywhere except the farm.

A woman in charge at the library service desk recognized me, but declined my request to see the video surveillance tape from any of the library cameras.

"Someone sent a comment to Channel 3 from the library's computers," I said. "I'd like to find out who." Because I had the time of day of the transmission, I figured it might be easy to track.

She shook her head like that would never happen. "Patron

library records are all private. Whenever books are returned the file is erased and not even staff can tell who has checked out what."

"But what if one patron jumps in another's Internet account? That would seem to be an invasion of privacy."

"I'm afraid we can't help you, Ms. Spartz. We only deal with court orders. Library patron privacy is essential to the exercise of free speech and thought. If you feel like this is a matter of grave importance, contact the police."

She turned and went back to work.

I went over to a bank of library computers to gauge how easy it might be to temporarily poach another's account. All the empty spots had been signed out, but I logged in anyway to check my email.

I found a reply from the Taunting Teresa account, puzzled about my remarks concerning an angel, discounting knowing anyone named Teresa, but delighted to hear from a real-live TV reporter. She mentioned living in some downtown apartments, included her name, phone number, and a request to bring her Red Hat Ladies Club to tour Channel 3.

CHAPTER 41

I stopped at the drugstore on Nicollet Mall near the station for some lip balm. The customer in front of me paid at the cash register with a hundred-dollar bill. I waited until he was out the door before acting nosy.

"Can I see that hundred-dollar bill?" I asked the clerk.

I could tell she thought my request odd. "Do you want to give me change for it?"

"Heaven's no," I said. "I don't carry that much cash. I just don't get to hold too many hundreds."

"Are you worried it might be counterfeit?"

I felt silly answering. "Well, as a matter of fact, I am interested."

She rang up my purchase, opened the register drawer, pulled out the bill, and held it up to the light. "See the watermark?" She pointed out a faint image of Benjamin Franklin. "When I see him, I know it's legit."

I thanked her, marveling at how easy it was to gain her cooperation, and thinking about how much fun it might be to take a counterfeit money survey. Having a camera along would be best, but I decided to attempt another trial run on my way back to the station.

I stopped at Hell's Kitchen, a popular downtown restaurant

that promises "damn good food," to dine on a half order of their house salad and famed ham and pear crisp sandwich. I made sure I snared a table where I could watch the cash register.

After my quick lunch, I talked the clerk into opening the till and holding the twenty-dollar bills up to the light and trading me one of mine for a suspicious-looking Andrew Jackson without the watermark. I might want to hold a bogus bill up on the air should I pull a story together on counterfeiting.

"But if it ends up fake," the cashier asked, "aren't you out the money?" She understood the principle of the last one holding a counterfeit bill loses.

"No, I'll expense it to the network," I said.

We laughed together and as I turned to leave, I noticed the man who saved me from the wrath of Buddy's owner sitting in a back booth with a cup of coffee, a bowl of soup, and a notebook.

Him being there was just a happenstance, I knew that in my head, but in my heart I wanted to believe he sat alone in the corner of the restaurant on protection detail for me. The man appeared unaware of my presence, but I remembered Father Mountain quoting a Bible verse about being nice to strangers because they might be angels testing us.

Test or not, I decided an expression of gratitude was appropriate. So I walked over to him and sat down. "I never got the chance to thank you the other day for stepping between me and that lunatic. So thanks."

He didn't act confident like he did the other morning when he threatened the egg man with calling the cops. Sitting across the table from me, he seemed tongue-tied and insecure. Yet days earlier, he had been my white knight.

"You're my guardian angel, aren't you?" I asked, trying to lighten the mood.

The man's jaw tensed. He left a ten-dollar bill next to his plate, before brushing me and mention of his good deed off with an excuse about being late for an office meeting. I figured he knew

who I was—not because I was vain, but because most people recognized me from TV, though I introduced myself anyway, handing him a business card.

"Let me know if I can ever do a favor for you," I said, preparing to walk out with him and maybe see where he worked.

But he waved me off, saying he needed to stop at the rest-
room. Only close friends wait for each other outside the bathroom, so I let him go. I genuinely hoped our paths would cross
again because it was refreshing to meet someone who expected
nothing in return for helping another.

As I returned to my desk, the investigative journalist in me
realized that he'd dodged my guardian angel question. When
that happens during a television interview, reporters try to gauge
what about the question the subject is trying to avoid. Sometimes an award-winning story pivots on discerning that answer
at that moment.

I'd expected him to laugh at my angel line and tell me not to
be silly, that chivalry wasn't dead in Minneapolis. I'd also assumed that when I said my name, he'd tell me his—but perhaps
it was Gabriel or Michael—and he was guarding his spiritual
identity. Angel law probably forbade their kind from either confirming their earthly mission or lying about it.

I smiled for the first time all day, and made a mental note to
call Father Mountain and share my heavenly wit.

She suspects, he thought. No, she knows. Why else would she
throw the word "angel" at him? She must lack evidence and was
attempting to get him to incriminate himself. Don't engage her,
just walk away, he told himself, and walk away he did. But he felt
her eyes staring at his back, and for the first time since he began
pursuing his avocation, he was unsure who was watching who.

Following her into the restaurant was a mistake. But he'd relished the idea of observing her and recording his impressions in

his notebook. Her obsession with the cashier's money puzzled him, but his real worry was how much she knew about him.

Now she'd seen him three times. A trilogy of sightings that had a symbolic sensation. The egg attack. The skyway crowd. And now, Hell's Kitchen—a suitable name for a showdown, especially because the restaurant's logo was dominated by an angular raven.

Letting his victim Kate know he was coming had added suspense to the chase. In this instance, the TV reporter was letting him know she was coming. He vowed not to wait any longer, but to act.

She would see him a fourth time . . . and it would be her last.

CHAPTER 42

By the time I got back to the station I had two suspicious twenties in my wallet that I reminded myself not to spend unless I wanted to risk being arrested.

The counterfeiting story got a green light from Noreen because I assured her it could be shot without fuss and air the same day. Malik and I set off to grab interviews and cover.

We learned how slick money rings bleach the front and backs of five-dollar bills and reprint a higher denomination so the paper feels genuine. And we saw up close that border and portrait edges are blurred on phony cash, distinct on the real McCoy.

"We tell stores to be wary of customers who make small purchases with big bills," said the Secret Service field agent. "Small businesses are more likely to be victimized because their staff is often untrained."

"What about counterfeit detection pens?" I'd heard their ink turned black when marking bogus bills.

"They are designed to detect starch and are not foolproof. If employees become familiar with how money is supposed to look and feel, they'll be able to tell what's counterfeit themselves."

He complained of losing investigative leads when stores simply pass the money back to other customers instead of calling police. "No one wants to be caught with the hot potato."

We even heard a fun story about a couple of meth dealers who called the cops after getting paid with a big stack of bad money, some printed only on one side. Ends up, they got booked for dealing drugs, and the counterfeiters never got caught.

I started off the script with an anchor lead in talking about how counterfeiting sounded like an exotic crime, but was really quite common.

> ((SOPHIE CU))
> IN FACT, THOUSANDS OF DOLLARS
> OF PHONY MONEY IS PASSED
> AROUND THE TWIN CITIES MOST
> WEEKS.
> RILEY SPARTZ EXPLAINS WHY
> COUNTERFEITING IS BECOMING
> A BIGGER PROBLEM AND HOW TO
> TELL WHAT'S REAL AND WHAT'S
> NOT.

But I was most proud of my standup.

> ((RILEY STANDUP))
> IN THE OLD DAYS OF
> COUNTERFEITING, THE CRIME
> REQUIRED A REAL INVESTMENT . . .
> WITH PROFESSIONAL PRINTERS
> AND PHOTOGRAPHERS. NOWADAYS,
> ANYONE WITH A SCANNER AND
> COLOR PRINTER CAN MAKE BOGUS
> BILLS LIKE THESE.

To dress up the video, I demonstrated the ease of counterfeiting by scanning real twenties and printing a phony page right before the eyes of the viewers. Malik shot the standup wide, then reshot it tight on the action and edited sequences together. At the end, I held the fake money toward the camera lens making it look close-up.

"Cute." While Noreen pretended to share my enthusiasm for the counterfeiting story, what she really wanted was to know what progress I'd made on the pet custody story we'd discussed earlier and how soon that could air.

"My gut tells me viewers haven't tired of it," she said.

The divorce file of Keith and Barbara Avise documented a complicated legal battle over their pet dog, Buddy. I had talked to family court judges and attorneys about such custody decisions and briefed Noreen on what I thought we could broadcast.

Noreen deemed the story "promotable"—her highest praise. "What's holding things up? Grab a photographer tomorrow and start shooting."

I slept better that night than in a long time. No bad dreams. No second thoughts. No phone calls.

Two men in dark suits and sunglasses were standing outside the station next to a black sedan with government plates when I got to work. I looked at the pair curiously, wondering whether a VIP with heavy security was due for an interview at Channel 3. Then one of the men approached me, flashing a badge.

"Secret Service. Are you Riley Spartz?"

"I think you know I am." Otherwise why would they be waiting here? Maybe they'd come to thank me for last night's story educating viewers about money.

"You're under arrest," one of them said, as the other opened the back door of their vehicle. Each grabbed one of my arms, lifting me off the sidewalk, all the better to fling me into their backseat.

"What are you talking about?" I yelled, shaking myself loose. My tush hit the curb and my foot kicked the door shut.

"Counterfeiting." The taller one loomed over me.

"What are you talking about?" I repeated. I thought it was all a gag and didn't take them seriously.

"We have video of the evidence."

I refused to come peacefully, insisting instead on speaking with my attorney.

"Time for that later," the bossy one said. "When we get downtown."

He tried to pull me up from the sidewalk while his buddy opened the door again. I shifted away, keeping my butt glued to the concrete, and my fingers across the keyboard of my cellphone.

URGENT. SEND MILES OUTSIDE ASAP. I texted Ozzie because I knew he constantly monitored his line.

WHAT'S UP?

UNDER ARREST. GET CAMERA. STOP WASTING TIME.

Noreen would be plenty disappointed in me if I let myself be taken into custody right outside the station without a camera present.

"I have to let my boss know where I'm going," I told the other fed as he tried to pry my phone away.

Just then Malik came through the door and hoisted a camera to his shoulder. His presence stalled the action until the arrival of Miles Lewis, the station media lawyer, seconds later.

Miles mustered enough indignation to ask, "What seems to be the bother here?"

The Secret Service team explained that I was guilty of counterfeiting for copying money on camera in my story that aired last night.

"Guilty?" Miles said the word in his legal scorn tone.

"Technically, yes."

"Well, *technically,* I can't believe your agency actually has time for jokes like this. Say what you need to say and let's finish up here."

As a compromise to hauling me off to jail, they agreed to settle for confiscating the paper money I printed for the standup. I wasn't sure where the pages even were, and envisioned having to crawl through the Dumpster in the alley behind the station.

The Secret Service team followed us into the building to observe. After leafing through my desk and several wastepaper baskets, I came up with a handful of copy pages of twenty-dollar bills.

"Is this all, Ms. Spartz?" one of them asked.

"You can't possibly claim these could pass as counterfeit," Miles said. "They're only printed on one side. And it's cheap copy paper."

They ignored Miles to lecture me about crime and punishment. "Are you sure this is all?"

I had no idea how many copies I'd made. I have a reputation of having to shoot multiple standups just to get a decent one. So there could have been lots more.

But Miles assured them they had the complete set, offered mea culpas, and agreed to call if any more should turn up.

"Why wasn't this story run by me?" Miles asked, after the men in black left. He was supposed to review any stories that might have possible legal entanglements.

"Because I didn't think there were any legal issues. We weren't defaming anybody. These guys got more dangerous crooks to chase than me."

After this, Miles told me, I needed to send all my scripts to him before air.

CHAPTER 43

I know. I know," I told Noreen as she too came up to scold me about the money printing mess. "I don't need to hear more."

I reminded her that if she wanted the pet custody feature finished, I had to start working on it pronto.

At the end of the day, she loved the script and wanted to hold pet custody a couple of days to promote the story before a big network audience.

> ((SOPHIE BOX W/ BUDDY))
> BY NOW MANY OF YOU ARE
> FAMILIAR WITH THE STORY OF
> BUDDY, THE DOG WHO DIED AFTER
> BEING LEFT IN A HOT CAR.
> WHAT YOU MAY NOT KNOW IS THAT
> BUDDY CAME FROM A BROKEN
> HOME. REPORTER RILEY SPARTZ
> HAS MORE.

Buddy's situation was unusual. Because pets are considered property, not family, courts typically don't assign visitation. But in their affidavits, both spouses said they'd rather share Buddy than see him given to the other outright. So the judge approved a week-by-week custody arrangement.

((JUDGE SOT))
PET CUSTODY CAN CAUSE
EMOTIONAL TURMOIL BUT COURTS
ARE BACKLOGGED AND CAN'T MAKE
THAT A HUGE PRIORITY.

My story explained how the court looks at whether an animal was purchased during the marriage; who handled the chores of feeding, walking, and vet visits; if children are involved; or whether one party has a fenced yard and the other a tiny apartment.

But the piece was missing one element.

In most cases, I never voluntarily give up a slice of any story I deem mine. But when it came to Keith Avise, I wasn't sure he would agree to answer my questions, or that I would be comfortable interviewing him. Besides being a journalist, when it came to him, I was both a witness to and victim of his various transgressions.

"I'm not sure my objectivity could go unchallenged," I told Noreen.

My boss startled me by suggesting someone else should handle that part of the story.

"You stick to the nuts and bolts of the issue. I'll get someone else to interview Buddy's family as a sidebar."

I was so gleeful at ducking that assignment, I didn't bother asking, who? But I should have. Because that might have made a big difference later on.

"Hey, Riley, Fargo wants a word about your angel killer," Ozzie yelled out to me from the assignment desk.

"What about it?" He was talking about our network affiliate in

Fargo, North Dakota. Television market rank 120, compared to Minneapolis–St. Paul at number 15.

"They think they might have one."

"A killer?"

"A murder."

I took the call at my desk and learned that a couple months earlier, Bonnie Brang had been beaten to death and left on the blacktop driveway of her fenced house on the outskirts of town. The station covered the homicide as big news. Still no arrests. But after the police had cleared the scene, the local reporter shot a standup in front of the open gate, and where the body had lain, a chalk outline could be seen.

"Until I saw your story, I just figured the cops made it. Now I'm not so sure. And they won't talk."

He emailed me the news link and as I watched the video, I saw that the outline resembled the one drawn around Kate. "What did the victim do for a living?"

"A waitress."

My murder map gained a star at Fargo, North Dakota, along with a photo of the victim. This latest case had more in common with the others than Kate. Staying objective, I could see Kate was the least attractive of the dead. The others were blond waitresses. From smaller cities. Madison was market rank 85 and Ames shared Des Moines's TV market at number 71.

If the homicides were the work of the same killer—and the chalk outlines inferred that scenario—it suggested the maniac's motive might have shifted.

The map was quite visual, and as a television reporter I prefer laying out my investigations in charts, graphics, and pictures. That technique helps me tell the story to viewers and see for myself where the case might be heading.

Some serial killers select their victims from the same geographic area, terrorizing a single city. Others enjoy traveling and staying undetected. Each of these homicides happened in cities more than two hundred miles from Minneapolis. All different states—Minnesota, Iowa, Wisconsin, North Dakota—another technique for a smart thug to evade attention.

But that observation was fairly obvious. I didn't need a custom map to calculate distance and borders. What really struck me was the shape of the murderer's route.

I traced a line between the slayings and saw the Black Angel appear before me. Let Minneapolis be her head. Ames, her feet. Fargo, the top wing tip. Madison, the lower wing. The killer was leaving an even more subtle signature than his chalk outline. The big picture.

I paged Noreen on the overhead speaker, asking her to come to my office.

She tilted her head and squinted her eyes at my wall. "I see what you mean, Riley, but don't you think that's stretching things a bit for crazy? Even for a serial killer?"

I reminded her about the wild college student about a decade earlier who planted pipe bombs in mailboxes across the Midwest in a path shaped like a giant smiley face.

"I'm not saying psychopaths make sense, Noreen. I'm just saying we have another murder that fits and we ought to build a graphic for tonight's newscast. Think exclusive."

So she did.

((SOPHIE CU))
CHANNEL 3 HAS LEARNED THAT A
FOURTH HOMICIDE—THIS TIME IN
FARGO, NORTH DAKOTA—MIGHT
BE TIED TO THE ANGEL OF DEATH
KILLER.
RILEY SPARTZ IS FIRST WITH THE
DETAILS.

((RILEY TRACK))
THE BODY OF A WOMAN
MURDERED IN FARGO WAS
ALSO FOUND WITH A CHALK
OUTLINE THAT RESEMBLED THE
SILHOUETTE OF AN INFAMOUS
BLACK ANGEL STATUE IN IOWA.

((RILEY GRAPHIC))
AND WHEN WE LINED UP THE
FOUR CITIES WHERE THE KILLINGS
HAPPENED . . . THIS IS WHAT YOU
SEE.

Then we froze the video of the Black Angel and dissolved in the four Midwest cities simultaneously. The statue's head, feet, and wing tips matched perfectly—and that shape spooked me.

CHAPTER 44

He deemed his progress acceptable.

Through patient observation, he'd learned that Riley Spartz typically left through the back door of Channel 3 at the end of the day. She bought monthly underground parking at a small hotel near the station. While no specific space was reserved, now that he knew she drove a gray Toyota, it was a simple matter for him to keep vigil on the street, watching for her car to exit.

The wild-card factor was the unpredictability of her shift. He must remain flexible. Once he discovered where she lived, he could plan around his schedule.

His first try, he lost her on the way home when she zipped through the stoplight off the 46th Street exit ramp, leaving him stuck behind two other vehicles. But he was able to see that she turned east. The next night, because he knew her route off the freeway, he was in a better position to chase. He passed ahead of her to drive through the stoplight first, then followed her for a few minutes toward Lake Nokomis.

He had expected a more affluent neighborhood with better security. He wished she had an attached garage, but he could make do. He had before. He was content to watch her shape pass in front of the windows until he was certain where her bedroom was located, and that she owned no dog.

He would make no move tonight, in case a neighbor had noted his vehicle, but more important, to allow himself anticipation time. He wouldn't have the inconvenience of tailing her from work. Now he could just show up, perhaps waiting in the covered porch of the house for sale next door. His surveillance convinced him it was uninhabited.

Back at his apartment, he switched on Channel 3's late news, hoping to watch Riley Spartz on the television screen and fantasize about their encounter to come. When she showed the Black Angel murder map, he knew he had to act soon.

CHAPTER 45

The ringing phone roused me at just after midnight.

"Hello?" Ten seconds later I was alert enough to recognize Laura on the line, crying.

"What's wrong?" I asked. "Are you all right?"

"I'm at Kate's," she sobbed. "I'm freaking out."

"Laura, what are you doing there?"

"I was trying to stay overnight, Riley. The motel was getting so expensive. I told myself to just fall sleep and not think about what happened to her. Except that's all I can think about."

"Doesn't surprise me. I can't believe you even thought you could make that work."

"I'm afraid to be alone here, Riley. Can you come over?"

Alone or not, I sure wouldn't want to sleep in a murder house in the dark. So I offered her my couch.

"Really? You don't mind?"

"Once a roommate, always a roommate." I gave her my address, and twenty minutes later she was at the door holding a suitcase.

"Thank you, thank you, thank you." She kept repeating herself as I got her settled on the hide-a-bed in my home office.

"It's no problem," I assured her.

"I'm so sorry," she said. "Right now cash is tight. I spent a lot on the plane and hotel and rental car. I've switched to Kate's car now, and I'm fine driving that. But I can't live in her house."

"I understand, Laura." As she rambled, I heated up enough hot chocolate for two, hoping we could both get a few hours sleep before I had to be at work.

"I'm meeting with Kate's attorney tomorrow morning," she said. "Her estate won't be settled for months, but he's seeing if I can get an advance on my inheritance to cover all the expenses."

Her attorney. Of course. I gave myself a mental kick for not thinking of it myself. From the time I'd theorized a connection between Kate's writing and her murder, I'd guessed the killer would be someone who knew Kate Warner was also Desiree Fleur. Kate's attorney would certainly have known her alias.

"Would you like me to go with you, Laura?"

"Oh, would you? Lawyers make me nervous."

No trouble, I assured her. And then I suggested we get some sleep.

Peter Marsden was a probate and tax attorney for one of Minnesota's largest law firms. Working among more than four hundred lawyers would allow him to stay under the radar of curious colleagues.

His office was four blocks from Channel 3, so I gave Laura a spare key to my place and told her to follow me downtown. Marsden escorted us into a conference room of dark wood furniture and landscape oil paintings, a more suitable setting for briefing CEOs than us.

He and I had never met, probably because none of his clients had ever made news before. But he immediately recognized me, and warned Laura about the perils of getting too close to the media.

"I'm here as a friend, not a reporter," I assured him. "I want to support Laura." I tried making both of them feel at ease. "As far as I'm concerned, this meeting's off the record."

Still suspicious, Marsden frowned at me. "How many days old is this camaraderie of yours? Laura, you've been under enormous stress. As your sister's attorney, I consider it my professional responsibility to point out that you might be mistaking manipulation for friendship."

He was all lawyer. I'd never want to face him during a deposition—or in a courtroom. And I wondered if his attack on me was to protect Laura or to isolate her. I'd expected him to be the kind of attorney who was good with numbers, not words. He was smooth, but was he also a killer?

"Actually, Riley and I went to college together."

In a more composed tone than I expected, Laura explained that she trusted me completely, and hoped he would as well.

So without him responding one way or another, we got down to business.

Besides her church and a few charities, Laura was the sole heir. After taxes and probate fees, Marsden estimated she would receive just under a million dollars from Kate's estate.

Laura was stunned. He detailed that the money would come from a life insurance policy, home equity, investments, and book royalties.

"Did she enjoy being an author?" I asked, wanting to hear more about Kate's life than net worth.

Laura nodded, encouraging him to answer.

"One of the conditions she insisted on before having our firm represent her was that her professional life and personal life remain separate and secret. She would decide who and when anyone else would be told. We followed her instructions. Ours was a business relationship."

"Do you know who else might have known?" I asked.

"It's not something I ever inquired about."

"Do you know anyone who might have wanted her dead? Did she ever mention being afraid?"

"Excuse me, Ms. Spartz, but right now you're sounding more like a reporter than a friend. In what capacity are you asking these questions?"

I apologized, because I didn't want to be banned from the discussion.

"I've already answered these questions with the police, and don't feel I need to go over that ground with you." He turned away from me and toward Laura. "However, you and I should stay in touch, and if you have any questions, please call me."

Marsden handed her a business card, but not me. I reached for one and while he conceded, he mentioned nothing about calling him with questions. Nor did he thank me when I gave him one of my own cards.

I was distracted from his rudeness by Laura's next announcement. "I want to sell the house."

After last night, I wasn't surprised.

"We can certainly arrange that," he said, "but the estate needs to be settled first and, frankly, that will take months."

"Isn't there a state law that sellers have to disclose if a murder took place in a home?" I'd always wanted to do a story about people moving into homicide houses and whether they knew the history.

My question displeased him. "Yes."

His answer disturbed Laura. "Won't that make the house hard to sell?"

"It's possible. But the more time that passes, the more people forget. Less publicity helps." He looked at me, and I got his message. I just hoped Laura didn't.

CHAPTER 46

On that night's late news, my pet custody story aired in the second block. After my outcue of "Riley Spartz, Channel 3 Television News" came a close-up anchor shot of Sophie.

> ((SOPHIE CU))
> YOU'VE GOT THE BACKGROUND,
> NOW YOU'RE GOING TO GET TO THE
> HEART OF THE STORY.
>
> ((THREESHOT))
> JOINING ME ON THE SET ARE THE
> NOW EX-HUSBAND-AND-WIFE TEAM
> OF KEITH AND BARBARA AVISE.

The lead in sounded a little circusy to me, but it was nothing compared to the actual interview to come. Keith had agreed to a live interview because his attorney had assured him that it was the best way to get his side of the story out—especially when guaranteed that Sophie, rather than me, would ask the questions.

Sophie had little experience interviewing live guests with opposing views. She was masterful at chitchat between weather and sports, or softball Q-and-A sessions with real-life folks thrust into the media spotlight. Give her the hero who rescued a child from a burning vehicle or the woman who became an overnight millionaire with a lucky lottery ticket, and Sophie could give viewers three mesmerizing minutes.

Sophie, like many anchors, had been shielded from controversy, but Noreen felt this interview was worth the risk because it could be a blockbuster and attract a whole new audience to Channel 3.

Sophie was excited about proving herself as a real journalist.

"I'm not sure, Noreen," I said, "to me, this setup feels better suited for the *Dr. Phil* show."

"I know," she answered proudly. "We're going to promote it heavy during *Dr. Phil* and *Oprah*."

Noreen assigned me to coach Sophie on interview techniques. "Your two guests could get surly, but you must stay calm. Cordial but firm is the way to go. You always want the audience to think you're the reasonable one."

"Cordial but firm," she repeated, while writing the words in a narrow reporter notebook.

"Exactly."

My "cordial but firm" philosophy has served me well whether taping an interview in which I had to point out that a particular politician was indeed a liar or ambushing a business owner who'd been ducking me on a consumer story. *Cordial but firm.*

"Never gloat on camera," I continued. "Always give the impression that you regret this unsavory part of the job, but your interviewee has given you no choice."

No gloat, my protégée wrote down under my watchful eye.

"During a few interviews, Sophie, I've actually said, 'I'm sorry it's come to this, but you give me no choice.' Then, I pull out the hidden-camera video that proves they're a crook."

I explained to her that live interviews can be more difficult because time is limited and guests may have agendas.

"Whose interview is it?" I asked Sophie as we recapped the fine points of interviewing.

"Mine."

"Yes and no. Certainly the interview belongs to you, but it also belongs to the viewers. Figure out what the public wants from the exchange and try to give it to them. Don't worry so much if a guest spins out of control, the audience will see that and form their own opinions. The important thing is for you to keep your cool."

"Cordial but firm." She gave me an enthusiastic thumbs-up.

My last advice to Sophie was to think up a few questions to start off and even fall back on, and load them in the teleprompter, but to also listen to the guests and form questions relating to their answers.

"Don't make the questions too long," I said. "Viewers want to hear the guests, not you. Don't ramble."

"Short questions," Sophie said.

"Live guests sometimes play off each other's answers, without even waiting for a question," I said. "And that's fine as long as this interview stays on track about divorce and pets or Buddy, and they don't start harping about forgetting anniversaries or disliking in-laws. Because remember, Sophie, whose interview is it?"

"Mine. And the viewers'."

In retrospect, it was a mistake to let both Keith and Barb sit on the set at the same time. Usually when conflicting guests share an interview segment, one or even both are interviewed from other locations in a TV news technique called through-the-box. They hear the questions in an earpiece, but can't see the anchor or each other.

Critics are always whining that TV stations do this to put the guest at a disadvantage, but no such conspiracy exists. The reality is that it's done for production values. A through-the-box interview looks more visually interesting than having all the guests in a newscast on the same set where the rest of the news is read. That's why reporters are often live in the field, which typically adds nothing to the story content, but looks cool.

However, Noreen was adamant that letting former spouses glare at each other in person would be good TV.

"What if one of them tries to punch the other?" I asked. "Or throw an egg?"

Noreen's eyes got bright and shiny at the prospect of two guests wrestling on Channel 3's news set. "Sophie can sit in the middle."

And so she did. As the floor director clipped microphones on the two guests, he reminded her she had four and a half minutes for the entire interview.

> ((SOPHIE THREESHOT))
> BARB . . . MOST DIVORCING
> COUPLES FIGHT OVER WHO GETS
> THE HOUSE . . . THE MONEY . . . THE
> KIDS . . . HOW DID YOU TWO END UP
> FIGHTING OVER A PET?

The question was neutral; the answer set off a verbal storm.

"Keith never really loved Buddy," Barb said. "He pushed for custody just to hurt me."

"What are you talking about?" Keith cut in. "I cared more for that dog than you, that's for sure."

I wasn't sure if he was talking about caring in the vein of feeding and walking Buddy, or caring meaning he liked the dog more than he liked his ex. Sophie didn't pursue that angle but smoothly played off his answer to another question.

> ((SOPHIE CU))
> YET BUDDY DID DIE IN YOUR CARE,

KEITH. HOW DO YOU EXPLAIN
WHAT HAPPENED THAT DAY?

The question was obvious and shouldn't have surprised him, but Keith seemed to have difficulty framing a response. Clearly his attorney hadn't coached him like I had Sophie.

"I'd like to hear that answer, too," Barb said.

"Let him talk," Sophie said.

He stammered something about how we all make mistakes.

His angst seemed to embolden Sophie, who traded her perky persona for one of power. "That doesn't really address my question, Keith. Let me explain how a news interview works. I ask, you answer—Yes?"

That wasn't anything close to cordial but firm. That was rude and condescending.

Keith tried explaining about the car and Buddy and how he lost track of time, I couldn't gauge his sincerity because Sophie kept interrupting him to say things like "none of that will bring Buddy back."

Barb chimed in, "If custody had been awarded to me, Buddy would be alive today."

"She kind of has a point, Keith. Do you think you might owe her an apology?"

"Sorry won't cut it," Barb said. "I don't think Buddy's death was an accident, I think he was murdered! You left him in your truck to die to punish me for leaving you."

Even though the four and a half minutes weren't up, the floor crew was giving Sophie a frantic wrap per instructions from the control booth. But the signal came too late. Barb lunged at Keith, knocking Sophie off her news perch and out of camera view. The floor director jumped between the two guests before they could exchange blows.

Sophie raised her head from behind the news desk—her perky personality back in play.

((SOPHIE THREESHOT))
THANKS FOR JOINING US HERE AT
CHANNEL 3 . . . COMING UP NEXT,
A LOOK AHEAD AT THE WEEKEND
WEATHER.

The newscast faded black into a commercial break. Sophie used the two minutes of advertisements to powder her face and assure everyone in the newsroom she was fine.

As the guests were escorted out of the building through separate doors, Barb beamed while Keith scowled. Noreen approached me, presumably to commiserate over the interview debacle. Instead, she blamed me.

"Riley, this is your fault, you were supposed to prep her better."

"I did. She didn't stick to the plan, Noreen. She went rogue."

We continued to bicker through weather and sports about why Sophie turned into Nancy Grace until the ending music rolled and Sophie signed off with a vivacious, "Good night, everyone."

She waved us over to the news desk. "How did I do?" She grinned, seemingly in anticipation of compliments. "I was reasonable, they were crazy."

Noreen looked at me and I looked at Noreen. Because she was the boss, I let her go first.

"It wasn't quite what I expected." Noreen's tact was certainly more than I expected.

"Didn't know I had it in me, huh?" Sophie interpreted Noreen's diplomacy as praise. "I'm proud that you're proud. How about you, Riley?"

Not having taken management classes, I was blunter. "You seemed to forget our cordial-but-firm plan. I fear you made the viewers feel sorry for a dog killer. And that's not easy to do."

"No way," she protested. "You said, figure out what the public wants from the interview. I figured they wanted to see him squirm."

"You and the ex-wife both came across as hostile," Noreen said. "Frankly, I'm afraid to look at the viewer call sheet and on-line comments."

"I was trying to be a serious journalist," Sophie said, "and not just a pretty face. I wanted to prove I can think fast and act tough."

Sophie got nailed, and not just by viewers. Bloggers, Tweeters, and other news outlets basically said she deserved to get knocked on her butt for her unprofessional conduct.

I was used to people hating me, but this was a new, unpleasant experience for Sophie. The next time she went on the air, her smile lacked its wow factor and her eyes their sparkle.

She was learning news hurts.

CHAPTER 47

The lights were on, so Riley Spartz must be inside. He was torn whether to wait until the house was dark, or surprise her at the door. Crouching in the neighboring house's porch, he eyed her silhouette as she moved from room to room.

He had taken his nanna's car for repairs, telling her the work might be a couple days. Now her vehicle sat a half mile away on a dark side street near Lake Nokomis Park. Far enough not to be linked to this crime; near enough for his escape to the freeway.

Just then he grew baffled and paid closer attention. As he watched, he realized two distinct female forms floated before him through the windows.

Who was the other woman? He was tempted to go for both, but didn't have the confidence or experience. More significantly, he didn't have permission.

He would wait them out.

This plan could work well. After her friend left, he would go to the door and the TV reporter would abandon caution and simply assume something had been forgotten. He could pounce.

An hour later he grew restless. Why was she still entertaining company? Didn't she have to be at work in the morning?

Then the house went dark and he was forced to consider that she might have a roommate or a houseguest. In his case, a witness.

He left to ponder alternatives, vowing to return to consummate the crime.

CHAPTER 48

I pretended not to see Ozzie flagging me down from the assignment desk the next morning, but he left his newsroom perch and intercepted me on my way to my office.

"No story," he said. "The GM wants you upstairs."

One-on-one time with the general manager can be really good or really bad. I deserved praise; after all, I'd delivered stories and viewers. But I'd never gotten any personal kudos from upstairs before, so more likely than not I was in for a second tongue-lashing about the pet custody interview, or another cyber consult from Fitz, this time under the watchful supervision of the big boss.

"Where's Noreen?" I asked, surprised she wasn't the one to fetch me and scold me about what to say and not say.

"Not sure," Ozzie shrugged. "But he's waiting for you."

His assistant, Lynn, waved me inside the big office with the windows overlooking downtown. I tried catching her eye for a cue, but she seemed to be avoiding my gaze.

Inside I saw why.

The GM sat behind his mahogany desk with Noreen in front of it. Both of them waiting in ambush.

"Hello, you two." I stayed casual.

He motioned me to take a chair. The air stayed still, as if he and Noreen were both waiting for the other to start talking.

He decided to go first. "I got a call from Nielsen. The ratings monster."

"Are we winning?"

"We were. Now they're going to flag our numbers."

Flag was a dirty word in broadcasting—unless it was directed at a competitor. I looked at Noreen, but she was no help. She seemed intent on his words and oblivious to me.

"Nielsen talked to one of their Minneapolis households, Riley. A viewer named Charles Heyden. He told them how interested you were in seeing him demonstrate how the people meter remotes and boxes work. And how helpful you've been, alerting him to certain stories, and finding him a good lawyer who knows how to file a subpoena."

He paused, presumably for me to respond. I considered myself an ad lib master, but this was a real jam. Nielsen pretty much had me nailed. All that remained was whether I took Noreen down with me.

"Your behavior has been so blatant, I must take appropriate action to appease Nielsen and send a lesson to other newsroom employees."

Noreen suddenly spoke up. "Certainly Riley suffered a lapse of judgment. But she belongs to us, not them. And I don't want to be bullied by the ratings machine any more than we already are. Charles Heyden's been dropped from the Nielsen family. I think our best course is to prove for the rest of the month that our numbers were not a fluke, and we can maintain our viewership."

"Not good enough," he countered.

I felt awkward, them arguing about my crime and punishment in front of me. But I feared saying the wrong thing. After all, I *was* guilty.

But I had an accomplice.

Sometimes you have to chose between two bad things: damned versus doomed. Damned if I do; doomed if I don't. I decided to keep my mouth shut and make Noreen pay another time. She would owe me.

I tried explaining that my relationship with Chuck came from the fact that he was a murder suspect and I wanted to stay tight so I'd land a jailhouse interview.

Noreen liked that answer; the GM didn't buy it. They compromised on a one-day unpaid suspension. Effective immediately.

We both left the general manager's office together. Around the corner, I guided her away from the stairs.

"Let's take the elevator, Noreen."

"This way's lots quicker to the newsroom, Riley. The elevator's way down the hall. And the photogs will probably be holding it to load gear."

"I don't care." I whispered each word low and with drama.

She followed me down the hall where we waited for the lift. Once inside, doors closed, I pressed the Stop button for privacy, so we could speak somewhere other than her glass-walled news director office.

"What do you mean throwing me to the GM like that with no warning?" I didn't push her up against the elevator wall, but I stood close enough to breathe heavy in her face. "You're my boss, you're supposed to protect me."

"What do you think I was doing in that office? I could have let you fend for yourself. But I argued him out of firing you."

"You were in there protecting your own job. You didn't want me alone with him or I'd rat you out."

"Then we'd both be out of work. Here you're just off a day. If you want, come in anyway, we'll just keep you off the air and I'll tell him you were gone."

"Forget it," I said. "I need a day off."

Then I let the elevator go and we dropped one whole floor to the ground level. Door open.

"Does this mean you're not going to watch my animals this weekend?" Now she was the one whispering. A full house menagerie like hers would make it hard to find a sitter. She might have to cancel her trip.

"No, I'll watch them, Noreen."

A promise is a promise. As a journalist I pride myself on keeping my word, even to people who might not deserve that courtesy.

The elevator door shut behind us. Noreen walked toward her office; I walked toward the building exit. When I got to the door I turned to look back at her in case she had turned to look at me. Somehow I thought if we exchanged an understanding glance just then, that would be a sign that things were okay. But she never looked back.

CHAPTER 49

I went home in a funk, forgetting I wouldn't be alone. Laura was thrilled to see me. I didn't mention anything about being suspended, just that I was taking a day off.

It didn't occur to her that kind of flexibility might be unusual in the news business because she had something else on her mind.

"I'm sorry to even bring this up," my old college pal said, "but I sort of need another favor."

"What's wrong, Laura?" She was becoming a high-maintenance friend, but I continued to cut her slack because of her murdered sister. I wondered what more I could do for her besides putting a roof over her head.

"Kate's editor just called. There's a problem, Riley."

"There sure is. Her author is dead. But I don't think there's anything you or I or he can do to change that. It's sort of like that dragon tattoo writer from Sweden."

"Well, apparently Kate was contracted to turn in another book and Mary Kay Berarducci says if she doesn't get it, Lascivious Press is going to sue the estate to get the advance back."

My first reaction was that a deal was a deal and the publisher was probably entitled to either the manuscript or the money. But I didn't see what any of this had to do with me.

"The deadline is in two days," she said. "The book must be finished. I just have to find it."

Days earlier, Laura was horrified by her sister's covert occupation. Now she was taking a business approach. I'd seen this before, money helps shift the focus away from grief.

"Well, the most likely place is on her computer," I said.

So we headed over to the murder house to look for the manuscript. On the way I asked Laura how her sister ended up owning their parents' home.

"She bought it from them when they decided to downsize. I never wanted to move back to Minnesota, so that was fine with me. I've enjoyed calling different cities home."

"Where have you lived?" I asked.

"Omaha, Phoenix, Houston, Des Moines, Chicago." She rattled off a list of cities.

"You're kind of a vagabond," I observed.

"I don't like being tied down," she responded.

One thing I noticed from my recent conversations with Laura was that she never inquired about me. How was I doing? Was I seeing anyone? How were my parents? And she never volunteered much about herself, except what I pried out of her.

I decided not to dwell on that because if her pattern held, she'd be on the road soon enough. And frankly, I wasn't sure she'd bother keeping in touch. So hearing the story of her life post-college might be a waste of time.

Kate's laptop computer was in her home office. I opened it and tried logging in, but found myself locked out.

"Any idea what her password would be?" I asked her sister.

Laura shrugged. No clue.

I tried the obvious ones. Birthday. Address. *Incorrect Password* flashed across the screen each time. "I think we should take it to the station and let my computer expert see if he can crack it." Then I remembered I was banned from the station until tomorrow.

On a sudden hunch, I typed in D-e-s-i-r-e-e-F-l-e-u-r.

A few seconds later, I was inside. Xiong would be proud.

I saw a row of files. "Anything look promising?" I asked Laura.

She shrugged. So I opened the first one and found a steamy book cover with the earth surrounded by naked bodies. It was titled *Sexpocalypse*. Kate's novels were still strewn across the floor from the rant the other day. "Laura, do any of those books match this cover?"

She looked distastefully through the stack, and shook her head. Seemed to me a good chance *Sexpocalypse* might be the work in progress. I used the finder feature on Kate's computer to search for the title and pulled up a file with that name and clicked to open.

I skimmed the first several pages.

The opening scene, England, boy meets girl. Almost immediately Kate, or rather, Desiree, had the couple coupled in a university broom closet. A similar scene unfolded in Australia where two characters ended up between the sheets one page after meeting in a Laundromat. Then cut to a subway train in Japan where passengers started making out with their seat mates until a hint of orgy at the end of the scene.

The action shifted to a laboratory where scientists concluded that a world pandemic was in play leaving its victims addicted to sex. The best global medical minds were trying to develop a vaccine, but a terrorist country was working to thwart them because a world preoccupied with sex would be easy prey.

The manuscript ran just over sixty-five thousand words. I hooked up the laptop to the printer to make a copy. As the pages printed, I emailed myself the file as an attachment. I asked Laura to keep the paper tray filled and the printer unclogged.

While we waited for last page, I noticed Kate hadn't logged out of her email account. I loaded her account and scanned her files. I first checked messages she'd sent, starting with the most recent, and found one telling Chuck how safe he made her feel.

That seemed an unusual compliment for a boyfriend, but Kate, I was learning, led an uncommon life and might have had good reason to feel unsafe.

She had also sent a note to her editor at Lascivious Press, promising to make her deadline, but bemoaning she had yet to lock in on a stunning conclusion.

Berarducci, eager to see the manuscript, reassured her, "Keep writing, this idea of yours has potential to be a Big Book."

Most of the mail Kate received seemed to be fan letters, from men and women, appreciative of such passionate writing. Some raves had even arrived after her murder, the aficionados unaware their erotic idol had fallen. As I searched for clues on her computer, I learned more than I wanted to about what turns readers on in sex scenes.

One thing I noted, Kate had not sent any messages to Laura, nor vice versa. "Hey, Laura, I don't see any sisterly chat here. Were the two of you not speaking?"

She seemed miffed by my question. "I prefer talking on the phone than with computers."

"Fair enough." But it occurred to me that perhaps the two of them might not have been on the best terms. Laura might be carrying some guilt.

I was at day three before Kate's death when I found what I was looking for, though I didn't actually know I was looking for it until I found it.

I opened an email, expecting to read another compliment about Kate's vivid imagination or a question on where she gets such sensual ideas . . . instead I read, "Taunting Teresa is tempting death."

Just then the last manuscript page printed, Laura straightened the stack of paper, and stood to leave.

"Before we go, try and find something that has your sister's handwriting on it," I asked.

"Like a diary?"

"That would be too good to be true, Laura. I'd settle for a shopping list."

"What for?"

"I'll explain later, I think there's a chance we might need it."

While she searched drawers, I focused my attention on the computer screen. This email address was different from the one that posted the "Taunting Teresa" comment on the Channel 3 website. I forwarded the message to myself, and to Xiong, with a note asking him if he could determine where the original email was sent from.

"Does this line mean anything to you?" I asked Laura.

"No, who's Teresa?" she asked.

"I can't be sure."

But I couldn't shake the name Teresa Dolezal Feldevert from my mind.

CHAPTER 50

We took the laptop, the manuscript, and the entire set of Desiree Fleur books back to my house. Laura asked me to email *Sexpocalypse* to Kate's attorney so he could send it to Mary Kay Berarducci at Lascivious Press.

"That will make it seem professional," she said.

"Do you want to read it first?" I asked.

"Heaven's no. I just want to hand it in and be done with it."

So I forwarded the attachment, and then curled up with the pages on the couch to see what all the fuss was about.

"You're not going to read it, Riley, are you?"

She looked so horrified, I told her I was looking for clues to Kate's killer. "Maybe your sister was trying to tell us something."

Laura looked unconvinced. I owned an extensive home library of fiction—bestsellers from yesteryear—but had never read a book before it was published and thought it might be fun to form my own opinions before any official reviews. Reporters also like being first, and I saw this as another way to capture that feeling.

Now I found myself wishing my roommate would go for a walk.

"Don't you find reading all those sex details embarrassing?" she asked.

Before I could answer, my cell phone sounded with an email from Xiong telling me the latest "Taunting Teresa" message was also sent from the Minneapolis downtown branch of the Hennepin County Library System.

The timing and location of the comments came days before and days after Kate's murder, suggesting that unlike the police theory that the serial killer had moved on, perhaps Minnesota was home.

The date and time sent were on the email. If surveillance video at the library computers showed the same person online during both times, that could yield a picture of the killer.

"I think I might need to go back to work, Laura."

"You're suspended." Noreen's greeting as I walked into her office lacked any twinge of delight at seeing me, or regret at dismissing me. "Don't make things worse, Riley, just leave."

"I thought you said I could hang out and just pretend to be blackballed."

"Since you left, I've rethought my position."

While the rest of the newsroom couldn't hear our exchange, they had been informed of my transgression and the meted discipline. They kept glancing in our direction.

"I think we might need to take a rain check on that suspension," I said, briefing her on what I'd found.

"You've put me in a difficult position," she said. "And I don't appreciate it. Either I wait until tomorrow to air this story, or assign it to someone else."

"I'm not handing over the details to anyone else, Noreen. See how far you get without me."

"I'm going to pretend I didn't hear that. I don't like either of my options, but I don't have much choice."

"You could stand up to the GM and tell him this suspension thing isn't working out."

"Then my job is on the line."

I could see from the tilt of her chin that debating the issue would be unproductive. "Then I guess we'll have to resume this conversation tomorrow."

My boss didn't express any qualms or reassurances. She kept her eyes glued to her paperwork and her mouth glued shut as I left the newsroom.

A voice mail message flashed on my phone. I could see from my missed calls that it was from Laura.

If I don't answer my cell, I wish people would just hang up, and simply wait for me to call them back. Then I wouldn't have to go through the mechanics of pressing extra buttons just to hear them ask me to return their call.

"Riley, I've got another problem," her message said. "This is a biggie. When are you going to be home?"

Even though I suspected I would regret it, I hit redial. I was prepared to tell her I was working late and not to wait up until I realized that, banned from the station, I had nowhere else to go. And neither did Laura.

When she answered, she sounded almost hysterical.

"Kate's editor says the book isn't finished, Riley. There's no ending."

I didn't know what to say. All books need endings. The author can't just stop writing and call it done. Except for some literary fiction, and no one could accuse Kate of crafting that kind of novel.

"Didn't you hear me, Riley? Here's the worst part. Mary Kay expects me to finish it. A sex book."

I wished her luck, especially given the tight deadline looming.

"What are talking about, Riley? You know I'm no writer."

"Well, somehow you must have given her editor the impression you could do the job."

"I had no choice," Laura admitted. "She was going to bring in a ghostwriter and pay them the rest of the advance."

Somehow, that bit of news didn't surprise me. But her next words did.

"I can't write the ending," Laura persisted. "I don't even know the story. At least you've read the book, Riley. And you're good at writing fast. I think you should complete it."

I pointed out to Laura that I never actually finished *Sexpocalypse*. "That part about the handcuffs brought back some bad memories about me and the local jail."

"But you read fast, Riley. You could catch up. You could be a ghostwriter."

The idea of ghostwriting had a certain panache. And all journalists believe they have novels hidden deep inside them. Maybe this would be a way to find out if I had a flair for fiction. I told Laura we'd talk when I got home.

I took my laptop and a sandwich into my bedroom, locking the door for privacy as I tried to brainstorm an ending.

"Let me know if there's anything I can do," Laura said. "Would you like something to drink?"

I told her to stop bothering me, although I phrased it a little more diplomatically.

I spent the next hour skimming through one intimate scene after another and saw what the Lascivious Press editor meant about the lack of closure. While *Sexpocalypse* explored an intriguing theme about society's obsession with sex, the manuscript had no real conclusion. I searched Kate's computer, but found no outline or hint of how she wanted the book to end.

She and Mary Kay Berarducci had exchanged emails about what types of food create an appetite for sex, but I hadn't seen that worked into the plot and wondered if it might just be girl talk.

Often while cranking out news stories, I found myself wishing I didn't have to stick to facts . . . thinking what a tale I could spin if I wasn't bound by reality. But rules are rules. Now as I tried to write fiction, I found myself craving facts because after a career in journalism, making stuff up felt like cheating.

"Hey, Riley, do you want any coffee?" Laura must have wanted to give me a caffeine boost so I wouldn't fall asleep before completing the job.

"Stop interrupting me," I told her.

To get me in the mood to write erotica, I decided to seek a male point of view. So I dialed my beau. I started off telling Garnett about the "Taunting Teresa" messages, which he found riveting.

"You must be crashing to make air tonight, Riley. I'm surprised you even had time to call me."

That's when I told him about my suspension. And my ghost-writing plan to finish Desiree Fleur's latest book.

"So you're writing pornography instead of news?" he asked.

"No, erotica," I said. "There's a difference. Porn is just sex. Erotica is emotion and art." At least that's what I told myself. "Listen, Nick." Then I read one of the hot manuscript pages to him.

"Well, maybe you should fly out here to DC and let me help you with your research." Garnett's voice had a husky tone that I recognized from our close encounters.

"You know how much I hate flying." It was probably unfair, but most of the travel in our long-distance relationship fell on Garnett because it was easier for him to find a business reason to come to Minneapolis than for me to fly out to our nation's capital. "Maybe you should come here to collaborate, Nick." I tried uttering the invitation with a come-hither tone.

"As much as I'm tempted, Riley, I have a security meeting dealing with all the controversy over the new full-body airport scanners. Hey, that might be an interesting segment for your novel. The X-rays are quite explicit."

Those naked images would certainly make the book topical. I told Garnett I'd consider that idea. I summarized *Sexpocalypse* for him, how global economies, politics, and military powers stalled because of the sexual chaos. Garnett made some intriguing suggestions for the terrorist characters, and I took down notes.

"Something big and unexpected has to happen next in the plot," I said. "I think the ending needs a burst of spontaneity."

"If you were more spontaneous, Riley, you'd be on your way to the airport now, counting the minutes until we, well, you know what I'm alluding to."

"I'm much more spontaneous than you, Nick. No job is more impromptu than covering news."

"Well, spontaneity has its time and place."

And while I didn't say it out loud, I never forget that I once married a man I barely knew for a week. And those vows were the height of spontaneity.

Garnett and I didn't talk much about my deceased husband, Hugh Boyer. They'd known each other casually in law enforcement circles, and he was among the hundreds of uniforms who drove bumper to bumper to his funeral. Bringing up Hugh would bring up the topic of marriage, and that wasn't something I wanted to discuss over the phone.

"Since you're suspended from work," he said, "you have more flexibility to travel right now. You could research those body scanners on your way to see me."

"But tomorrow I'm back in the news saddle, so I guess our fantasies are going to have to play out a thousand miles apart. In the meantime, I'm back to ghosting sex."

"Well, you know what they say, women need a reason for having sex," he said, "men just need a place."

"Well, as much as I'd like to use that adage in my erotic prose, I believe Billy Crystal in *City Slickers*, 1981, said it first."

And then I suddenly came up with the perfect steamy outcome

to *Sexpocalpyse.* I promised Garnett to read it to him when I finished. And he whispered a few sweet nothings to me before wishing me a productive night without writer's block.

So I wrote and rewrote.

"How's it going, Riley?" Laura tapped on the door to make sure I was still typing.

I ignored her because I was in the middle of a tense scene.

"Are you still awake?"

"Leave me alone, Laura."

I had a feeling book clubs might enjoy discussing my ending and even sharing private passions.

I only hoped my parents would never find out I wrote it, nor any of their church friends. Or my bosses at Channel 3. They'd probably invoke the unsuitability clause in my contract to fire me. I didn't think they'd settle for a one-day suspension.

CHAPTER 51

I stayed up much too late. Laura was zonked on the couch when I finally wrote The End. I was tired of typing. I was tiring of her company. I was just plain tired.

Crawling under the blankets, I think I fell asleep before my eyelids shut. By the time I yawned and stretched myself alert, the newsroom huddle was long over. When I arrived at the station, I pretended thinking I'd been scheduled for the afternoon shift. The bosses couldn't really yell at me because my story was marked for the late news, and the producer wanted me live on the set.

That made a plenty full day.

((SOPHIE BOX))
CHANNEL 3 HAS DISCOVERED
A POSSIBLE CLUE IN A FOUR-
STATE SERIAL KILLER CASE THAT
SUGGESTS THE MURDERER MIGHT
HAVE TIES TO THE TWIN CITIES.

((SOPHIE TWOSHOT))
RILEY SPARTZ JOINS US WITH
MORE ON THE INVESTIGATION.

Even though Chuck's ratings value as a viewer was gone, I had called him to watch anyway, hoping his girlfriend might have mentioned the email threat to him.

((RILEY CU))
CERTAINLY ONE OF THE
VICTIMS . . . KATE WARNER . . . IS
LOCAL, HOWEVER, POLICE HAVE
MAINTAINED NOTHING SUGGESTS
THE KILLER IS.

((RILEY NAT))
BUT CHANNEL 3 WAS SENT AN
ONLINE MESSAGE THAT MIRRORS
AN EMAIL MESSAGE SENT TO
WARNER BEFORE HER MURDER . . .
THE TEXT OF BOTH READS
"TAUNTING TERESA IS TEMPTING
DEATH."
BOTH WERE SENT FROM
COMPUTERS AT THE MINNEAPOLIS
PUBLIC LIBRARY, PRESUMABLY
FROM TWO ACCOUNTS WHERE
PATRONS FORGOT TO SIGN OFF.
THE STATION'S MESSAGE
APPEARED IN A VIEWER COMMENT
FOLLOWING A STORY I REPORTED
NOTING THE SIMILARITY BETWEEN
THE SHAPE OF THE BLACK ANGEL
STATUE OF IOWA CITY AND CHALK
OUTLINES AROUND THE BODIES OF
THE THREE HOMICIDES.

To get viewers' attention, I like holding up props on set and explaining their importance. Noreen's favorite props are baby animals. For this story, I used the *Black Angel Lace* book. The cover would have been considered too risqué for the early newscasts, but this was past ten PM.

> ((RILEY HOLD UP BOOK))
> THE SAME MESSAGE, "TAUNTING TERESA IS TEMPTING DEATH" ALSO APPEARED HANDWRITTEN IN THE FRONT OF A BOOK KATE WARNER WROTE TITLED *BLACK ANGEL LACE* . . . THAT I FOUND IN HER HOUSE . . . WHERE SHE WAS MURDERED.

Sophie and I had gone over a couple of questions for her to ask me on the set, so news control cut to a twoshot of us.

"Riley, have you been able to compare the handwriting in the book to Kate's?"

"Yes, Sophie, we found known samples of her handwriting and it appears quite different from the inscription in the book."

"Any idea who Teresa might be?"

"The only Teresa reference I've come across in this entire investigation is the name of the woman who commissioned the Black Angel cemetery marker nearly a hundred years ago: Teresa Dolezal Feldevert."

My phone was ringing as I reached my desk. Chief Capacasa was on the other end of the line . . . furious. He was yelling so loud it was hard to hear what he was saying, but finally he quieted enough for me to understand him. But even then I could feel his anger from the other end of downtown.

"Listen, you should have come to us with that information rather than blasting it all over the air."

"Why, Chief? So you can feed my work to the competition?"

I was looking for assurance that that was all a misunderstanding and would never happen again, but he ignored my question.

"I am putting you on notice, Ms. Spartz, that my team is drawing up a search warrant right now and will be demanding the murder victim's computer and inscribed book first thing in the morning, just as soon as we can get a judge to sign off on it."

I was about to tell him not to bother with a warrant, that I'd just hand the items over to the homicide department. But I remembered Miles, the station attorney, was firm on not giving up tapes, notes or any evidence without a subpoena or a warrant. And sometimes not even then.

Channel 3'd been involved in First Amendment court battles before. We'd won some, lost some. As a compromise, I decided to recommend to Miles that we simply comply with the search warrant and turn over the items. If we appealed, the cops would argue they had no other means of obtaining this specific evidence. They'd be right, and the judge would order us to acquiesce. Viewers might assume we were thwarting law enforcement and protecting a killer, all in the name of freedom of the press. At least that's what the police would argue to the public.

So I told the chief, "Fine, I'll be waiting."

CHAPTER 52

Dolezal watched as Riley Spartz waved the book with his handwriting on television in front of a world of admirers. He smiled at the recognition of his effort, especially grateful his work was not attributed to an undeserving.

He remembered mailing the package to his victim on a trip to Iowa City as a signal to expect him. The book proved that he knew Kate Warner was Desiree Fleur. The inscription and postmark warned of his wrath over her disrespect of his dear Black Angel.

He had arrived at Kate's house after dark. He'd been observing her long enough to know she sometimes had a male visitor, but not this night. She opened the front door for him when she saw he held a legal document from the office, supposedly requiring her signature. He followed her inside, hitting the lock behind him while she hunted for a pen.

"I have one here," he assured her, as he pulled the blood-stained bat from his briefcase.

That's when she understood why he came wearing gloves. Kate tried fleeing, but found the legend firm. No escaping the curse of the Black Angel.

CHAPTER 53

After Chief Capacasa's tirade, I called Noreen and Miles at their homes to brief them about the sudden police interest in our story.

Now we were sitting in the news director's office before most of the rest of the staff had arrived, except Xiong. I'd asked him to come in early and download everything from Kate's computer so we'd have a copy.

Black Angel Lace and the laptop were now sitting on top of Noreen's desk. She turned the cover facedown, confirming my belief she had issues about sex.

"I agree," Miles said. "If the police have a legal subpoena, we will comply and turn over the items they seek. If we balk, they may approach the sister and technically the material belongs to her."

"We can report handing the stuff to law enforcement, can't we?" Noreen asked.

"Certainly," he answered.

I ad-libbed a news lead so we could all be on the same page.

((RILEY SOT))
CHANNEL 3 HAS PROVIDED
EVIDENCE TO THE MINNEAPOLIS

POLICE THAT AUTHORITIES
BELIEVE MIGHT BE CONNECTED TO
THE MURDER OF A LOCAL AUTHOR.

Noreen looked at Miles for approval as he nodded at the gist of the script. Over the loudspeaker, we heard a voice call out, "Riley Spartz, you have a visitor at the back door."

"I'll escort them here," Miles said.

"Let me get a camera in position first," I replied. "I want video of them carrying out the book and computer."

I had hoped they'd send a uniformed officer for better TV, but instead Detective Delmonico, in plainclothes, showed up with a badge and paperwork.

Miles reviewed the subpoena with lawyer eyes, and signed the correct line. Malik rolled the whole encounter on video while I tried to chat with the homicide detective about the direction of the murder investigation.

"Do you think this message connects the killer to the Black Angel statue or to the Twin Cities?" I asked.

Seeing he didn't have to be polite to gain cooperation, he ignored me. He did sign the subpoena, indicating the station had complied with the request. Then he handed a copy to our attorney, and picked up the computer and book. He had also wanted the "Taunting Teresa" comment from the Channel 3 website, but Miles told him it was available to the public online.

Malik and I trailed him out the door until he climbed into a unmarked vehicle, me asking questions, Malik shooting tape.

"Did he tell you anything?" Noreen asked when we returned.

"No," I said, "but let's see how far they get without the password."

The neighborhood mother-in-law called me an hour later to report the police were back on the street in front of Kate's house.

They'd stretched yellow-and-black crime scene tape around the property again.

"Did they say why?" A murder investigation stays open until the case is solved. But once a crime scene is cleared, the cops are generally finished with that location.

"They just told me to keep my eyes on the block and call if I noticed anything unusual," she said. "But I have to go now. I hear Johnny crying."

Access to the crime scene via Laura was the main advantage I had over the other media. That relationship had gotten me the angel chalk outline and more. The police were unlikely to talk to me about the current situation with the property. But as the homeowner, Laura had rights. They might be forced to discuss it with her.

"I'm uncomfortable around the police," Laura told me as we sat at my kitchen table. "I don't want to meet with them."

"I'll be with you," I assured her. "Remember, the longer that crime scene tape stays up, the harder it's going to be to sell the house."

That argument convinced her.

"It's best we get this resolved before the weekend," I said, telling her to grab her purse and I'd drive downtown. She fumbled with an oversized bag stuffed with papers and climbed into the car. On the way, she thanked me for writing the ending to her sister's book.

"Did you read it?" I guess I was fishing for praise as a novelist, rather than a journalist.

"No. I sent it to her editor and Mary Kay said the part about the afterlife was just what the story needed."

"Did you tell her about me?"

"No, you're the ghost." But she promised to pay me something for my time once money settled.

I was starting to think this ghost business wasn't so glamorous after all.

Not sure what kind of reception Laura and I would get at the cop shop, I pulled into the Government Center parking ramp rather than risk getting ticketed at a street meter. The station might pay for the fine and tow for a photographer's vehicle because of all the heavy gear it carted, but never a reporter's.

Prepared for a waiting game, the last thing I expected was to be settled outside the chief's office and told he'd be with us shortly. We were even offered coffee while we waited. The chief was a known chess master and I amused myself by moving carved pieces around an antique board he kept on display in the reception area.

When Laura and I were finally shown in, I greeted the chief, introduced Laura, and asked if the homicide squad had any luck obtaining surveillance video of the library computer banks from the days the "Taunting Teresa" emails were sent.

"The video was erased." The chief was pissed, more at me than the library. "The latest tape, the day before our request. Perhaps if you'd come to us right away, they might have proven useful."

I wanted to answer with something like, Perhaps, if I hadn't been suspended by idiots at the station. But I thought it best to keep quiet about that happening.

Instead, I changed the subject by mentioning Laura had some questions about how long her sister's house would remain a crime scene.

"The homicide team is working on that," he said. "But I'm also interested in how long you're going to remain in Minneapolis, Ms. Warner." He stared at Laura. He knew I wasn't going anywhere, though he probably wished I'd leave.

Laura squirmed, but stayed silent. It seemed an unwelcoming question from a Minnesotan.

"I'm only asking," the chief said, "because trouble seems to follow you."

"What are you talking about?" I asked. "Laura's been nothing but cooperative throughout this homicide investigation. Her sister's death has nothing to do with her."

"Probably not." Then Chief Capacasa explained that they'd received a call from a local man who saw Laura on the news and claimed she had filed a false police report many years ago. An allegation of rape. "And he still harbors quite a grudge."

Clearly the chief was looking to surprise us. And it worked.

Laura said nothing, so I figured I had to speak up for her.

"She made a mistake, Chief. That was a long time ago, and really has nothing to do with the current situation."

Laura looked grateful for my mediation and mimicked my answer. "Yes, a mistake that I've regretted ever since."

The chief leaned over his desk toward her, like a dare for her to pay attention. "Did you make the same mistake in Omaha, Des Moines, Madison, Phoenix, and Houston?"

I was much more confused than Laura by his implication.

The chief kept talking. "We've done some digging on your background, Ms. Warner. While there's a national crime database of suspect arrests, there's no such record of victim reports. Which makes tracking such information difficult. So instead of one-stop checking, we had to contact law enforcement in towns where you've lived. In most all of them, you've claimed to have been raped. I don't buy those odds."

He explained that sometimes she'd accused men by name, and they'd land in a legal jam, their reputations a mess, before being cleared. Other times, she simply reported an assailant's general physical description and various men would be hauled in for questioning. Once she had even been found guilty of falsely reporting a crime. No jail time, but the judge had urged her to seek help.

"That and your old college pal got us on track," he continued.

"I don't know if you're looking for sympathy or revenge. But you're not getting either here. Because we're on to you."

His speech stunned me. I didn't buy those odds either. And knowing Laura, I could believe she was disturbed about sex. Her lies confirmed it. So did her attitude toward her sister's writing. What the chief outlined was a suspicious pattern of misconduct.

The chief turned to me with a gleam of triumph. "Don't say I never give you a story."

Laura didn't talk much during the car ride back to my place. She mostly just cried. "It's not like he said, Riley."

Though his lecture humiliated me, I believed the chief's words more than I did Laura. She may have felt betrayed by life, but once again I felt betrayed by her.

I found myself wondering what's up with the Warner women, sex and secrets? One sister felt comfortable enough with the subject to write erotica. But only under a pen name. The other appeared to be trying to settle an old score by crying rape. Over and over.

I dropped my old college friend off at the curb outside my house, told her I needed some space, and that our roommate arrangement must come to an end.

"I want you gone when I get back," I said.

CHAPTER 54

That night Dolezal watched from outside long enough to be convinced the TV reporter was alone inside. One shadow only. The house grew still, as did the rest of the street. He picked up his bag of tools and crept from the neighboring porch across the backyard, tingling with expectation and confidence.

As a journalist, she might try to get him to open up about his feelings. Perhaps to convince him to abandon his mission. To stall the preordained. But he had made a promise that no slick reporter could subvert. So there seemed little point in listening.

When the prime crime moment came, she would probably have little to add that he hadn't already heard.

CHAPTER 55

Usually I snooze through the early-morning newscasts. Most of the time, the stories are just a rehash from the night before. The real news of the day hasn't happened yet unless you count an occasional overnight fire or a preview of scheduled events.

Restless animal noises woke me. Dogs whimpering. Cats hissing. Birds scratching. Also, sleeping in Noreen's bed creeped me out, and I had nightmares that my boss lay curled on the mattress next to me. Waking up, I realized the snoring shape was Husky.

I clicked on the TV remote thinking the news might bore me back to sleep. Instead a picture of me dominated Channel 3's screen. I turned up the volume and heard a recitation of all the national investigative awards I'd won and how much the world was a better place because of my stories. A few seconds later, news control cut live to a dark exterior of my house with police cars parked in front.

That's when I found out I'd been murdered.

CHAPTER 56

I turned on my cell phone I'd powered down the night before because the vibrating noise kept the animals up, and saw numerous missed calls from the station, Garnett, and my parents. While I was far from dead, I feared this news could kill them.

I didn't bother listening to any of the messages, but speed dialed my mom and dad and heard a raspy, exhausted voice on the other end. I couldn't tell who was speaking or what they were trying to say.

"Mom? Dad? It's Riley."

Frenzied sounds came over the line. "Calm down," I urged them. "It's me. Your daughter."

"Riley?" I still couldn't be sure who picked up the line.

"I don't know what anyone told you, but I'm fine. There's been a misunderstanding."

"They told us you were dead," I now recognized my dad's voice. "Father Mountain is on his way down from the Cities to pray with us. We called him when we got the news."

"They were wrong, but I can't talk long. I need to straighten out this blunder. Is Mom there?"

"She fell asleep."

"Well, wake her up and tell her you have some good news."

"No, you better tell her yourself, she'll think I've been dreaming."

"Then put her on the other line."

She thought she was dreaming. Then she made me prove my existence by quizzing me about the name of my favorite doll when I was a little girl. Finally, convinced I was alive, she started going on about how this horrible ordeal would never have happened if I'd let them get me a dog like they wanted.

"Then we'd know you were safe," she said.

Being surrounded by a trio of dogs who all wanted to go outside, I insisted that her idea, while thoughtful, was unnecessary. My last words to her before I hung up were, "Don't bring me a dog."

They had just suffered an incredible shock, but so had I; hard to believe we were finding time to argue about pets. Then I called back, trying to be more positive.

"Tell Father Mountain hello from me." He would be glad not to have to bury me in the country cemetery with all the other Spartz descendants, though I was curious what he would have said about me from the pulpit.

"Tell him yourself, Riley, he just pulled into the yard." Then she passed the phone to the priest with the message that I was not dead after all.

"You must have a powerful guardian angel, Riley," Father Mountain said. "You must never take his work for granted."

And I had to admit, he had a point. "I have felt his presence around me, Father."

Then in thanks to my protector, he urged me to recite with him his special prayer. *"Angel of God, my guardian dear, to whom his love commits me here; ever this day be at my side to light and guard, to rule and guide."*

Then on a less spiritual note, I let Husky, Blackie, and Speckles out to do their canine business while I tried brushing animal hair off my only set of clothing while searching for my car keys. Because it was early in the day, and being a weekend, traffic was light. As I drove toward my house, I called the assignment desk and demanded a retraction.

• • •

Dolezal could have killed her while she slept amid a tumble of blankets. But he needed to see the look of recognition in her eyes before the blow fell. Eliciting that wide-open fear was part of his mission—the money shot. So he stood over her, held the club high, and whispered, "Taunting Teresa is tempting death."

She lifted her face from the pillow, glanced in confusion toward the source of the noise, and within seconds, was literally screaming for her life.

On his end, his past pursuits were always hushed, but now a crazed wail, in harmony with hers, escaped his throat simultaneously.

The woman was not Riley Spartz. But he had to kill her anyway.

In a frenzy, he pounded her head until he could no longer tell he'd attacked the wrong target.

Her blood dominated the bedroom. The spatters ricocheted across the covers, floor, and ceiling. Seeing his image reflected in a full-length mirror on the wall, Dolezal felt more like an angel of death than on any of his previous missions. Damp and sticky, he stripped his clothing. Then he spread his arms and tilted his head downward in his well-practiced cemetery stance, but felt no pleasure because he knew he had failed his dark icon.

He turned his shirt and pants inside out, wiping the blood from his face with his underwear. Then he dressed and prepared to leave the grisly scene behind.

He longed to pose this woman's body like his beloved matriarch and give her corpse wings for eternity like the others. But he knew better than to draw the powerful shape; he did not have permission and the Black Angel would be angry.

CHAPTER 57

My street was crowded with law enforcement and media, roped off to gawkers. I parked around the block and walked toward the pandemonium, a scarf shielding my face. The officer in charge of crowd control would not let me pass.

"Behind the line," he barked.

"But I live here," I shouted. That made no difference. He figured I was one of many residents of that block and would just have to hang out elsewhere until the police gave the all clear. I needed to be more specific. I dropped the scarf. "I'm the deceased."

That got his attention, but he just thought I was some wacko.

"I'm Riley Spartz," I told him.

He flashed a light in my face and that was one of those times when I wished I hadn't left the house without makeup. Because of my disheveled appearance, he seemed unsure of my identity. I reverted to my broadcast voice. "Riley Spartz, Channel 3 news, reporting."

That did it. He grabbed my arm and marched me past the police tape and up to my house where I crashed into Detective Delmonico, who was just coming out the door.

"Hey, what's going on?" he yelled. He could tell I wore no

badge or uniform and thus did not belong near the crime scene. "Get her out of here."

"I think you better take a look," my escorting officer said. "Inside." He pushed me into the foyer and out of view of the media.

The detective's face grew pale when he realized who was standing in front of him. He grabbed my shoulders and pulled my face close to his. "What's going on?"

"That's what I want to know." I shrugged his hands off me. "How come everybody thinks I'm dead?"

"Because we got a body inside your house that's been identified as you." He emphasized the words "body," "your house," and "you."

A body? He could only be talking about Laura. I feared she must have killed herself after all the converging events. I wished I hadn't confronted her so harshly, adding to her turmoil.

"Her name was Laura Warner," I said. "It must have been suicide."

"Heard her name, but can't confirm the victim's identity," Detective Delmonico continued. "But I've seen the remains, and this was absolutely no suicide."

"Well, somebody clearly messed up on the identification, so I wouldn't be surprised if you guys messed up cause of death, too. By the time I get off the air, you're all going to look like idiots."

"You want to call someone an idiot, start with him."

Delmonico pushed me into the dining room where a man sat in the dark, seemingly in a stupor, his face to the wall.

The detective motioned with his head that I should approach. So I walked over and found Nick Garnett holding a framed picture of the two of us, arms entwined, that normally rested on my fireplace mantel.

He didn't seem to realize anyone, much less me, stood behind him. So I rested my hand on his shoulder and murmured his name. "It's okay, Nick. I'm here." He didn't respond. I knelt in front of him, cupping his chin in my hands, and kissed his lips. "I love you."

He seemed mystified. "Were you right about angels, Riley? Are you a visiting angel even now?"

I shook my head and my dark hair fell loose, over one eye. "I'm no angel and you know it."

"Zombie is more like it." Delmonico came over to our corner. "Garnett, you ID'd the wrong broad with the crushed skull. Your girlfriend is alive and as big a pain as ever. The guys and I are drawing straws over who has to tell the chief."

Garnett looked from one of us to the other, not believing the apparent miracle.

"I'm fine," I assured him. "Does this feel like a kiss of death?" I planted another one across his mouth and this time he responded, desperately.

"I'll give you two lovebirds a couple of minutes for crime scene courtship," Delmonico said, "then I need a statement from you." He was pointing at me. "But first, I better confirm to your media pals you're most definitely still alive and kicking, though I'm sure some will be disappointed by the news."

"Are you going to tell them the name of the real victim?" I asked. Laura was still on my mind.

"I see no need to rush down that path again." He glared at Garnett. "We'll verify the identity of the deceased first."

Through the front window, we watched Delmonico approach the row of cameras. We couldn't hear what he said, but less than thirty seconds later, he was walking back toward the house, not taking any questions. Flashes from still cameras lit his moving shadow.

Garnett and I had less than a minute alone. "What are you even doing here, Nick? You're supposed to be in Washington."

Garnett stood, pulling me tight against his chest. My head tucked under his chin. "I was being spontaneous, like we talked about while discussing your ghostwriting adventure. So I caught a plane to Minnesota to prove I was the more impulsive one."

Instead, he was the more tormented one. "I let myself in with my key and found you, well, not you. Her. Horrible."

His face looked grim and pained—unusual for a veteran homicide investigator. Of course, he'd never handled the murder of anyone he loved. I started to explain about the other woman in my bed, but he put his finger on my lips to stop me.

"Later. Tonight has taught me a lesson about delaying happiness. Waiting is wasting. Never again. Spontaneous forever."

He reached into his jacket pocket and pulled out a small jewelry box. Inside, a ring—a large, deep-red, oval stone surrounded by small diamonds. "It's a garnet," he explained. "So we can always be together."

Then he got down on one knee and took my hand in his. "Riley Spartz, will you marry me?"

CHAPTER 58

Fancy restaurants. Beautiful scenery. Exotic locations.

Many married couples revisit the romantic settings where they pledge their devotion to each other and officially become engaged. What was I supposed to say?

A cadaver lay in the next room. I smelled blood. I smelled like dogs. My lover and I were surrounded by guns inside and paparazzi outside. Was this a day we would ever want to remember as the start of our lifetime together?

But Garnett had been through hell, and seemed to need proof I was actually back from the dead. Seeing me walking among the living didn't appear real enough to his tortured mind. The proposal seemed his way of cementing the present with the future. Might accepting his offer of matrimony be a means of finding good in evil, and making the day bearable?

I couldn't bring myself to speak, so I simply smiled. He took my gesture as affirmation and slipped the ring on my finger.

"Now you can live the life of Riley," he said.

Then Detective Delmonico stepped back in the room and Garnett scrambled to his feet, possibly not wanting to seem too sappy in front of another homicide cop. I put my hand in my jacket pocket so the sparkle of the gem wouldn't attract attention.

The detective pulled up a chair at the dining table and motioned that Garnett and I should join him. He pulled out a tape recorder, hitting the Play/Record buttons. He was being nicer to me than normal, probably because Garnett was present.

"So tell me what you know about the unfortunate lady in the next room, Ms. Spartz."

"I'd like to see her first." It seemed the decent thing to do.

"No," said Garnett. No hesitation.

Delmonico agreed with him. "I wouldn't advise it. In fact, I won't allow it."

"Then how are we going to avoid another case of mistaken identity?"

"We'll use fingerprints and DNA to verify who you say she is. Trust me, looking at her won't help. So tell us why you weren't here last night and why she was."

I explained I hadn't been home because I'd been dog-sitting for my boss outside of the metro area. I hoped I wasn't being considered a suspect, because my alibi witnesses could only bark.

Explaining my relationship with Laura Warner was more complicated. "The more I learned about my old college roommate, the less I wanted to stay in touch. It was a reunion gone bad. And yesterday I had told her this was the last night she could stay here. Laura was supposed to be gone when I got back today."

"You two had the only keys to the house?" Delmonico looked at Garnett and me for an answer. "None hidden outside?"

I shook my head. "Laura had a spare so she could get in and out." That's when I realized I should be mourning for Laura, instead I was relieved not to be dead myself. I felt selfish, wearing an engagement ring while she wore a body bag.

I twisted my new jewel nervously, wondering if her death had anything to do with the choices she made in life. Then the obvious question occurred to me and would probably make headlines across the country.

"Why do you think the killer decided to go after them both?" I asked. "Did he develop a sister fetish?"

Neither man answered. Garnett finally spoke up. "We can't be certain the same person murdered both."

"Two sisters murdered by two different killers in barely two weeks?" I asked. "I don't believe it."

"Forensics might tell us more, but the crime scenes had differences," Delmonico said. "We'll have other questions later, but you can leave while we finish in here."

I asked about grabbing some clothes from my closet, and was told nothing from the bedroom. I settled for a makeup case from the bathroom. And then on the dining room table, I noticed my yearbook, wide open. Two pages torn out, crumbled in a tight ball of paper. Unfolding them, I found my photo and Laura's on one page. On the other, a picture of the man she'd accused of rape.

Garnett looked at my discovery and motioned for Delmonico to come over. Had Laura, infuriated, ripped the pages as a hurtful message? Or had her killer?

"Speaking of murder motives," I told the detective. "You might want to ask your chief about this man."

Then I saw Laura's giant purse on a chair by the table, threw it over my shoulder and, not wanting to discuss the subject further, left with Garnett on my heels. We disregarded my car since it was parked far away and raced to his rental, which sat in front of the house.

I saw the rear lights of his vehicle flicker, signaling the doors were unlocked. Then the media swarm hit. We pushed through to try to reach the car. Photographers stuck high-definition cameras in my face and I was again aware how bad—and old—I would look on-screen without airbrush makeup. I was glad Noreen was out of town and not watching the news.

Reporters yelled questions like "How come you aren't dead?" "Is anyone dead?" "Are you the killer?"

I wanted to just drive away, but I figured they'd only chase after us in their media caravan and I didn't want to end up like Lady Di, crashing in the Lowry Tunnel, paparazzi on my heels. So while Garnett climbed into the driver's seat, I decided to throw them a sound bite.

Turning to the mob of microphones, I said, "As you can plainly see I, Riley Spartz, am alive. Quite alive. The reports of my death are greatly exaggerated."

Then I scrambled inside and shut the door. Garnett turned the engine over and said, "Not bad. *The Adventures of Mark Twain*, 1944, though I can't remember who played the title role of Samuel Clemens."

"Me neither." I was about to compliment him anyway when Jenny from Channel 8 jumped in the backseat demanding an interview. We'd been too slow to hit autolock.

"Get out," I said.

"Just one more question, Riley, is that an engagement ring sparkling on your finger?"

My mouth opened wide, but before I could stammer an answer, Garnett pulled out his Glock. "You heard her. Get out. And when I shoot I'm talking bullets, not video."

Now Jenny's mouth was open wide. She hurried out the door and we took off down the street before she could close either.

I motioned toward my car parked up ahead, but Garnett said we'd come back for it later. He slowed enough for me to reach back and shut our car door tight before we entered the freeway.

"Where are we headed?" Garnett asked.

"The station."

"Police or television?" he asked.

"TV," I responded. "I want to stay clear of the cop shop."

I had noticed a Channel 3 rookie reporter getting pushed around at the scene, so I texted him an exclusive. "MURDER VICTIM IS LAURA WARNER NOT ME." I added that he could meet me downtown for an interview, but to give me at least an hour to look decent.

I realized the police had their own reasons for holding off releasing Laura's name, but decided Channel 3 deserved the scoop much more than Channel 8, and even though I couldn't cover the story myself, I could be a source.

My cell phone rang almost immediately, and I figured it was him wanting more details, so I answered. Instead it was Noreen.

"Oh Riley, I heard you were dead. Then I heard you weren't. And I was so relieved. I thought, Thank God she's alive."

The depth of my news director's emotion touched me. I wasn't taken aback that my parents, lover, or childhood priest would grieve my death, but that my boss gave a damn was unexpected and gratifying.

Before I could respond, Noreen continued. "Because if anything happened to you, who would take care of the animals?"

With that, I disconnected her.

"Who was that?" Garnett noted I hung up without saying anything.

"Nobody important."

CHAPTER 59

I let my fiancé wander around the newsroom while I headed for the basement to shower. Usually only photographers used the on-site facilities, but I was beyond dirty. I needed to wash away all of the morning.

Garnett made the same claim. "It's okay, Riley, we're engaged." But I turned down his offer to join me under soap and hot water. "Wouldn't be professional." The last thing I needed was to be caught showering with my boyfriend at the station. As an internal matter, it probably wouldn't get me fired, but it would get written up in my personnel file and future bosses would think I was a slut.

Luckily, I always kept an extra on-air outfit at the station for emergencies, so when I walked into the green room, I was presentable neck to toe. I let Garnett sit on the stool next to me as I tried to make my face and hair decent.

"Tell me about the crime scene," I said, as I ran a hot-air brush through my hair. "Delmonico said it was different from the others."

"In some ways it was different, in others similar. She was also clubbed to death."

"Was there an angel chalk shape?"

"That was the biggest deviation. The body wasn't posed or outlined. But the killer might have been spooked and left in a hurry. Or might be trying to throw us off. Or might have been someone else entirely with a personal motive."

I shook my head at the latter, still not buying into the two-killer theory. Although I had to acknowledge that after what I'd learned about Laura recently, others might have motive to want her dead.

"Why did you think Laura was me?"

"Well, she was in your bed." He seemed to hesitate, so I prompted him. "And?"

He looked away when he answered. "And basically, her face was gone."

I didn't like that image and wished I hadn't asked and he hadn't told me.

"Overkill," Garnett continued. "Someone was very angry."

"I'm glad he wasn't angry at me."

"I'm not sure you can be sure he wasn't."

"What do you mean, Nick?"

"I don't think we can rule out *you* being the killer's target."

"I might buy that if we didn't have two dead sisters. That connection seems too strong to discount."

"Regardless, Riley, me and Saint Glock are going to stay by your side until things look clearer."

No argument from me. Though I hadn't yet shared with him whose roof we were going to crash under tonight.

As for the place I called home, I was glad I rented on a month-by-month basis, because I swore never to sleep there again. I wouldn't want to touch anything a killer touched.

Except his story.

My face looked normal again—for television, that is. A layer of loose powder over airbrush makeup gave me a uniform complexion for the critical lens of high-definition cameras.

My fiancé—I rehearsed the word in my mind, because I wasn't

sure how easily it would roll off my lips—kept telling me how I didn't have to go to all that cosmetic fuss for him.

"I'm not, Nick. I'm doing it because viewers are more likely to believe I'm alive if I don't actually look dead."

The large mirror, bordered by Hollywood lights, made the finishing touches to my face easy. I was inches away from lipstick when Garnett stopped me for a smooch.

As our lips parted, he whispered, "Just wanted to practice kissing the bride."

"Maybe we need another try," I replied.

Then from down the hall, in the newsroom, I heard my name being called. A shrill and wild soprano. "Riley, where are you?"

Garnett looked confused. "Is that your boss?" After all, I'd already told him she was out of town.

"No. Worse," I replied. "My mother."

CHAPTER 60

When she saw me coming around the corner, my mom rushed toward me with her arms open and her eyes tearing. "Oh, Riley, you are safe. We had to be certain."

"Mom, you two didn't have to drive a hundred miles just for a hug."

"Oh yes, we did."

I almost told her she could have just watched the news, but realized that wouldn't have been motherly on her end or daughterly on mine. While we embraced, I saw my dad out of the corner of my eye, waiting for his turn.

And he was holding a black-and-white puppy.

Just as I saw fur, my mother saw glint. We both yelled our discoveries concurrently.

"A dog!"

"A ring!"

I hadn't meant to share my engagement news with my parents yet. But you can't carry classified information on your ring finger. Especially during a parental ambush.

Mom and Dad starting gushing about how happy they were for us and glancing around for the lucky chap. They spotted Garnett by the news desk, abandoning me so they could thrust the pup into his arms.

"Congratulations, son! We brought you an engagement present," my dad said.

"His name is Max," Mom said. "He can grow up to be a guard dog."

Garnett seemed delighted by their joy, and anxious to join the Spartz family as son-in-law.

They were full of questions like when is the big day? And will Father Mountain perform the ceremony? I explained that we'd only been engaged an hour and had lots of details to work out. Weddings and dog ownership had to be among the last things I wanted to talk about just then. Because I'd been thinking about Garnett's theory that the killer might have come after me. If true, he was likely to have been enraged that I wasn't home. But that wasn't the kind of conversation my parents needed to hear.

"About the dog," I said. "That dog can't be a newshound. It has to be a farm dog. Nick and I have no place to keep the animal."

I explained that he lived on the East Coast and I was homeless at the moment. So we couldn't have pets.

My parents lavished Garnett and the pooch with a group hug while I looked on and around in puzzlement.

"How did they get in here?" I asked. Access to the building, especially on weekends, was difficult for nonemployees.

"I let them in." Channel 3's rookie said sheepishly. "They showed up at your house looking for you. The police told them you were gone. No kidding. That's the word they used. *Gone.* Your mom panicked and said, 'No, she's still alive, we talked to her on the phone. Let us in.'"

I could see the whole scene unfolding poorly.

"Then your folks saw the Channel 3 logo on my jacket. So they sort of latched on to me, and I had to invite them to follow me downtown to find you." He smiled apologetically. "Here they are."

I couldn't really blame him. I knew my parents could be formidable when it came to family. "It's okay. Best they not be running around loose here in the Cities."

"Now how about a quick sound bite?" He reverted back to the news mode. And because I knew what he needed we wrapped it fast.

I rounded up my parents and fiancé—it was getting easier to say, maybe because it wasn't so secret anymore. The gang was hanging out by the assignment desk getting a head start on the day's news. I remained the lead story. But that's how they found out Laura Warner was the murder victim.

"Wasn't she your college roommate for a while?" my mom asked. "Such a nice family. I didn't know you two were still in touch."

I glossed over Laura's other troubles with them. Her being dead and all made them seem unimportant.

That's when my dad told me he and Mom were too tired to drive back to the farm. "We were up all night grieving for you, Riley."

"Yes," Mom chirped in. "I think we better just all stay in the Cities together tonight. Safety in numbers."

"Together where? My house is a crime scene." If the homicide squad was clamping down on media access to Kate's house, they sure weren't going to let me inside mine anytime soon. Especially not for sleepovers.

"Well, where are you staying?" Dad asked.

So I explained I was house sitting for my boss who was out of town until the next day.

"Is there room for us?" he wanted to know.

"No. If I'm squeezing anyone in with me, it's going to be my fiancé." There, I said the word.

Nick looked pleased at the prospect of a night together—just the two of us—before he had to head back to Washington. Wait until he saw Noreen's house.

"Is there a hotel nearby?" My mom is fond of staying at hotels, especially ones that include a free breakfast.

I told them to follow us and we'd look for a place, but that we had to stop at my news director's house first.

"I have to check on the animals." Being farmers, that made sense to them.

My parents dislike urban driving, especially freeways, so even though no weekend rush hour existed, we decided Dad would ride shotgun with Garnett and I would drive the other car with Mom. I led the route to Noreen's, heading west into the sun.

Max was riding with the men.

My mom wanted girl talk, like whether I was going to have a church wedding and if Dad would be allowed to give me away. I found myself wishing for heavy traffic, so I could hush her.

She noticed a hotel off an exit, and writing down the particulars distracted her enough from wedding questions that I was able to get her to talk about how the town lutefisk supper went. In Minnesota, codfish preserved in lye is considered a delicacy. Mention the Scandinavian tradition elsewhere and it's a joke.

"Good turnout," she said. "People will drive far for tasty lutefisk."

She was surprised when we left the metro area for rural roads, especially when we pulled into Noreen's long driveway. A fence surrounded the yard. A pet door allowed the dogs in-and-out privileges from the house.

"Your boss lives here?" Mom said. "Why can't you live here? It's like the farm without the chores."

Noreen had fixed the place up since she'd gotten married and divorced, but there were still plenty of chores. That's why I was there.

"Wait until we get inside," I warned.

The men parked beside us and were taking Max to the bushes to do doggie business while I unlocked the front door.

The animals could hear us and those not sleeping started their greetings.

When my parents counted up all the pets inside, feather, fin, and fur, I think they were glad not to be staying overnight. And Garnett didn't look thrilled to be bedding down with me in a domestic zoo.

"One problem," Dad said. "The hotel isn't going to let Max stay with us. Would you mind one extra till tomorrow?"

The pup was starting to squirm to get down from his arms, but I held off making any commitment until I saw how the big dogs and the newbie got along.

"Hey, look, they like each other," he said.

And they sort of did. Blackie touched noses with Max and that puppy peck paved the way for Husky to accept him too. Speckles seemed a little standoffish, but she'd spent most of her life coddled by Noreen as an only dog and was still adjusting to the swarm.

The cats weren't happy, but they seldom were.

My parents promised to swing by and pick Max up in the morning. "Maybe we'll even bring you doughnuts," Mom said. I wasn't sure if she was saying that because Garnett was a cop or because she could snag them free at the breakfast buffet.

And then, not counting creatures with tails and wings, my fiancé and I were alone in my boss's bed.

CHAPTER 61

Garnett's fervent whispers stopped. "Did you hear something, Riley?"

"Just you blowing in my ear."

"I thought I heard something."

"Well, pay more attention to me and less to ballyhoo."

I reminded him there were a couple dozen animals in the house, and all but the fish made night noises. I could definitely hear dog sounds in the other rooms. Garnett had insisted Blackie, Husky, Speckles, and Max all sleep outside the bedroom to give us more privacy and less panting.

"I'm worried someone else is in the house." And because another woman had been murdered the night before, he reached along the floor, feeling for his gun.

Our clothes had been enthusiastically discarded moments earlier so he had to leave my smooth side and warm bed to find his weapon. That's when the bedroom door opened.

"Freeze!" he yelled. Just as the light went on.

Naked, in a well-practiced cop crouch, he pointed his Glock at Noreen. I pulled the blankets over my head because I couldn't bear to watch.

I still heard her scream.

"It's okay, Noreen." I held my ring finger out from under the covers. "We're engaged."

"In what?" she asked.

Garnett and I checked into the hotel down the road. Neither of us was eager to resume where we'd left off, maybe because we both knew my parents were staying under the same roof and now kept thinking What If They Walk In On Us?

We'd apologized to Noreen; she'd apologized to us. I hoped the incident could be one of those things neither of us ever mentioned again. Especially not during job reviews.

"You weren't supposed to come back until tomorrow." I felt that certainly put me in the right.

She explained that with all the day's upheaval, she wasn't sure I could keep my word to pet sit. "So I came back early. If you were gone, I'd be glad I did. If you were here, it wouldn't matter."

She glanced at Garnett who, by now, was holding my sweater as a shield. "I wasn't expecting you to have company."

"That's complicated," I replied.

The two of us dressed as quickly as we could and Garnett left without looking Noreen in the eye. I tried keeping things casual by telling her I'd see her at the station . . . and she winked.

My cell phone rang the next morning on the hotel nightstand. I expected my parents calling to check our whereabouts. Instead it was my boss wondering why she had one more dog than when she left, especially since none of hers were pregnant.

"That's even more complicated," I said. "Can I get back to you?"

Then I dialed the front desk and asked to be connected to my parents' room, and was told no guests were registered by that name.

"Did they already check out?"

"No one by that name stayed here last night," the clerk said.

And then I realized I'd been scammed by my own mom and dad. And once again I was left holding the dog.

"You sure your boss is going to be okay with Max?"

Garnett and I were driving by my house to gawk at crime scene tape and pick up my car.

"I told her it was a misunderstanding. She said he can stay for the week until I find a new place, but that's all. She doesn't want the other dogs growing too fond of him."

We unloaded my junk, and while we kissed good-bye, I caught him looking at his watch because he had to return his rental car before catching his flight.

"Why don't you fly out with me for a couple days, Riley? I think you could use a break."

"I'd love to, Nick. But no way can I get time off on this short notice. And I haven't the nerve to ask Noreen after . . . you know."

He knew. And he didn't have the nerve either.

"Besides, you have a busy workweek, Nick. You were just telling me about that hearing before the Senate committee. How much time would we really have together?"

He got my point. I waved to him as he drove off, leaving me wondering where I'd be sleeping that night. I also wondered if my fiancé could see my ring flashing in his rearview mirror.

In the neighborhood of Ed's liquor store, I wasn't sure if I needed a drink or a friend, but I left with a gun and bullets.

"I insist, dearie." Ed handed me the revolver he kept hidden and handy. "You're traveling around a mean crowd."

"But what about you, Ed? You're the one up against a strange face every fifteen minutes."

He snorted with amusement. "The only time I've fired this gun in the last twenty years, you watched. My gut tells me you could need this old six-shooter before I do."

He emptied the bullets on the counter, encouraging me to practice pointing the firearm at the smoke alarm and pulling the trigger. Then he showed me how to load and unload the ammunition until I could do it myself.

Ed had only fourteen cartridges, and urged me to find a quiet spot out in the country and fire a few.

"Get the feel for this Saturday-night special," he said. "But make sure you save six bullets. So you've got one in each chamber. More options then."

"I don't think I'll ever need it, Ed. But I'll hold on to it for a while. Thanks." I tucked the gun into my purse. Just having it close might make me feel safer.

"Oh, sweetie," Ed called after me. "No registration, so best you not show off."

My heart wasn't really into being armed and dangerous. Maybe if I went legal and got a conceal and carry permit. But that legit stuff took time. Maybe if I named my gun. But Saint Saturday-Night Special didn't have quite the flair of Saint Glock. Neither did Saint Six-shooter.

CHAPTER 62

Locked out of my house, I bought new socks and underwear, as well as jeans, two crew shirts, and a corduroy blazer to tide me over until I grasped what was ahead. I dropped most of the stuff off at the station because I didn't want to buy a suitcase.

Delmonico had left a message at my desk asking where I was staying in case the police needed to reach me. The chief probably wanted him poised to make an easy arrest.

"I haven't decided yet." None of his business, I figured. Telling him I was likely to crash on the couch in the Channel 3 green room made me sound pitiful. He settled for my cell phone number.

"Anything new on Laura's murder?" I didn't expect much of an answer and didn't get one, other than that the autopsy had confirmed blunt force trauma as the cause of death.

"Your boyfriend still in town?"

"No, he needed to fly back to the job."

I had noticed the detective being much nicer to me when Garnett was watching, but I didn't want to call Delmonico on his behavior. Plenty of time for that later—after I became a cop's wife again. So I asked Delmonico to keep in touch if he heard anything; he made the same request of me. But I suspected neither of us really thought the other would stick to our deal.

• • •

I found Ed's revolver settled on the bottom of my purse as I rooted for change at the pop machine. Carrying the weapon around made me feel nervous and guilty, so I unloaded the gun and filed it in my desk drawer under *G*.

I decided not to tell Garnett. He actually favored me owning a firearm, and had even taken me to the shooting range once, but the timing for me and gun ownership was never right. Maybe it could be a marriage present. A wedding-night special.

Buried in the mess on my floor was Laura's tote bag. I sorted through my dead roommate's wallet and papers, telling myself I was investigating, not snooping.

In a folder was Kate's will, spelling things out just as her attorney explained. My eyes fell on her signature, and again I noted it was quite different from the inscription in *Black Angel Lace*.

We all know a day will come when our last will and testament moves from theoretical to actual and our heirs get all. Our only consolation? We won't be there to watch.

The will was drawn up two years ago by her attorney, Peter Marsden. Kate's signature was witnessed by two other people. Usually law firms use employees because most clients don't want friends or family to know their final wishes until after they're dead. I glanced at the names and drew a sharp breath.

One name meant nothing to me, the other read Karl Dolezal.

Dolezal. An unusual name, shared by the Black Angel's Teresa Dolezal Feldevert. An Internet search told me only 142 people in Minnesota shared the same last name. Did he share Black Angel blood?

I couldn't shake my wariness over coincidences, and working on her legal matters would put Dolezal in position to know her pen name and her address. So he shot to the top of my suspect list.

I considered going straight to Delmonico. But the cops had already denigrated my Black Angel theory and this was admittedly more of the same.

I needed to find out more about this man.

CHAPTER 63

Dolezal was right. With her house off limits, Riley Spartz gravitated to Channel 3. He found her vehicle in the hotel parking ramp; if he watched the exit long enough, he'd discover where she had moved.

By now, he was more amused than aggrieved by the mistaken-identity murder. Apparently he hadn't been the only one expecting to find the TV reporter at home.

Watching the late news, he learned that the woman he'd beaten in her bed was the older sister of his previous victim. He wished he would have known of that relationship at the time of her death. It would have made the killing more meaningful. He was now optimistic that the Black Angel would absolve him because of that connection.

The news story about the blundered beating had included an interesting bit of background about Riley Spartz: her parents.

((PACKAGE TRACK))
RILEY SPARTZ'S MOM AND DAD
DROVE UP FROM THEIR FARM
ALONG THE MINNESOTA-IOWA
BORDER TO ASSURE THEMSELVES
SHE WAS STILL ALIVE.

((SPARTZ DAD))
TO GET NEWS THAT YOUR
DAUGHTER HAS BEEN MURDERED,
WELL, THERE'S NOTHING WORSE
THAN THAT.

((SPARTZ MOM))
HEARING HER VOICE TELL US IT
WAS ALL A MISTAKE WASN'T GOOD
ENOUGH, WE HAD TO TOUCH HER.

He made notes of their names, then checked computer property tax records of counties along the Minnesota-Iowa state line to determine their homestead location. It charmed him that their land straddled the two states for which he felt such affinity. He might even get a head start on the Spartz family tree.

While sitting in his car, he pretended to be reading the newspaper, but was really just fixated on the front-page headline about the murder. Rain started to pound against the windshield. That pleased him because he would be less noticeable.

CHAPTER 64

I called the law firm and a computer voice told me to punch in the first three letters of the last name of the person I was trying to reach. D-O-L. A click, then a recording: "You have reached the desk of legal assistant Karl Dolezal. Please leave a message and I will return your call."

Because it was a weekend, I hadn't expected to reach him. I was just fishing to know if he still worked at the firm. Landing my answer, I hung up.

I let loose a jubilant shout as I gazed at the murder map on my wall. Dolezal could have been watching us the day Laura and I came to the law office to review the will's details. That visit might have put Laura on his radar, dooming her. He might have stalked her to my house, then moved in for the kill when he saw she was alone.

Because Dolezal worked at an esteemed law firm where the human resources department conducted employee background checks, I didn't harbor much hope of discovering a damning criminal record.

I'd settle for an arrest, not a conviction. A misdemeanor instead of a felony. My goal was a mug shot of the guy. Then I could show it to neighbors and ask if he looked familiar.

"Hey, Xiong, it's me." I called our cyber geek at home for

computer help. Normally he would have complained, or maybe even not picked up, but seeming glad I hadn't been murdered, he walked me through the mechanics of his computer data system.

"At least he has an unusual name," Xiong said of Karl Dolezal. "The only one in the state." Xiong often bemoaned having a very common name himself and the problems it could cause because of name-alikes with bad credit.

Xiong and I called up the details from Dolezal's driver's license. License photographs aren't part of the public record pool, but we were able to skim his date of birth and learn our guy was in his midtwenties. From there we checked criminal records. No arrests, thus no mug shots.

Dolezal listed his work address on both his vehicle and driver's license. Nothing illegal about that—I do the same thing, so do many law enforcement officers. We searched for hunting and fishing licenses in his name as even cops put their home address on that because they don't want to risk those renewals getting lost in the mail.

Without a mug or a home address, it's hard learning what a person looks like, particularly if they work in a large office. When trying to eyeball one woman out of hundreds, I'll sometimes send her a dozen yellow roses on a Friday and watch to see who carries them out the door to take home for the weekend.

I didn't think that technique would work this time.

Dolezal was growing impatient with his stakeout when he saw a figure rushing toward him from the direction of Channel 3 and recognized Riley Spartz as she ran through the rain to the hotel's revolving doors.

Knowing he might not get a second chance if he lost her, he started his engine so he would be ready to follow. But her car didn't exit. Ten minutes passed. He turned off the engine to think. Was she meeting someone? Eating in the restaurant? As long as her vehicle remained inside, she had to be there, or at least nearby, because the building was not part of the downtown skyway system.

Then he realized why the TV reporter hadn't left. She was a hotel guest.

CHAPTER 65

Would you like to go for a car ride, Nanna?" She liked being asked, but was weary, and had already settled down in front of the television for the night. She wanted to watch the reality show about dancing.

"You look cold," he said. "Let me find you a sweater or maybe a blanket."

"You're such a good boy," she murmured.

But that was only a ruse to hunt through her closet.

He would not need her car tonight, the hotel was within walking distance of his apartment. But there were other items he would require that she would not miss.

Even though I had promised myself I would live the life of Riley and order room service at the hotel, I couldn't bring myself to justify the perk when I saw the prices and realized there would be no expensing the bill.

So I ate a mac-and-cheese supper downstairs at Café Luxx while a jazz trio played. Comfort food and comfort sound. After buying a few snacks at the lobby store, I was ready to head back upstairs in a mood to watch cable television.

I held the Door Open button for an older woman in a dated

sweater since we were both exiting the elevator on the third floor. Balancing a granola bar, mints, and Pearson's Nut Goodie in one hand, I fumbled with my key card in the other outside my door.

I'd requested a room near the elevator because I don't like lonely hallways. The front desk gladly complied because those rooms are usually noisier and less popular. The occupancy rate was low that night anyway.

I like bragging that I see life two seconds faster than most people, and that gives me an edge. This was one of those times.

As my lock clicked and door opened, something curious made me turn my head before I landed hard on the floor of my room. I wasn't sure if I tripped or fainted until I looked up and realized I'd been shoved.

I heard chanting of "Taunting Teresa is tempting death." And while I had assumed the angel of death killer to be a man . . . he was actually a she. I shook my head to focus my brain, and still saw the woman who had been in the elevator standing over me, arm raised.

I had fallen with barely a thud, though it was enough to knock my breath away. Trying to muster a kick, I could hear a knock at the door and a voice calling my name.

So could my attacker.

The knock grew insistent so she replied that she didn't need anything. I couldn't seem to speak loudly enough to contradict her.

"Police, Ms. Spartz. Please open the door."

The woman complied, peering through a crack, then lurching forward.

Not until later, after my head cleared and Detective Delmonico arrived, did I find out that the woman had bolted past the plainclothes officer and down a stairwell. Rather than pursue, he called her description to his partner downstairs, then came to check on me. My attacker was not seen leaving the building.

While standing over Laura's body, the cops had become concerned that Kate's sister might not have been the murderer's target. Perhaps I was. After all, while she died there, I lived there.

"So we decided to guard you." Delmonico explained they'd used a global position satellite to track my cell phone, then verified I was registered for the night at the hotel. "We rented the room next door."

One officer had watched me as I finished dining, then texted upstairs to her partner that I was on my way. "If a man had gotten on the elevator with you, we would have boarded as well. But we figured you could only see us once before getting suspicious. So we were trying to stay concealed."

They were probably right about that assessment. And if I had caught the cops tailing me, well, they would have had some explaining to do.

Delmonico continued, "The chief warned that anyone who got made by you would be fired."

"What if I got killed on your watch?" That seemed more of a fireable offense to me.

No answer. Knowing the chief, that might merit a day off duty, off the books.

The first clue there was trouble at the hotel was a shuffling noise coming from inside my room. Then the officer stepped out of his room and noticed candy scattered in the hallway outside my door.

"That's when the scrutinize mode started," the detective said.

Sure, the cops were making themselves sound smart and tough, but bottom line, they lost the perpetrator.

"So where did she go?" I wondered if they even knew how my assailant slipped through their fingers.

Delmonico looked like someone who was hoping not to be asked a certain question. "We found a sweater, dress, and wig in the ground floor stairwell."

"So *she* simply walked out the front door a free man," I said.

"Probably," he agreed.

"Any surveillance cameras?" I asked.

"Nonfunctioning in the stairwell." I must have looked irked because he quickly added that they had video from inside the elevator. "Matches the clothing. But your attacker had his back to the camera and the image is pretty fuzzy."

Oh, the cops talked a good talk, all this protection business. But I knew exactly what had happened. "You weren't guarding me, you were using me for bait."

When my fiancé heard about that, he was unhappy.

"I'll call you back, Riley."

I should have started at the beginning of the story with the old lady in the elevator, instead of the ending with the me-as-bait punch line. Now Garnett wanted to yell at them more than he wanted to console to me. "Do you want to guess what my attacker said to me? 'Taunting Teresa is tempting death.' What do you think of that?"

"We'll talk later. I promise."

I don't know what exactly he said to them, but he encouraged me to head to the airport and catch the next flight to Washington. "I'm not convinced you're safe in Minneapolis."

"Believe me, Nick, I'm checking out of this hotel, ASAP. I'm going to sleep at the station tonight. The green room couch never sounded so good."

"My bed has to outrank any couch."

"There's no flight leaving until morning, unless I want to make two connections and take ten hours to get there." Besides I hated flying even on direct flights.

"A woman was killed in your house, Riley, and now you've been attacked. Pretty clear you're someone's target. I'd feel better if you drove to your parent's farm and holed up there until I could join you."

That was crazy talk. I told him I was overnighting at Channel 3, where we have round-the-clock security. Then I told him I loved him and wished him a pleasant good night.

When Noreen heard the news of my assault, she invited me to room with her and the animals. "The dogs will be excellent protection."

I knew those dogs and knew them to be as much protection as marshmallows. Any intruder who petted them and talked pretty would get a welcome lick.

Me? I was through with pretty talk. When I got back to the station, I headed straight to my file marked *G*, grabbed Ed's gun and bullets and practiced uttering "Freeze, sucker" and other words the FCC doesn't let us say on the air.

CHAPTER 66

I called Malik at home, interrupting him in the middle of a backyard landscaping project involving laying sod on wet dirt. My message that I needed him to come in early the next morning for a hidden camera assignment met with no zeal on his end.

I was scruffy-looking when Malik arrived. My neck was stiff. I hadn't eaten. And I'd slept poorly because the morning crew kept forgetting I was in the green room.

"I hate this spy stuff." My photographer was pouty even though he'd climbed out of a cushy bed to a hot breakfast. "Why can't I just set up the camera and you wear it?"

"Because they'll recognize me, either from TV or being in the office the other day."

My plan called for Malik to wear a hidden camera—his choice: glasses, baseball cap, or watch—and deliver a package to the law firm and ask Karl Dolezal to sign for it. "Barring technical difficulties," I said, "that should get us our picture."

"Good luck there," he said.

Malik grumbled that Channel 3's covert devices were not the most current. They were clunky compared to the sleek digital models on the market, but hot hidden camera gear wasn't a high priority after the station reduced the emphasis on investigative stories.

"It doesn't bother me as much as you, Malik. I guess I don't necessarily want my hidden camera video to look perfect, otherwise viewers won't believe it's undercover."

Channel 3's devices had pros and cons. The glasses provided a pinhole lens in the nose of the frame and shots wherever the wearer looked. But the frame resembled something out of a Buddy Holly movie, and didn't allow the photographer to be inconspicuous.

The hat also offered good sight lines, but if the brim turned slightly, the shot could miss. And undercover often didn't get a second chance. Both devices had noticeable cables that ran down the back of the wearer's neck and allowed the video to record in a fanny pack.

The watch was harder to aim, but the cables ran under the photographer's sleeve and were less noticeable.

Malik put on the hat, adjusted it in the mirror, then flung it on the floor. "Forget this, I'm just using my cell phone."

"What?" I said.

"I'm going to turn on my cell camera and record the shot. Watch."

He clipped his phone to his belt and pressed a button. "Stay where you are, Riley. We're going to test this." He backed up, walked forward, then stopped a yard in front of me.

He called up the digital video and showed me a well-framed in-focus shot.

"Can you do that more than once?" I asked.

"I guess we'll find out," he said.

I gave Malik a padded manila envelope addressed to Karl Dolezal, and a receipt that required a signature. I knew there was a good chance that the front-desk receptionist would simply want to sign for it herself. On the walk to the law firm building, we went over strategy.

"Try playing dumb and say you were told to have him sign," I said. "Pretend you're worried you'll get in trouble if he doesn't."

"I'm an artist not an actor," he replied. "I find it insulting you think I can play dumb convincingly," he said.

"I'm going to ignore that to avoid a fight."

Once on the street outside the building, I called Dolezal's phone number. When he answered, I acted flustered.

"Sorry, sir. I must have misdialed." Then I hit the End Call button.

"Nice lesson in playing dumb, Riley. So natural."

"I'm going to ignore that, too."

The important thing was we knew our target was at his desk. So it was time to move. Malik positioned his cell phone in a belt holster and checked to make sure the camera lens was visible.

"How long can you record?" I asked.

"Hours. I'll run out of battery before it runs out of memory."

I wished him luck and found a nearby coffee shop to wait. I ordered a hot chocolate and found a table and an abandoned newspaper in the corner. The cops had been excited about grilling Chuck Heyden on where he was when I was attacked, but I had told them not to bother.

"Too tall," I said, eliminating Kate's lanky boyfriend from any suspect pool.

Five minutes passed. Dolezal worked on the eighteenth floor, so I expected Malik might have an elevator wait. But when ten minutes passed I grew uneasy. I hoped he hadn't done anything strange that would attract the security staff.

After fifteen minutes, I was agitated and tempted to call him to check his status, but knew interrupting an undercover shoot could be disastrous. I patted my purse where Ed's gun was hidden. Just in case.

I gazed out the shop window at the crowd hurrying by and noticed a now familiar figure, my guardian angel, glancing up and
down the street. I chose to interpret it as God's way of reminding
me I was not alone. Having violated angel etiquette once already,
I decided not to engage him, but simply take note of his appearance and disappearance.

And recite a quick prayer. . . . *Ever this day be at my side . . .*

At the twenty-minute mark, I left my seat to pace on the sidewalk in front of the law building. I texted Malik to reply "OK" if
all was fine, but then he walked through the revolving door with
a big smile spread across his face.

"Did he sign it?" I asked. "Did you get the shot?"

"At that distance, don't see how I could have missed."

"Show me. Show me."

He pushed a button on his phone and I watched a video clip of
him walking up to a woman at a desk. Then the shot moved and
for the next thirty seconds I watched his feet, tapping nervously,
before he headed back into the elevator, apparently shutting off
the camera.

"You missed it." I couldn't believe the gaffe. The phone apparently shifted and he missed the shot. I was so dismayed I almost
walked in front of a bus driving along Nicollet Mall, but Malik
pulled me back off the street.

"Relax." He held the phone to my face and I watched a new
clip of him walking up to a different desk. "I got off on another
floor to tape that on my way out to spoof you. Here's the real
thing."

"What?" I felt like pushing him in front of the next bus. "Do
you think this is some April Fool's joke? We have work to do and
you're messing around with gags?"

"Sorry. Sorry. Look. Here's your guy."

The phone screen showed a woman talking on the phone
briefly before hanging up the receiver. The scene stayed un-
changed for at least twenty seconds. I was getting bored, because

in television news, twenty seconds of not much going on is an eternity. If I'd been a viewer, I'd have clicked to another channel after four seconds.

"Here we go," Malik said. "Keep watching."

A man in a white shirt, tie, and dark pants walked into the shot and up to the desk. A hand (presumably Malik's) gave him an envelope and clipboard. The man's lips were pursed together in concentration while he took out a pen.

I handed the phone back to Malik. "Hey, don't you want to see the rest?" he asked.

I shook my head. "I don't need to see any more."

Karl Dolezal was my guardian angel.

All the times I credited God with placing him nearby to be my protector, he was stalking me.

Back at Channel 3, I found myself wishing I had stuck to my original plan of putting blank paper in the package Malik delivered.

CHAPTER 67

The torn envelope fluttered to the floor as Dolezal raced back to the lobby to catch the man who had handed him the package.

"The man who was just here? Did you see where he went?" He blurted the words out at the receptionist like an accusation.

She pointed helplessly to the elevator. He punched the button for the ground floor. Every time the lift stopped for another passenger, his heart beat faster. On the third floor, he changed tactics and took the stairs. He realized the move probably cost him time, but if he remained in that confined space with other people, he feared he might explode.

He didn't find the delivery man on the street outside the building. Whoever he was, Dolezal knew, his own anonymity was lost. He held the sheet of paper from the envelope up against his heart. Then he crumbled that picture of the Black Angel into a tight ball and dropped it in the gutter.

He should have just stuck to waitresses.

The Black Angel must be punishing him for the wrong kill. Unless he performed suitable penance, he might be sacrificed himself.

He couldn't risk going back to the office or his apartment. A trap could be waiting.

He called in sick to the office manager. "I thought fresh air might help, but I feel so nauseous."

She urged him to get some rest. It was summer flu season. "Lot of nasty stuff spreading around."

Phooey on guardian angels. That's all I could think about on the way back to Channel 3. But once there, no time to pout about spiritual disappointments.

Malik held out his cell phone so Noreen and Miles could watch the slick video of Karl Dolezal. I'd also printed a close-up of his face off the shot.

"We can't broadcast it," Miles said. "Whatever we say about him is bound to be defamatory at this stage. Your dead dog guy has already retained an attorney to make problems over that live interview. We don't need more trouble. And this Dolezal fellow works for a law firm."

"I agree we don't have context to air the video as is," I said. "What we have is coincidence after coincidence. But it might be enough for the cops to get a warrant."

"What do you think?" Noreen asked Miles.

He nodded. "Might be the difference between someone's life and death. Let's go play *Law and Order*."

While Nanna fixed him a baloney and cheese sandwich, Dolezal used a chair to climb to the top shelf of the bathroom closet. In the back, high out of her reach, was his stash.

Nanna's place was the perfect safe-deposit box. Easy access, no questions asked, and no records kept. Over the last year, he'd tucked nearly five thousand bucks in a rolled-up towel in case he ever needed to disappear fast. Mostly twenties, but some hundreds, fifties, and tens for variety.

He put about a hundred fifty bucks in his wallet along with

a fake driver's license and library card he'd obtained the year before by "borrowing" a client's name and documentation. At the time, the man's appearance and age seemed a good match. Whenever Dolezal visited his clandestine cash, he always fingered the plastic to make it look worn.

"Nanna, always remember, you did your best raising me."

His compliment seemed to please her, as did his kiss against her cheek. Squeezing his hand, she murmured something about nurture and nature that he couldn't follow.

"You stay seated," he said, clearing the table. "I'll let myself out."

This time, he took his grandmother's old Taurus out of the apartment garage without telling her. He left his own car behind, first cleaning out anything he might need. Like a hunk of chalk from the glove compartment.

When the media ran his name and photo, a call from her senior housing facility might tip police to their relationship. He wanted Nanna genuinely confused when the detectives came to interview her.

About a mile away, he imagined her pain and shame. The news of his sins would destroy her. He headed back to fix things.

When Dolezal finally left her place, he slipped a heavy brass candlestick from the fireplace mantel under his jacket. He felt naked without his trophy bat, but knew he could not chance returning to his apartment to retrieve it without jeopardizing his scheme. The bat, and all it stood for, would have to be surrendered.

He turned his cell phone off and drove south because south felt familiar. And also because Riley Spartz's parents lived on a farm in that direction.

CHAPTER 68

One by one, I laid out the list of suspicious connections concerning Karl Dolezal for Detective Delmonico. Miles listened and took notes.

First, surname Dolezal.

"That only works if we buy into your Black Angel conjecture, and we really don't," he said. "What else you got?"

Victim was client. Dolezal signed will.

"That helps. What else?"

Dolezal works near Minneapolis library.

"So do ten thousand other downtown employees," he said dismissively.

Dolezal stalking me.

Delmonico scrunched up his face. "That helps regarding your attack, but it really doesn't as far the murders go. Unless we can prove the same hand is behind both."

He promised to show Dolezal's picture around my neighborhood and Kate's and see if anyone recalled seeing him before. "We'll also bring him in for some questioning about his apparent interest in you."

"But won't that put him on alert?" I asked. "And give him a chance to destroy evidence?"

"I'm sorry, but there's nothing here to get a judge to sign a search warrant," the detective said. "It'd be different if you could positively identify him as your attacker. Then we'd have to act."

So that's all they needed. "Absolutely, Detective." I could play that game.

"The minute I saw the tight camera shot of his face, I recognized him as the woman in the elevator. His eyes. His nose. No doubt. Put him in a wig and dress, he's the guy."

"Really?" Delmonico seemed skeptical. Even Miles looked doubtful. "Why didn't you mention that fact before?"

"I was working my way up to it. Didn't want to make the interview all about me."

Like I said, I could play that game. And once I understood the rules, it wasn't hard to break them.

He went over my statement, and again I claimed that Karl Dolezal was my assailant.

When I got back to Channel 3, I briefed Noreen on the meeting.

"Will the police let us be there to shoot any arrest?" she asked.

"Doubtful," I answered. "But I told them if they give our video to any other media, there'll be another homicide to investigate."

"So we need to wait." As I nodded in agreement, she changed the subject from death to dogs.

"The puppy thing isn't working out, Riley."

"What do you mean?"

"I think it's time for Max to go home."

"He doesn't have a home, Noreen. I was hoping you'd decide to keep him."

She shook her head, claiming to have dogs aplenty. "You'll have to drive him back to your parents' farm." She held out a spare house key and told me I should pick him up now and take tomorrow off.

This show of consideration was quite unlike my boss.

Then I realized what must have happened. "Garnett called you, didn't he?"

Her face gave it all away. "If you don't head down there, he's going to call them and tell them you're in danger. What do you think will happen then?"

No good. My parents would show up in downtown Minneapolis to protect me. They would take turns standing watch while I slept. My dad might even bring along the old shotgun he used to hunt pheasants.

I agreed to leave town for a day until things settled down. After all, it wasn't like I could count on my guardian angel.

I texted Garnett. OFF TO FARM. YOU WIN.

After twenty minutes of sniffing the interior of my car, Max curled up in a ball of fur and fell asleep in the backseat. I hit cruise control and played with the radio reception as we got farther from the Twin Cities.

I hadn't called my parents about my visit. I decided to surprise them. Otherwise they might ask too many questions. Max would be my excuse.

Halfway to the Black Angel, Dolezal had to rely on memory to locate the Spartz family farm because he didn't want to ask directions. He took a few wrong turns, but luckily their name was posted on the mailbox.

He didn't pull into the yard because he didn't want them to know they had company . . . yet. Instead, he found a private dirt road that ran through the land and connected to the main road via a pasture. He hid his car between a grove of trees and field of corn, then made his way on foot toward the homestead. He listened for the sound of a dog, but heard nothing.

A barn loft, decorated with a wooden quilt painting, offered good sight lines around the property. So he hid inside, moving straw bails to an open window to watch for signs of activity amid the silos, sheds, and grain bins. He heard some pigeons in the rafters, and was starting to think this farm might be a good place to temporarily hide out.

After he finished.

Just as the sky was turning dark, large yard lights came on that cast mysterious shadows. He would wait several hours, maybe even nap first. He was in no hurry.

Then he heard voices. Two figures left the house, slowly making their way toward an outbuilding. A garage, he realized as they drove away in a pickup truck.

They would be back. And they had left the garage door open. He wondered about the house. Sometimes people in the country didn't lock their doors. He contemplated exploring, but decided to wait.

About ten minutes later, as his eyelids felt comfortably shut, a vehicle turned back into the yard. He shook himself alert, but instead of the truck, a sedan stopped near their front door. A woman climbed out and a small, barking dog followed.

It was Riley Spartz.

The Black Angel must have sent her. A sign. He put on plastic gloves.

Mom and Dad weren't home. No church service tonight, so they'd probably headed to town for a supper of tacos or fried chicken at the American Legion. I must have just missed them on the road.

Had it still been daylight, I'd have taken Ed's gun out behind the barn to practice. The yard lights shone deep enough for some visibility, but not enough for shooting.

Max wanted to explore and do his dog business, so I tailed

behind him as he nosed along the ground. He seemed to be following some kind of trail toward the barn. Likely a raccoon or possum. Because my parents were retired, they rented out the farm fields and had no livestock.

The puppy barked, running faster.

"I'm coming, Max."

The dog smelled him. Another sign. Dolezal believed in signs. The puppy would make her suspicious in a matter of minutes. And he realized it would be best to move now, before the truck returned and two more sets of eyes arrived.

The pup looked up and began growling at Dolezal's window, ten feet above the ground.

"Did you find him? Did you, Max? Go get him." The reporter stood just below his hideout, humoring the pooch.

Then she turned toward the house, whistling for him. "Come along, boy."

Dolezal jumped, knocking her to the ground. He could have kept tightening his grip, thus ending the mission there. But the Black Angel wouldn't have approved. She preferred blood to bruises. And he had promised her a visit from them both.

CHAPTER 69

This death endeavor was his riskiest. But it stood to be the most rewarding. Karl Dolezal kept his eyes on the road and his mind on his cargo.

Whether the reporter was awake or not would make no difference for hours. Until he opened the trunk, she was his. Once they arrived, she would belong to the Black Angel.

A sacrifice at her feet would make him historic.

He thought Riley Spartz's car more likely to be reported stolen than his grandmother's. So he loaded the reporter, unconscious, into her backseat and drove down the private farm road to switch vehicles.

The puppy raced after them, barking, but couldn't keep up.

Pawing through her purse while he drove, Dolezal discovered the gun. A loaded revolver. Nice. He put the firearm in the glove compartment to examine later. In her wallet, he found two twenties, and pocketed the cash.

He threw her purse and cell phone out the car window into a ditch and continued driving south.

CHAPTER 70

The last thing I remembered was barking. So much for my presumption of seeing life two seconds faster than everyone else.

Until I recognized road noise, I didn't even realize I was trapped inside a car trunk. Not a crack of light shone through the night. My neck ached, my ankle hurt, and coarse twine fastened my hands behind my back.

A blanket seemed wrapped around my body. I shifted my legs and rocked back and forth to loosen the cover. I tried locating something with a sharp edge, like a tire iron. But any tools must have been stored in the space under the floor mat along with the spare. I was probably lying on top of prime gizmos, but didn't have enough room or dexterity to pry the compartment open.

My purse and cell phone were missing. No Saint Saturday-Night Special.

The vehicle was moving fast; no point in kicking against the sides or yelling for help. That would only tell my captor I was alert. Best he think me dazed and helpless.

Our speed increased. Most likely we were traveling on a freeway. No idea what direction, or how far, but I decided to stay quiet until the car stopped.

I had no doubt Karl Dolezal was behind the wheel. I wondered why he hadn't just beaten me to death instead of slamming the trunk shut. Clearly he wanted to take me somewhere. But why not simply kill me first? He could draw an angel around my body any time.

He might be using the blanket to avoid traces of my DNA in his vehicle. That made me determined to leave something of myself behind in case searchers found the car and needed proof it had carried me to my death. While that strategy might not save my life, it could doom his.

I scratched my wrist until I felt wetness. Blood, I hoped. Sticky. Pushing the blanket aside, I rubbed my arm against the carpet. Then I spit on the floor of the trunk. Again and again. Until I felt thirsty.

To take my mind off lying in my own saliva and blood, I started tearing off my fingernails and shoving them in corners of the trunk to be discovered during a forensics search. I knocked against an edge of metal along the back. It wasn't razor-sharp, but felt honed enough that it might cut through my binding.

Rolling on my side, I held my wrists up against it and rubbed back and forth. My position was awkward, and I had to pause to rest, but already I could feel the fastening loosen.

I had no idea how much time had passed. The tire hum was making me drowsy. I tried to stay awake by sawing through my ties and thinking of Nick. Briefly, I fingered my engagement ring.

And because I could think of no one else to turn to, I prayed to my guardian angel. *"Ever this day be at my side, to light and guard, to rule and guide."*

CHAPTER 71

His gas gauge was low.

Dolezal would have rather waited to fill up the tank after his mission, but didn't think he'd make it to their destination. He pulled into a service station and parked at the pump farthest from the cash register. Then he remembered not to use credit cards because his movements could be tracked. Dolezal also couldn't risk playing pump pirate and driving off without paying because gas stations always videotape license plates.

He had plenty of cash, thus the bill was no problem. Riley Spartz didn't seem to be awake, so he decided it was safe to leave her for a few minutes. His disappointment would be to open the car trunk and find her dead.

Dolezal walked inside the convenience store, and handed two twenties to the clerk. The young woman took the money, fingered the bills and then looked at him without making eye contact.

He didn't like that look. But he also didn't want to be remembered, so he took his receipt and left without saying much beyond "thanks." Glancing back from the car, the clerk seemed to be holding money up to the light. And that made him nervous.

He made sure he drove off slowly. But a couple miles later, flashing lights came up behind him. The officer gave a short burst of siren, indicating he should pull over.

Dolezal wasn't speeding. He thought about hitting the accelerator but didn't have much hope that Nanna's old Taurus could outrun the cop's Ford Crown Vic in a chase. He hoped he was being stopped because small-town cops like ticketing out-of-state drivers instead of their neighbors.

He pulled over, and the officer parked behind him on the side of the road. The cop sat in his squad for a minute, probably checking Dolezal's plates to make sure the vehicle wasn't stolen.

Dolezal opened the glove compartment and went for the gun. If the officer asked him to step outside the vehicle, he would fire. He watched in his mirror as the uniform approached, carrying a flashlight which he shined in Dolezal's face.

"Driver's license, please."

"Excuse me, Officer, I do not believe I was exceeding the speed limit."

"You weren't. Now may I see your license?"

He handed over the plastic, confident it would pass muster—both visually and through any computer crime check. Dolezal had made sure the identity he'd lifted came from a client with a clean criminal record.

"What probable cause do you have to pull me over?" He thought a little lawyer jargon might speed things up.

"Counterfeiting," the officer said.

Dolezal couldn't believe the accusation. "What?"

"You paid for that gas with two counterfeit bills."

"This is some misunderstanding," Dolezal said. "If they were fake, I had no idea." Then he realized the twenties were the money he took from Riley Spartz's wallet. Damn her.

"Wait here for a moment." The cop headed back to his squad car to run the driver's license.

Dolezal still thought he might slip out of this mix-up by offering to pay for the gas. Until he heard a woman screaming for help.

Riley Spartz was awake.

• • •

The car had slowed, then halted. Smelling gas, I realized we must be filling up at a pump. I was tempted to call out then, but knew I would only get one chance. I had to be sure a rescuer was within earshot. I heard nothing, so I stayed quiet.

A few minutes later, we started moving again and I knew my opportunity was lost. I resumed trying to cut through my binds. I felt some give and knew I was close.

Then I heard an unusual noise, and we stopped again. The sound might have been a siren blast. I listened carefully and thought I heard footsteps. Then voices. Definitely more than one. That's when I knew the time had come to scream for my life.

Dolezal could see that the patrol officer was not prepared for the scream. While the cop glanced around, fumbling for his weapon, Dolezal stuck his head and arm out the car window and fired.

The cop fell down, injured but not dead.

Then Dolezal, in his Angel of Death mode, tossed the gun on the passenger seat, started the engine, and floored reverse, backing over the officer.

Dolezal climbed out of the car to retrieve his driver's license. The officer still seemed to be breathing, but was in no position to call for assistance. He had apparently dropped the driver's license. His assailant spread his hands across the cold ground, crawling on his knees, searching for the lost plastic or at least the flashlight.

He knew he didn't have much time. Another officer would soon be dispatched to check on this one. And his vehicle license plate had already been radioed to police headquarters. But nobody knew his final destination. He would take back roads to Iowa City.

And then he found the license, and got back on his feet.

The reporter was still shrieking; he banged his fist on the trunk to silence her.

CHAPTER 72

When Dolezal reached the Iowa City town limits, he was ready to execute his plan. And the TV reporter, Riley Spartz, would be the only victim he slew in the open. With the others, he'd always taken care to act behind fences or walls.

The time was just after midnight, so he wasn't worried about witnesses. He knew he was trespassing, but he especially enjoyed driving through the cemetery in the dark.

He parked next to his dear Black Angel, shutting off the engine and lights before meditating a moment. Then he reached for the candle stick because he appreciated the personal contact and wanted to get used to the grip.

I heard the car door open and suspected he was coming for me. When the trunk opened, I was startled by the face of the Black Angel staring down at me. Even though my hands were free, I kept them behind my back so he would think me vulnerable. He dragged me to the cement slab in front of the statue, and slammed me down. Then stood over me, arm raised.

I rolled and ran, taking him by surprise.

Dolezal knew the general direction of my hiding place, and proceeded to search methodically from headstone to headstone.

The full moon offered enough light for his hunt. If I moved, he would see me. If I stayed still, he would find me.

Cat and mouse in a dark cemetery. I tried not to squeak.

Dolezal held his breath. If he listened closely enough, he might hear her pant or wheeze. She must be trying the same trick, because he heard nothing.

While he could not see her, he was certain she could see him. That gave her an edge. He decided to replace suspense with shock by rushing toward a nearby crypt. If she was crouched there, she would be his. If not, she might be startled into giving away her position.

Then the chase could commence.

He never doubted the outcome. Before dawn, a freshly dead body, outlined in chalk, would pantomime the statue of his beloved.

A shriek left his throat as he made his wild blitz.

My ankle was too sore to count on consistently. So I needed a place for a last stand. I decided on Dolezal's car because I was closer to the automobile than he was.

If the keys were inside, I could escape. Otherwise, I would buy time by locking the doors, leaning on the horn, and praying for a neighbor to call 911 and complain about the noise. The vehicle seemed too old for autolocks.

My confrontation with him would take place there. I was trying to decide when to up and run when he made an odd noise and raced in a direction away from me. My only chance. But almost immediately, he perceived my destination and raced me.

I got there first, but once inside, my plan changed because waiting on the seat to rescue me was my true guardian angel—Saint Saturday-Night Special.

"Drop it, or I'll shoot." I cocked the hammer like Ed showed me, then climbed out of the car carefully. "I mean it."

I had intended to order him to "Freeze, sucker," but even though I'd practiced, the words did not come.

Dolezal let his weapon, a candlestick, fall to the ground without any fuss. Daylight was hours away. I couldn't stand watch over him that long. The cemetery was empty, except for us. I thought about firing in the air as a call for help, but wasn't sure how many bullets remained. And couldn't risk running out of ammo.

The trunk was still open, and seemed like the ideal place to keep him until I could get assistance. Let Dolezal experience the tight quarters.

"Toss me the keys," I said.

Instead, he flung them far off into the darkness without saying a word. He folded his arms across his chest in defiance.

"Okay, climb in the trunk." I motioned with my gun that I was serious.

Instead he moved backward, away from the vehicle, to pose in front of the sculpture, his arms mimicking her wings. I could no longer see his face, and that's when I noticed he wore plastic gloves.

"Fine, Dolezal. Say your good-byes to your Black Angel. Where you're going, you won't see her again. You'll live the rest of your life behind bars. Prison can be hell on earth. And I will pray that you suffer misery for all the pain you've caused."

He made no move toward the vehicle, merely shrugged as if my remarks were irrelevant. Then apparently changed his mind and decided I deserved a lecture. For such a quiet guy, he surprised me by being articulate.

"The Angel of Death was my destiny. I'll be more famous than Ted Bundy or Charles Manson. Son of Sam. The Zodiac. Maybe even Jack the Ripper."

He certainly was well versed on notorious serial killers in history. I detected no shame in his voice, only pride.

"Behind bars, I'll be a star. A real-life Hannibal Lecter. Law enforcement officers will want to interview me. Psychiatrists will want to study me. They'll scan my brain. And examine my motivations."

He was probably right about that. For cooperative research sessions with him, authorities would make his prison stay palatable. Just then, I regretted Minnesota didn't have a death penalty. Then I realized that neither did Iowa, North Dakota, or Wisconsin. He'd done his murderous homework, and realized he could dodge execution.

I was starting to worry that as an inmate, he might be smart enough to escape from prison; or as a defendant, beat a murder rap by pleading insanity.

"Get in the trunk, Dolezal."

He didn't seem to fear me or my gun. In this spooky graveyard, I was uneasy that he might catch me off guard. I could still end up dead before morning.

"My trial will be the trial of the century." His spiel continued with enthusiasm.

He smirked in anticipation of his celebrity. During our other encounters, I couldn't recall him ever smiling. His face, once stoic, now beamed like salvation was his alone. Under his breath, I heard snickering.

He was right about his destiny. He would become a champion of evil. And I couldn't stand it.

Society would grow more fascinated with him each year. Anniversary stories would appear. No one would remember the names of his victims, but Karl Dolezal would become a household word. And when he finally died, headlines across the globe would publish clever lines like *Grim Reaper Finally Claims Angel of Death*. For generations, his grisly deeds, like those of his bloodthirsty idols, would be glamorized.

To reward him with infamy seemed so wrong.

And I could see only one way to prevent it.

I took two steps forward and pulled the trigger.

In the past year, I'd seen too many people die up close. But this was very different. They had wrought their own demise—by their own hand, own carelessness, certainly by their own demons.

Now, Karl Dolezal lie bleeding across the cement slab at the foot of the Black Angel. And I was culpable.

His eyes locked on those of the statue. Hers black as stone, his black as glass. He struggled to throw wide his arms as if embracing her wings. All the while, his chest wound gushed blood that looked more black than red.

He muttered, "Do not weep for me, dear mother, I am at peace in my cool grave." It took a second for me to realize he was quoting the inscription from the tree-stump marker over the buried son.

Then I heard a final word slip from his lips. "Teresa."

As his life slipped away, I had an overwhelming sense Teresa Dolezal Feldevert was transporting his soul to hell.

CHAPTER 73

In a midnight instant, I, too, had become an angel of death.

I told the Iowa City police how I acted in self-defense using Karl Dolezal's revolver. That seemed more prudent than a long-drawn-out explanation of why an unregistered firearm belonged to me.

The police had questions about the events leading up to me blowing a hole in my abductor's chest. So I outlined a complicated scenario about disarming my foe, and how he had then resisted my plan to lock him in the car trunk by charging at me in the dark with a candlestick.

They wondered why the candlestick was so far from the scene of the shooting.

I shrugged. "It happened so fast, I don't remember even pulling the trigger."

Certainly, that part of my statement was a lie. Pulling the trigger is something I will never forget. Strange how an action that took a mere split second is now one of the paramount memories of my life.

Neither the police nor the media wanted to dig too deep. After all, Dolezal was a most unsympathetic victim—a delusional young man who believed a cemetery statue was urging him to kill.

They confiscated the firearm for forensic tests and determined from gunpowder residue and fingerprints that I had indeed fired the lethal shot. What puzzled them was that my fingerprints were on the remaining bullets in the gun. So I lied about empty- ing the firing chamber afterward to check whether any ammo was left, just in case my attacker had an accomplice lurking be- hind another tombstone.

Everyone told me how lucky I was to be alive.

Yet I wondered if I had become another pawn of Teresa Dolezal Feldevert. Perhaps I wouldn't have fired the fatal shot if our confrontation had not happened on her turf. Might I have fallen under her power? Or was I just making excuses, telling myself it was really her spirit that pulled the trigger? Maybe I was seeing ghosts to avoid accountability for my own actions. Or perhaps she was determined that someone, anyone—Karl Dolezal or me—die on her grave that night.

I shook those ideas aside, because I believe in news. I believe in facts. The paranormal has no place in my world.

Regardless, the episode changed me. Because when I killed Dolezal, a little bit of me died inside.

I supposed I shouldn't have been surprised. What was the in- famous quote from the German philosopher Nietzsche? *He who fights with monsters should look to it that he himself does not be- come a monster.*

So was I a newshound or a hellhound? I was no longer sure.

Father Mountain was the only one who knew the truth of what happened that night, but he was bound by the confidentiality of confession.

Not even Garnett suspected my sin. I wasn't sure I'd ever tell him. The fewer people who know something, the easier it is to pretend it never happened.

"I've never killed anyone," he said. "All my years in law enforcement and I've never actually drawn my gun in the line of duty. I can only imagine what you're going through."

I shook my head. No, he couldn't. What I was going through was beyond his imagination. I worried about trying to build a life with someone while keeping that big a secret from him. And not just a secret, a lie. But I didn't see much choice. I didn't want to put him in the position of choosing between me and the law. I had no doubt he would chose me, but I also feared a choice like that might change him. And us.

I'm not denying what I did that night in the graveyard; I took responsibility in the confessional. "Oh my God, I am heartily sorry."

And I meant it.

I just didn't feel the legal system needed to be involved in my contrition. A life sentence in prison can easily cost taxpayers more than a million dollars per inmate. So I argued in my mind that I had saved the state money that could be better spent educating children and caring for the environment.

Perhaps one day God would judge me, and I might be punished. But until that happened, I would pray for a merciful God, and hope He would understand the extenuating circumstances that night in Oakland Cemetery when I violated the sixth commandment.

I had no idea fire and brimstone waited just around the corner.

CHAPTER 74

I took a couple days off work after pulling the trigger, and holed up at my parents' farm with my fiancé. I did an interview with Channel 3, but ignored all network requests and other media.

Nothing seemed normal, especially not my first day back at the station. Garnett dropped me off, then left for a meeting with state officials before he needed to fly back to Washington.

The assignment desk had just gotten word about some bootleg booze found hidden in the walls of an old house once owned by the Gluek brewing family in northeast Minneapolis.

"Sounds like it might have been a Prohibition hideaway," Ozzie said.

I wanted to run on the story because I enjoy local history and because this assignment seemed to hold a minimal chance for bloodshed, but Noreen had put me on standby in the newsroom.

Keith Avise wanted a word with my boss about our coverage of his dead dog and deceased marriage. He was bringing his attorney along to weave terms like "libel," "defamation," and "reckless disregard for the truth" into the discussion.

"Money we spend on legal costs means money we can't spend on news," Noreen said.

My boss thought it best Miles participate in the meeting instead of me. That way she'd be armed with a lawyer too. And maybe, behind closed doors, they could make all of this go away without hysterics.

"I sure don't want to meet with him," I said. "But I don't think you two should meet with him either. The guy's nuts. If he wants to sue us, bring it on. Let's handle it in court."

"Clearly we're in the right," Miles said. "No way would we lose the case before a judge. But we'd like to avoid having it get to a jury because there are viewers who felt sympathy for him during that live interview with Sophie."

"Even more reason to keep me out of it. This is more Sophie's fault than mine."

"But we're all part of the Channel 3 news team," Noreen said. "We stick together."

"If you have to talk to this jerk," I said, "go to his attorney's office. Remember this is the dude who egged me just outside the door."

"I think there's an advantage to meeting here," Miles said. "Gives us the home court advantage."

Noreen agreed. "We may have you join us in the meeting later, Riley, but we'd like to speak with him first and see where he's at. Wait in your office until we call you."

I didn't like the sound of that. Seemed like I might get dissed out of earshot just to appease a crazy newsmaker. But honestly, I no longer cared. Anything was better than that night with the Black Angel. Dodging eggs was easier than dodging death.

Those memories remained troubling, so I lay my head on my desk, trying to let my brain go blank and escape the haunting that happened in my mind when I wasn't focused on news.

I told myself that while Noreen was definitely the worst boss I had ever had, she might also be the best.

Then my phone rang; when I opened my eyes, I saw the black feather pinned to my bulletin board. That boded ill. The front desk called to say Garnett was out in the lobby. The receptionist put him on the phone.

"How about a quick farewell lunch before my flight?"

If he'd called before showing up, I would have told him I was busy, because I didn't feel like I could handle another round of good-bye. But I didn't see much choice with us under the same roof.

"Send him back," I told the receptionist.

I walked down the hall and waved him toward my office. He closed the door, planted a deep kiss on my lips, and pressed my body against my desk.

"Not here." I pushed him away. "The last thing I need is for Noreen to walk in on us making love. This time she could nail me for unsuitability on station property. So cherish your kiss and call me when you land."

He noticed a photo of us on my desk, taken at my parents' farm, and I could tell that pleased him.

"I just wanted to show you some spontaneity, Riley."

Spontaneity. I remembered that conversation. "I've been re-thinking what I said, Nick. I've had enough spontaneity to last a lifetime. I'm starting to treasure predictability."

He laughed, wrapping his arms around me. "I'm going to spend the rest of my life making you feel safe without abandoning spontaneity."

"Those might be contradictory goals." I stared into his eyes, feeling guilt over what I wasn't telling him about that night by the Black Angel. "Are you sure about us?"

He gazed back at me and paused. "This kind of certainty comes but once in a lifetime." And he kissed me like he wanted our lips locked forever.

I knew I'd heard those words before. Then I realized he was quoting a movie line. "Clint Eastwood, *The Bridges of Madison County*, 1995."

I remembered the year because TV anchorwoman Jodi Huis-entruit was abducted soon after the film was released. Both the on-screen romance and the real-life crime happened in Iowa. I really didn't want any reminders about Iowa.

But what bothered me most was *The Bridges of Madison County* didn't have a happy ending. Clint Eastwood said his final line to Meryl Streep, then walked out the door and out of her life. And she just let him go. I felt like that scene was putting a hex on us.

"Say a different line, Nick. Say something where the hero and heroine ride off in the sunset together. Quote me something from *Pretty Woman* or *Sleepless in Seattle* or *Romancing the Stone*. I want a comedy, not a drama."

He shook his head, puzzled at my outburst.

"Please, Nick. I need a happy ending."

"You complete me."

I recognized the line. "Tom Cruise, *Jerry Maguire*, 1996."

"Will that do?" he asked.

I thought back to Tom Cruise and Renée Zellweger. Their work and love overlapped, but all eventually ended well. Kind of like us. I hoped, anyway. "That will have to do." This time, I kissed him.

"I suppose I should tell you, Riley, that lunch was just a ruse. In the interest of spontaneity, I booked a hotel room across the street. Don't worry, not the same place where the angel killer came after you."

"Hotel sex? Nick, I can't leave. I'm waiting for Noreen to get out of a legal meeting that sort of involves me."

He handed me a hotel key card. "I'll head over there now, and maybe you can catch up with me later." He winked, looking at his watch. "I don't have to catch a cab to the airport for another hour, maybe longer since I know a shortcut through security."

His optimism brought tears to my eyes. He trusted I would keep our rendezvous. Instead, I was contemplating breaking his heart. I could not marry him, carrying such a bleak secret. And he could not marry me, knowing the truth.

Then another film came to mind with the line "You complete me," and I remembered that version did not deliver a happy ending for any of the characters, not even Batman.

"Heath Ledger, *The Dark Knight*, 2008."

Garnett smiled ruefully like he'd been expecting that answer all along. He offered no comeback, simply kept eye contact with me before mustering a Mona Lisa smile. His gaze was so intense, I had to look away.

Breathing deep, I slipped the engagement ring off my finger, sticking it and the key card in his shirt pocket.

His shock seemed genuine. Whatever he might have imagined could come from my cemetery encounter, this wasn't it. "Riley, is this the end of us?"

"I'm really confused right now, Nick. Can we call it the middle, and sort things out later?" I turned away so I wouldn't have to look at him, but he pulled me back.

"I don't want what we have to be over, Riley." He paused, lips pressed together with determination. "I know what happened in Iowa rattled you, but we can work through this."

Before I could answer, a banging sound interrupted our conversation. While I was shrugging it off as some construction noise outside, Garnett was drawing his gun. Seconds later, we heard a scream.

"Stay here," he told me. "Lock the door and don't open it again until I tell you to."

More banging. More terror.

"No matter what happens," he demanded. "Don't open the door. Promise me? Riley?"

I nodded.

"Remember, I'm holding you to your word." Then he left me.

Immediately after my door closed, he pounded on it, reminding me to hit the lock button and ordering me to call 911. "Tell them shots fired. Tell them I'm on the scene and ask them not to shoot me."

I made the call and told the dispatcher that someone at Channel 3 was firing a weapon, and gave her the message about Garnett. She told me my call was the fourth they'd received in the last fifteen seconds and that squads were en route to the station.

"Stay calm and take cover."

I wasn't surprised to discover evil in a dark graveyard, but none of us expect to find danger at our desks. I had to see what was happening. I remembered the station's closed-circuit house feed and turned on my television monitor. One of the floor cameras was rolling. The view was stationary, but I saw a person crumbled on the floor.

Suddenly a figure walked through the shot, and I recognized Keith Avise. He was waving a gun and shouting. He wasn't wearing a studio microphone, but his muddled audio must have been picked up by a wireless microphone left on at the weather wall.

"Where is she?" he ranted.

He pointed the gun and another shot echoed, followed by a scream. "Find her!" he ordered someone standing off camera.

I knew he was talking about me. And I wanted to rush out and end the whole ordeal, even if it cost me my life . . . because I believed I deserved to die. I even wondered if God had sent Avise to deliver my punishment.

"Promise me?" My promise to Garnett stuck in my mind as I debated my guilt.

Suddenly I realized a way I could get the psycho's attention and perhaps distract him. I grabbed my phone and activated the overhead paging system.

"Looking for me, Avise?"

He glanced right and left trying to figure out where my voice was coming from.

"Better ration those bullets," I advised. "Or you'll run out before you and I face off."

"I'm coming for you, bitch!"

"Better hurry, the police are on their way. I suspect you're not going to want them to take you alive. Your kind seldom do."

I knew rescue was not as simple as the first cop on the scene walking in with gun blazing. With spree killers, officers would assemble a SWAT team and plan their entry. I figured Garnett was in touch with them, giving them instructions about the building floor plan and shooter's location.

My immediate mission was to draw the shooter's attention away from my coworkers. "Hey, Avise, I can see you, but you can't see me."

He looked confounded, then raised his gun, walked toward the floor camera with the tiny red light. The last video I saw was the flash of his demented grin before the screen went black. Then a loud bang. Pulling the trigger on the robocam had destroyed my window to his rampage.

"Open up, bitch." His voice was clear now, just outside my door. I hoped my colleagues were all fleeing the building while he was in this back hallway. He hammered against the door. "I know you're in there."

My name was on a sign outside my office. But I stayed quiet so he couldn't be certain I was indeed inside. I longed to push a bookcase against the door, for another layer of protection, but worried the noise would verify my presence.

Suddenly he started shooting. With every bullet fired, I sunk lower to the floor until I was cowering under my desk. I'd never paid any attention to whether my office door was wood or metal, but I put my hands over my ears and prayed the bullets stayed on the other side.

I contemplated letting loose a tortured scream, as if I'd been hit. Maybe that would satisfy him and he would place his weapon in his mouth and blow his brains out, like so many mass murderers do to avoid being taken into custody. More likely he'd be determined to break down the door to watch me bleed to death. I stuck with my strategy of silence.

A minute went by. I heard two more shots, this time farther away. Then five minutes seemed to pass without gunfire. Was it over? Why hadn't Garnett knocked? Or at least called? Where was he?

I wanted to open the door, but I'd promised. I called his cell phone, which rang into his voice mail. I dialed the assignment desk, but no one answered.

I counted back the number of gunshots I'd heard, and considered whether the stillness in the building could simply mean my attacker might be out of ammunition. If that were the case, Garnett would have apprehended Avise and handed him over to the authorities.

And come for me.

So I continued to wait, but no one came.

Seven minutes passed and I tried not to think that one of the bullets might have found him, though that now seemed the most likely explanation. I didn't want confirmation of that news, so I stayed under my desk, where I could continue to deny the worst.

My cheeks felt wet before I realized I was sobbing. I clenched my eyes tight to slow the tears, and started ruminating useless thoughts of "What if?"

What if Buddy's death had never made the news?

What if Noreen hadn't let Avise in the building?

But the real "what if" hinged on what if I hadn't killed Karl Dolezal? Because it was that decision I suspected turned Channel 3 into a war zone. A perfect storm of evil.

My own culpability now kept me on the floor of my office, rather than out in the newsroom soaking in the aftermath.

"Sorry. Sorry. Sorry." I kept muttering a useless apology that no one could hear.

Then a determined knock startled me, and I jumped to unlock the door for Garnett. Instead, Malik stood there.

So I had my answer on the fate of my once fiancé.

My cameraman hugged me and told me how glad he was that

I was all right. "It's a mess out there, Riley. The building has been declared a crime scene. Police are evacuating everyone and interviewing them downtown."

The last thing I wanted to do was talk about what happened.

Malik pushed me toward the back door. "They want everyone out this way to avoid the carnage."

"I need to see it."

"They won't let you back there. They're moving in body bags."

"I need to see his body. Don't you understand, Malik?"

What I wanted to do was take the engagement ring from Garnett's pocket and put it on my finger. An irrelevant gesture but one I needed to make, both for me and him.

"They're not going to let you anywhere close to that jerk. None of us are getting by his corpse. I think they're afraid we'll spit on it and contaminate the evidence."

"I'm talking about Garnett," I said.

"Garnett? He's busy with the homicide team. He sent me back to get you."

We looked at each other; Garnett was the first to speak. "Now we've each killed somebody. I guess that makes us even."

EPILOGUE

For the first time in more than half a century, Channel 3 did not broadcast the nightly news. Those time slots were filled by the network. But our local competitors crammed most of their news hole with details of the tragedy.

> ((CHANNEL 8 ANCHOR))
> FOUR DEAD . . . TWO WOUNDED
> IN A NEWSROOM MASSACRE AT
> CHANNEL 3.

Sophie Paulson's death got top billing. Beautiful dead television anchors are always lead stories. The media lumped Noreen in with the rest of the casualties because she was no household name.

Miles survived with a bullet in the stomach, and later described the spree to police, saying Avise went crazy when Noreen pointed out that Channel 3 was merely reporting the news about him, his dog, and his ex-wife.

"Are you going to let them talk to me like that?" he shouted at his attorney, who was trying to smooth things over and scare the station into a quiet financial settlement to avoid a public legal battle.

Avise apparently pulled out a gun and, without saying a word, held it against his lawyer's head and pulled the trigger. "Now do you see I mean business?"

Blood spatter and brain matter were on everyone. Miles said he couldn't talk or move or even breathe, but that Noreen tried to assure Avise that the station would retract everything they'd broadcast about him.

"Let's work on the script right away and you can approve it. You can watch us read it live on the air."

Avise smiled like he was satisfied with this triumph, then pointed the weapon at her, firing twice. Miles didn't remember anything else except waking up in the hospital the next day.

Ozzie heard the shots while sitting at the assignment desk, ducked underneath and was the first to call 911, reporting the attack. He told investigators that Avise wasn't aiming at just anyone. "He seemed to be looking for specific targets."

He found Sophie almost immediately and ignored her apologies, blowing away most of her anchor face. That's when he started asking newsroom staff about me. When no one answered, he shot Xiong in the leg. "Maybe this will get your attention."

Right away Xiong had volunteered directions to my office.

Karl Dolezal had bought a plot in Oakland Cemetery and left instructions and money for a small replica of the Black Angel to sit over his grave. Trustees of the cemetery were horrified and voted to deny his wishes.

Based on my trumped-up identification of him as my attacker, Minneapolis police showed up at his apartment with a search warrant. Inside, the cops found a broken bat coated in human blood, birth and death certificates of the murdered women, and a framed photograph of the Black Angel.

Channel 3 was cheated out of any news exclusive because I

was locked in a car trunk, and because the FBI immediately announced a national search for Karl Dolezal.

When my parents returned to the farm, they initially thought I had just dropped off Max and driven away in a huff. But the puppy led them to my car, hidden near the grove. They called Garnett, and a national search was announced for me.

Minneapolis Police asked their counterparts in Iowa City to put Oakland Cemetery under surveillance. That's where they found me, in the shadow of the Black Angel, standing over a bleeding corpse.

The next day, Dolezal's nanna was discovered dead in her bed, smothered with a pillow.

The patrol officer who stopped Dolezal for passing counterfeit bills survived the altercation, but requested a desk job.

The Angel of Death's body remains unclaimed at the Johnson County morgue in Iowa City.

Consultant Fitz Opheim was named acting news director at Channel 3.

Good homes were found for all of Noreen's animals. Barbara Avise took in Speckles the dalmatian. My parents adopted Blackie the Lab, to stay with Max on the farm.

And Husky now lives with me. I figured while a puppy would probably make me crazy, Max might keep Mom and Dad young.

Desiree Fleur's final book, *Sexpocalypse*, was a breakout bestseller. The book received critical acclaim for challenging mankind's overemphasis on sex. Reviewers especially raved about the ending in which the world explodes, yet the protagonists go on to make love in heaven with famous dead people like Einstein, Cleopatra, and Elvis.

Since the author and her heir were both dead, under Kate's will, all royalties passed to the Minnesota Library Foundation.

Kate's editor, Mary Kay Berarducci, went on to be hired by one of the top publishing companies in New York.

Because all Laura and I had was a handshake deal, I never saw a dime for writing that ending. No one besides Garnett ever knew about my role as a ghostwriter.

I tried getting reengaged, but this time Garnett was the one who held back. "Let's wait for a happier stretch. Too much pain surrounds us right now."

So I'm not sure whether I'll ever wear that deep red ring again or live the life of Riley.

ACKNOWLEDGMENTS

My apologies to Iowa City's stunning Black Angel statue and to the ghost of Teresa Dolezal Feldevert. I mean no disrespect to this historical character. If you haven't seen the sculpture, it is worth the trip to town.

My agent, Elaine Koster, had been enthusiastic about the concept behind this book but died before the manuscript was completed. I wish she could have read it. Her associate Stephanie Lehmann was supportive and kept me on track in her absence. I will miss working with her.

My publisher, Atria Books, did much for me and *Killing Kate*, but nobody did more than my editor, Emily Bestler, who encouraged me as I wrote from a killer's point of view and shook things up in my fictional newsroom. Her editorial assistant, Kate Cetrulo, deserves thanks for her attention to detail and her good sportsmanship in regards to the title.

Additional kudos to Mellony Torres for publicity; Isolde Sauer for production editing; Jane Herman for copy editing; Hillary Tisman and Rachel Zugschwert for marketing; Jeanne Lee for jacket art; and also to Richard Defendorf, Adrian James, Renata Di Biase, and Fausto Bozza for all the other tasks involved in bringing a book to print.

My loyal beta readers—Trish Van Pilsum, Kevyn Burger, and Caroline Lowe—contributed praise and criticism to make this a better book.

My thanks to those experts who shared specific knowledge with me: John Kirkwood, special agent in charge of the US Secret Service–Minneapolis, for chatting about counterfeiting; senior investigator Keith Stress of the Animal Humane Society in Golden Valley, MN, for discussing animal cruelty laws; Vernon Geberth, author of *Practical Homicide Investigation*; and Dr. D. P. Lyle, author of *Howdunit Forensics*, *Forensics for Dummies*, and *The Writer's Forensics Blog*.

My sister Teresa Neuzil I fear will endure taunting and teasing from family about being the evil persona behind the Black Angel. To minimize that I have named my other sisters—Bonnie Brang, Kathy Loecher, Maggie (Mary Agnes) Kramer—as murder victims, so she will have something to throw back in their faces.

I have spared my other relatives a similar fate, but they should not become overconfident because there's always the next book: Ruth Kramer; Mike Kramer; Richard and Oti Kramer; Steve and Mary Kay Kramer, along with Matthew and Elizabeth; Jim, Adriana, and Zach Loecher; Roy Brang; Galen and Rachel Neuzil; Christina Kramer; Jerry and Elaine Kramer; George and Shirley Kimball; George Kimball, Shen Fei, and Shi Shenyu; Jenny, Kile, David, and Daniel Nadeau; Jessica, Richie, and Lucy Miehe; Becca and Seth Engberg; Mary, Dave, and Davin Benson; Nick Kimball and Gannet Tseggai; numerous far-flung cousins and other kin, especially those who granted me gracious hospitality on my last tour—Mae Klug in Nebraska; Rosemary and Bruce Jacobs in Arizona; Amy and Dan Comstock in Texas.

Soon after this book is released, my husband and I will become empty nesters. I will see what that does for the writing process. I'm just glad to have raised a family of readers: Andrew and Alex Kimball—off to college; Joey and David Kimdon—with Aria and Arbor; Jake and Katie Kimball (take special note that while Kate may have been killed, Katie lives on).

And, as always, my soul mate, Joe.